Lars

UGLYBUGLY

Translated by Deborah Dawkin

Dedalus

This translation has been published with the financial support of NORLA and Arts Council England.

Supported using public funding by
**ARTS COUNCIL
ENGLAND**

Published in the UK by Dedalus Limited,
24-26, St Judith's Lane, Sawtry, Cambs, PE28 5XE
email: info@dedalusbooks.com
www.dedalusbooks.com

ISBN   978 1 903517 91 8

Dedalus is distributed in the USA by SCB Distributors,
15608 South New Century Drive, Gardena, CA 90248
email: info@scbdistributors.com   web: www.scbdistributors.com

Dedalus is distributed in Australia by Peribo Pty Ltd.
58, Beaumont Road, Mount Kuring-gai, N.S.W. 2080
email: info@peribo.com.au

Publishing History
First published in Norway in 2004
First published by Dedalus in 2012

Uglybugly copyright © Lars Ramslie 2012
The right of Lars Ramslie to be identified as the author & Deborah Dawkin to be
identified as the translator of this work has been asserted by them in accordance with
the Copyright, Designs and Patents Act, 1988.

Printed in Finland by Bookwell
Typeset by Marie Lane

The Author

Lars Ramslie was born in 1974. He made his debut in 1997 with the novel *Biopsy,* about the relationship between a son and his heroin-addicted father, which received the Tarjei Vesaas First Book Award.

Other novels include *Microchaos* (1999), *Destroyer* (2000) and *Fatso* (2003), which has since been made into a feature film in Norway.

Uglybugly marks a new departure in his work. It is his first novel to be published in the UK.

The Translator

Deborah Dawkin works as a translator of fiction, drama and non-fiction.

Recent publications include Johan Harstad's novel *Buzz Aldrin, Whatever Happened to you in the Confusion* and the co-translation of Ingar Sletten Kolloen's groundbreaking biography of Knut Hamsun for Yale University Press.

She also has an MA in Social and Cultural History.

I AM DYING. I, Earl Merrik, am dying. When I walk out of that door I know it'll be over. I'm done for, and I'm ready for that. If you're listening up there then you'll know I've made friends with death. It's been a few days now since my sister snuffed it, so we've had time to get acquainted. Death and I. And, if you haven't just plain forgotten me, I'm your next man. I'm just waiting for her to start stinking. Because when Betty starts to stink, I'll probably start stinking too. How else could it end, when you tacked us together the way you did? Flesh spliced to flesh, sibling fettered to sibling at the breast. All night I've been sitting up at Sugarcane View, the old folk's home, with the meat cleaver that I nicked from matron, trying to man myself up. Maybe it's not even such a big a deal. If that new doctor could just be arsed to help me with pictures from one of those new inventions, those new machines that see through your body, then I might know exactly where to chop. If I can just get rid of a little bit of my left arm and a little bit of my belly. Then I'll be free. If not, I'm as good as done for. Unlikely perhaps – there can't be too many people that have survived hacking themselves in two, can there? No, I'm a goner. And soon I'll go out of that church door. Like a cat, a little creature, that feels an icy premonition every time it slinks out of the kitchen door, that the end is lurking somewhere in the undergrowth outside. Like a dog on a chain, a never-ending cable tie-out. Death. You hear this hound behind you, hear the clank of its chain, and you think, believe, hope, that soon, soon the leash will tighten and bring the dog flailing to the ground. And you run and run, round the earth, but you can still hear this hound from Hell panting at your neck, and the rattling of its chain. Until you suddenly get the joke with this cable tie-out thing, you realise you're doomed to lose to this hound that God's set on your trail – the fight is fixed, and you're the one paid to stay down. There's nothing to do but wait for your cue to take the fall. Which comes just when you've finally escaped to Littletown and think – just for one lousy second – that God's hound has forgotten you. That's when he suddenly grabs your sister while you're asleep.

It's not easy to say exactly *when* you grow aware of it running behind you. You discover it suddenly, maybe you're nineteen, maybe twenty or thirty, but suddenly it dawns on you. Everyone realises it at some point, and one day it'll hit you, for *real*. From that moment hardly a day will pass without you thinking about it. But now I *know* death's standing right there. And I'll go down for the count, if I don't do anything – but, then again, there's nothing I *can* do. I'm in the Devil's mouth and his slavering jaws are closing around me.

So now you know, Big Guy. I know I'm gonna meet death, but not whether I'll meet you. That is, if you haven't, as I already said, forgotten me. Which would be fucking typical. You've made yourself known to my sister, alright – but just so you know, there are two of us here. If you don't believe me, look it up in that big book of yours. And if you need a clue, look for it under practical jokes. This is your last chance, you hear me?! I'm sitting here now waiting for you, and I honestly reckon this'll be your last chance. I'm not exactly in the habit of stumbling in here of my own free will. The statistics don't exactly stack in my favour, however you look at it. So if you've considered revealing yourself – now's the time, Big Guy. But then again, if you can't be arsed with me, you could at least give my sister a helping hand – she's the believer, not me. So I'll sit here a bit longer, and take a nap while the pastor does his preaching, and you can come here and poke me in the shoulder. Or however you choose to do it. I'm not in a hurry. Just you come. Or, I'll shuffle back up to Sugarcane View and dig out that meat cleaver. I'm not scared. I'm ready to shake off whatever it takes.

BIGTOWN

MR. KING

On the day Mr King, that no-legged pimp, entered our lives, we'd sat in our berth waiting until the ship was empty of passengers, and there was hardly any life left on the quay. But when we finally walked down the gangway and onto Bigtown's quay, with that bitter wind blowing against us, the door of the big black car swung open. And Mr King waved at us from the back seat with a broad smile. Next to the car door stood the tallest, biggest negro I'd ever seen. Smiling too, all teeth.

"Mr King would like to offer you a lift," he said.

"I ain't sure," I said, hesitating. "Who is this Mr King?"

"Mr King's there in the car," said the negro, pointing.

We wandered over to the car. On the boot was the word *Ambassador*, written in those fancy shiny letters that are almost impossible to read.

"Ladies!" said Mr King, flinging his arms wide open. His cane lay on the seat next to him, next to a bouquet of flowers and an outdated newspaper with a small notice announcing that we were on our way. Mr King in a grey-and-black striped suit with his hat in one hand.

"Excuse me, sir," I whispered, "but the fact is…we're actually a lady and a *gentleman*…"

Mr King looked up at me. Since we were without papers – they'd as good as disintegrated on our travels, before vanishing altogether when we were thrown out of our last hotel – I'd put on one of Betty's frocks so as to make things less problematic at immigration. Because it seems that whenever people come across a medical sensation like us, everybody always wants to play doctors and investigate whether we really are one of God's own fancies – a man and a woman spliced together. And without any paperwork to explain our tragic plight, there was no reason to assume the immigration officers would treat us any better – all, of course, in the name of science...No, it had seemed sensible to swallow my pride and don a frock, and look as normal as two co-joined twins could. And I hadn't had a spare suit for Betty to borrow, because I'd pawned it to buy a few bottles of booze to keep our spirits up during the journey...or for as long as they lasted.

"So it's *true*..." he whispered. "Fantastic! So you're Earl, I presume?"

I nodded. Mr King took off his glove and stretched out a hand. Cautiously I stuck my head into the car and took it. Which was when I noticed the missing legs.

"And this is Betty," I added as I took the obligatory step backwards so we could both turn and Betty could stretch a hand out with a tentative curtsey. She was as good as mute, as she tends to be when she's feeling awkward. Although it might have been because I'd accepted an offer of liquor the night before. There are plenty of people who want to drink with a man like me, and I'd drunk pretty heavily throughout the entire trip. To fight the seasickness and the fear of what might happen when we came into port. But then, Betty rarely talked much anyway, especially when she felt nervous or insecure. Except of course when God turned her tap on, then it could flow out of her for hours.

The sensation, faint as it was, of Mr King's lips against Betty's hand – her only hand incidentally, because we share my left – made my hair stand on end. Mostly because, with my back to them, I didn't see it coming. But also because,

8

just then, I was busy monitoring the movements of some uniformed men some distance from the car.

"The coloured feller mentioned somethin' about a lift," I said, when we'd finally turned ourselves round again.

"That's right. Hop in!" Mr King shunted sideways along the seat on his arms, his stumps sticking stiffly out in front of him.

"I'm afraid me and Betty will 'ave to wait till we've got everythin' in order. And that could take a bit o' time, I'm afraid. We ain't got any papers. It shouldn't really be a problem, but they vanished on the way, and it's taken us years to get back home…"

"Oh, don't you concern yourselves about that, Earl. We're just glad you're back. I'm sorry there's not been a better welcome arranged, we've been waiting so long for you, but what with this weather, it was hard to get everybody together. But I promise – before the day's up you and your sister will have had a reception you shan't forget in a hurry."

"Right…" I said, clearing my throat.

"Everything's in perfect order, Earl. But if you really must, and as a gentleman I understand your feelings on the matter, then we can wait for you to go through all the formalities. It'll be a shame, of course, to worry our guests for the sake of a few niceties that have already been taken in hand but by all means, we can wait. Although, I think we should send word to all our the guests waiting at the party."

"Party?"

"We've prepared a party for you both, of course!" Mr King looked up at us from his pocket watch.

Betty was getting very distressed. She didn't utter a word, but I could feel it by the way she shifted her legs and writhed about. Mute. Besides, waves of nausea were rushing through her body. Then I got a glimpse of myself in the glossy paintwork of Mr King's car – not a particularly convincing sight. The frock was one of Betty's shabbiest cast-offs, and my make-up had been applied with a less than steady hand. The whole thing looked like badly assembled fancy dress and the shoes were killing me. Eyes like two narrow, black-painted, swollen pig-cunts, a surly lower lip and hair tangled under the idiotic hat that Betty had shoved on my head at the last minute.

"Yeah, alright, Mr...Mr *King*. But I need to 'ave a word with my sister."

"Of course." He smiled, before craning his neck to squint at the uniformed men through this front windscreen. Then turned back to me. "Of course, Earl."

We tottered away from the car with me stumbling on my ridiculous high heels. But as usual it was impossible to get a peep out of Betty. She just stood there stiff as a poker, her knuckles white with fear. Then she started to cry. No huge surprise there.

"So, what d'yer wanna do?" I asked her. "There's somethin' fishy 'ere. I ain't sure what, but we've gotta decide pretty quick. I can't promise everythin'll go smooth at Immigration... we've been away too long and we ain't got no papers. And it ain't certain they've got our papers any more, either. D'you get me?! I don't get what this guy's talkin' about...perhaps he wants to help us...or perhaps he's just another sicko, another conman but I ain't gonna decide this on my own. D'yer hear me, Betty?!"

Betty barely uttered a sound. Just gasped. I gave a heavy sigh, and took a step in the direction of the car.

"No-no-no!" she whispered.

"What d'you mean *no*? Come on!"

Betty said nothing. One of the uniformed men pushed his cap further back on his head with his index finger, following us with his gaze. With Betty stiff as a post I hauled us back to the car and crammed her, suddenly struggling, into the back seat. The chauffeur closed the door. And with Betty between me and Mr King in the backseat, the car drove swiftly out of the harbour and in towards town.

"Excellent," said Mr King.

For a while we sat in complete silence.

"Awful sorry, Mister, but I think my sister's gonna puke. Perhaps we oughter stop. Wouldn't want 'er damagin' the nice covers in your car."

Pretty fast Mr King magicked up a bag from one of those little pockets on the back of the front seat. And Betty emptied her guts, while I did my best to hold the contents of mine in place. Mr King scowled disconcertedly as he clung to the handle over the car door with one hand and carefully stroked her back with the other.

"Our travel chest!" Betty screamed suddenly. "Our photographs and backdrop!"

"There's no need to worry about that, my dear, the chauffeur's put everything in the boot and everything's quite safe. Look! I've bought you some flowers."

True enough, we'd managed to get our suitcase and sailor bag into the car, containing our essentials and just a few of our dearest possessions but our biggest chest was still on board, in the cargo room. In it were our posters, our backdrop, the marriage proposal that Betty had never replied to, but always kept, some rings, and the note our parents had left for us when they disappeared. And, most important of all, our photographs – everything we'd experienced, for better or worse, in our time across the Pond. Without them it was almost as if we didn't exist.

"No reason at all for concern. I'll send somebody down to deal with it the minute we arrive."

But there was every reason for concern. The chest would

take its time. And however much the legless pimp wrapped everything in fine words and gestures, the thing he was really after was Betty's skirts. From the moment we'd walked off that ship and set foot on dry land. Not that I want to be too hard on him – he gave us a roof over our heads and food on the table. At least we didn't live on the streets under Mr King's protection, and we got nothing but the best in the beginning. Besides, if it hadn't been for Mr King, we'd never have had the pleasure of meeting Cougher, Frehley and Uncle Rust. And to be fair, I have to take some of the blame for the fact things went sour in the end between Mr King and us.

But right now, we were sitting in the car, on our way to all of these things.

Mr King peered over at me.

"Tell me Earl, do you suffer from the palsy?"

"No."

"So you're alright, are you?"

"Yeah, sure. What d'you mean?"

"Well...that hand of yours – it was going round like a propeller before you got into the car."

"Eh, yeah. It just 'appens now'n'then. I can't do anything' about it, Mister. That's just 'ow things are with us, now'n'then."

"Hmm, I'll have make sure a doctor sees you. You can't go around like that, you know. It can't be good. Maybe I can get some medication for you."

"Yeah, p'raps. But I'll 'ave to ask Betty first. She ain't too keen on doctors. We've 'ad some pretty full-on examinations – put it that way."

I hadn't noticed anything myself. But now Mr King mentioned it, I could feel the sensation slowly coming back into my left hand. I opened and closed my fist, and felt the blood flowing back into my fingers. It wasn't the first time it had behaved like this. It had drawn attention to itself increasingly often during the journey across the Pond, particularly when we had some liquor down us. But I had no intention of disclosing anything about the hand or *the thing* to Mr King. That, I thought, could wait until I knew more about him, and what he had planned for us. As it turned out, it was a long time before *the thing* would draw attention to itself like that again anyway. And, I may have done my fair share of dumb things during our stay with Mr King, but staying schtum about *the thing* was not one of them.

THE BORDELLO

AND IF IT HADN'T BEEN for the dreadful state I was in, what with Betty's tatty frock, the gruesome make-up and my hangover, I'd have said I loved it from the first moment. The welcome Mr King had laid on for us proved truly fabulous. Even though he did nothing during the entire drive to prepare us for what lay ahead. Nor to explain who he was, what kind of business he ran, where we were going, or why he was lavishing so much attention on us. Betty was too sick and scared to ask, and I was too tired and too busy thinking, to open my mouth. So we sat in silence throughout the journey. Besides, I was sitting too awkwardly, with my back turned towards him and Betty, to hold any normal conversation.

The car swung into a backyard and stopped. The black man fetched a wheelchair and placed it so Mr King could lift himself out of the back seat and into it. Moments later, two tall, slender, stunningly beautiful women, came running over with an umbrella to wheel him in, while the negro opened the car door for us and fetched what little luggage we had. Still ignorant of what lay in store for us, we were led through the back entrance. And while we went in the lift up to the fourth floor, the women and the black guy took the stairs. At the top the lift door was opened for us by another, equally stunning looking woman, and we were escorted into a large room, which, somebody explained later, was the ballroom and Mr King's legitimate business front.

There was hardly a sound in the room. There were mainly women. And most of the men present were black, wearing tuxedos and carrying instruments about. I'd never have imagined, negros in *tuxedos*. There was a steady hum of whispering, which stopped dead the minute we walked in. Everybody turned towards us. We still didn't know who these people were, ambassadors perhaps, or maybe a secret society of amateur scientists, though that seemed unlikely, or a circus troupe or some charitable organization – we'd met that kind before, for better or worse, mainly worse. We could but guess. But one thing was sure, there were enough women. Women of every size, colour and shape. So my eyes nearly popped out of my head. And all of them smiling at us.

Bit by bit, the picture was coming clear for me. And Betty must have been getting her suspicions too, though she kept her lips well buttoned.

"Mister," I said, "this is great, but…well, as you probably realize, this ain't my usual style of dress. D'you think I could get my own clothes on?"

"But of course."

"Cos as you know…me and Betty aren't the same…*sex*," I whispered.

"Really, Earl, there's no need," Mr King began.

"And it's not like I'm one of those blokes that gets the urge to wear his sister's clothes, either.

"No, of course not, Earl. But surely you, and your beautiful sister here, would like a little champagne first?" Mr King plucked up a bottle from the ice bucket and peered up at me. He raised his eyebrows and smiled.

"That's very generous, Mister King. I'm afraid my sister hardly drinks, though I'd be happy to have a drop when I've…"

But before I knew it, I was standing there with a glass in my hand, dressed in a tatty dress and Betty getting increasingly fraught at my side. As everybody rose to their feet, Mr King lifted his glass.

"Cheers!" he shouted. The orchestra struck up on a low

stage at the back of the room. When one of the women got up with a snake round her neck, and a tiny monkey simultaneously bolted across the dance floor in front of us – startled by the noise of the band – I felt the weight of Betty's body as she fainted and her legs slithered out behind me.

Mr King raised his glass again. I emptied mine in one, and then began, despite my better judgment and years of experience, to chase my limp sister round the room, like a dog chasing its tail. And the bloody high heels didn't exactly help matters, skidding on that shiny floor. To get a foothold I sought sanctuary (and I was about to regret this) on the large rug that lay under the sofa area by the bar.

The music stopped. The monkey chattered anxiously. I turned to look towards a trickling sound, which I took to be a bottle of champagne we'd knocked over in our mad waltz. Only to find it was no champagne bottle, but Betty urinating, with a sleepy and contented sigh. Mr King had given us a stupendous welcome, and this little Missy was repaying his generosity by pissing on his rug.

"I...we're...awful sorry for..." ...I was going to say for *this outrage*. But instead I felt the champagne rush to my head and a great grin spread across my face, followed by a bubbly snigger, which can't have gone down well. But hammered as I'd been over the last few days, it didn't take a lot.

Mr King smiled tensely and waved two oriental girls over to him.

"Could you please show Mr and Mrs Merrik up to their room." Mr King ran his finger up and down his glass, looked down at the stain on the carpet, and then back up at us with the same stiff smile.

The girls came over. One took me gently under my right arm, while the other struggled with Betty's sprawling body.

"Mr and Mrs Merrik?" I heard myself yell in the corridor. "We ain't exactly married!"

The Hotel

We were back. After years over the Pond, we were back where we'd begun. Where we'd first come into existence. Bigtown. Earl and Betty Merrik first came into being in a five star hotel suite in Bigtown. Although, when I say that, I don't necessarily mean we were born there. And though we ended up coming back here, Bigtown wasn't exactly our home. When I say *we came into being*, I mean that it was here Earl Merrik became Earl Merrik and Betty Merrik became Betty Merrik.

We were found in a hotel room with some fruit and a note that stated, in an unsteady hand, our names, what we liked to eat and drink, our approximate age, and that despite our smart clothes, we had lice. Our most precious possession – a note scrawled with our names and saying we had lice. Hardly something to flaunt when you want to impress or make new friends. Yet we frequently brought it out when we were kids. If people succeeded in deciphering this document that we presented to them so proudly as our dearest possession, they'd take a startled step backwards. And that would generally be the last we'd see of them.

My only memory of the hotel is of a man and a woman leaving the room. Betty still hadn't got her talking-tackle in order yet (and it would take time before she opened Heaven's floodgates with her prattling about God and angels and so on). The man, or perhaps the woman, I can't remember which, said we had to be quiet and wait. I must keep quiet so as not to wake my sister. And if she woke up, I must calm her down again. They were going to fetch food, but since food wasn't allowed in the hotel – not from outside at least – we must be quiet. They'd get food, and then we'd all have something to eat. But if we weren't completely quiet, there'd be nothing. No food for Betty and Earl. No, no, no. So there we sat, all day and all night. A chambermaid stuck her head in once or twice, after complaints about kids crying, but still managed to overlook the note and leave us. Perhaps she couldn't read. Perhaps the sight of us was too unbearable. So there we sat. With Betty sobbing inconsolably. From time to time I stuck her thumb in her mouth, but it only helped for a moment, since she soon spat it out. In the end it was impossible to get her thumb in at all. And if anybody else peeped in and asked after these people, who were presumably our parents, my poor brain must have managed to concoct some explanation or other – I couldn't say they were out to get food, of course. Then there'd be nothing to eat.

It was hard for most people to believe we were real. There we sat, spliced together by the Big Guy. Who could believe that? One doctor was drawn again and again to the question of how we were, as he put it, *fused together*. There's a visible difference where our skin overlaps. The skin that begins on my side of the body is far coarser and more wrinkled, with the occasional spot or growth. Betty is, to this day, as smooth as a baby's bottom. One specialist who examined us was so amazed, even he thought only the Devil could have stitched us together. This scared the pants off Betty, of course, and depressed her terribly. Another cruel rumour was that we'd been ripped out of some miserable whore and stitched together, to be smuggled around among secret scientific circles, before ending up in the hotel in Bigtown – the ultimate calling card to the world. We are a medical sensation. Neither more, nor less. An impossible impossibility.

And however much celebrity this brought, we benefited very little from it ourselves. They didn't like us at the orphanage where we were placed. Our teachers didn't like us.

And when we were transferred to the institute, there weren't many people who liked us there either. Every day we were poked at or abused in some way. I generally came off worst in their scientific investigations. They'd dunk *me* in cold water, and take Betty's temperature. They'd give Betty an anaesthetic injection in the arm, and then pinch *me* with the pincers. We suffered years of it, and who knows, they might have gone on until we were nothing but calluses and bones if the newspapers hadn't written about us. It was the journalists who caused us to be sent back to the orphanage. Only to be thrown straight back out again. Thanks to me making a complete nightmare of myself. So, due to my unacceptable conduct – and the fact we were no longer kids – we were given our liberty at last. With few other options available to us, but to exhibit ourselves to the world and his brother.

But even in these circles we didn't meet much goodwill. Even the touring freaks couldn't stand a pair like us. They looked at us with suspicion. And even when they made an effort – they could be friendly to our faces – things would go sour. We weren't proper freaks. We were fakes, frauds and though they could tolerate a little fakery, we were way beyond the pale. Even for people who should have counted themselves as kith and kin, and in the same boat as us. So despite a brief flurry of celebrity, rumours spread that we were the authors of our own misfortune. And these same rumours soon spread among the public. Rumours that we'd got ourselves sewn together of our own freewill – with the Devil's assistance – to make an extra buck. They decided Earl was a lazy wino and Betty was a screwball. Sick lovers who, in a moment of perverted inspiration, had got themselves stitched together so as to avoid working like ordinary people.

"Sickos!" they whispered or yelled. Audiences dwindled and applause turned to dissatisfied jeers and muttering. Some of the public shook their fists, before letting rip. So once the rumour was out, there was nothing for it but to get away before all hell broke loose. Whether it was Betty's pussy they were gagging to peer up, or my dick they wanted to pull out, or whether they wanted to prod our skin in search of scars from the stitches – it was a nightmare. We tried to get proper jobs. But what with my never being quick at school-learning, nor much good with my hands, and dragging a sister about with a head full of Jesus and angels, there weren't too many options open to me. Now and then somebody would turn up wanting to be charitable. But we only ever brought disappointment. It was useless to teach us anything, and the minute I hit the bottle, we'd be straight back out. In the end we were known as the ungrateful twins. As if all we'd been put on earth for, was to bow and scrape.

Which is why, for once, Betty and I were in agreement when we decided to cross the Pond and try our luck there. But now something else occurred to us – perhaps we might look for our parents. They had to be somewhere in the world, and they'd left no trace in Bigtown. Perhaps they'd crossed the Pond, like so many others. In the beginning things seemed quite promising. We got a passage over, and once we'd arrived we were soon involved with a travelling circus. And they reckoned that with all the publicity, our parents might surface. If nothing else, we thought, they'd turn up just to see us.

But just as the circus seemed more than pleased with us – publicity and all – we found ourselves caught up in rumours again. Spread this time by the selfsame newspapers that had shown us such goodwill. We were branded swindlers wherever we went, and people wanted us shipped straight back home. And when the circus themselves cooked up stories to defend us against the worst of these rumours, the press only got more poisonous. But then somebody in the troupe might have helped spread these rumours too, maybe out of envy for how things had gone so well for us at the start. It was our earnings from this period, when things looked so promising, that kept us going for the remainder of our time there. If it hadn't been for this cash, we'd have found ourselves on the ship back to Bigtown long ago.

"Sickos!" the crowds yelled again.

Or: "The Devil himself must have sewn 'em together!"

If anybody so much as looked at us, they would be struck down by some gruesome curse. "Set eyes on them, and you'll never be happy again. It's like bugs in your eyes, creepy-crawly-bugs." It was rumoured that people had been blinded by the sight of us. "It's like getting bugs in your eyes," they'd say: "Bugs in your eyes! *Foul* bugs in your eyes."

I'm pretty certain the circus themselves were to blame for some of this *bugs in the eyes* nonsense too, when they planted roadies in the audience to heckle us and crank up the mood. Whatever the case, the rumour was out and it refused to die. It followed us wherever we went. But worse, it had started to affect Betty and she began to believe all this garbage – that God could never have brought himself to create us, or anything like us.

"But what if it's true, Earl? What if we were stitched together by the...the..." she didn't dare say the word. "And if I'm the one with the heart, Earl, then what keeps you alive? What if it's the...*the thing?*"

Still, we tried to hold out a bit longer. Until one night we were woken up and thrown out onto the street with everything we owned. Nobody bothered giving us an explanation. Not that it was necessary. We'd seen it coming. We didn't need hollow excuses.

We found lodgings next day, with an elderly couple, who Betty managed to impress with her religious ranting. They'd pushed to the front of crowd of curious – and far from kindly disposed – onlookers, to find my sister down on her knees praying, and me straining to stand up and shaking my fist. With loving smiles, they rescued us from our plight. And soon we sat at a food-laden table, washed, brushed and saying our prayers.

"Earl, they want you to lead grace."

"You what? Ah, right…Oh Lord, for what we are about to receive…blah-blah-blah, and while we're on the subject of food God, it'd be nice if you treated us like we were more than just a fly in the soup."

The elderly couple smiled. And Betty smiled too, ashen faced, before continuing from where I'd left off. And since she had no right hand to put together with her left in prayer, she grabbed hold of mine, nails practically digging into my bones.

"You can put your hands together, but you never do," she whispered one evening.

That must have been the one thing Betty envied me – the fact that, unlike her, the Big Guy had given me the possibility of praying like other people. I suspect that it's the only worldly thing she'd ever have included in her prayers.

"How can He hear me if I can't fold my hands?"

"P'raps he don't want to hear your nagging, who knows? P'raps it's Our Lord's way of defendin' 'imself against all your complaints about His unfair treatment. 'Ave you ever thought abou' that?"

But with Betty at the controls for a change, and me saying as little as possible so as not to get on the wrong side of the old folk, things were looking up again. Until, that is, the same old thing repeated itself. Again, I got the reputation for being a useless, good-for-nothing wino, getting into scraps with people who didn't even speak in a language I understood. And when one of the girls next-door gave birth to a baby with a clubfoot, the whole district almost ran amok with burning torches and whatnot. It didn't matter how much Betty prayed for us now, it was no good.

"We'd have liked to keep *you* here, Betty my dear," the old woman said. "But seeing as you two are inseparable." She'd long ago stopped talking to me directly, instead I was meant to hear anything concerning myself, through Betty.

"They'd have liked to keep us..." Betty repeated, as though to keep me informed.

"Oh belt up," I said, "I've got ears..."

The elderly couple even tried getting us under the knife, but at the last minute – washed, brushed and dressed in her best – Betty changed her mind and told them that if *she* stayed, they'd have to count *me* in too. So that was that, however upstanding and Christian they tried to be. They gave us a tidy sum to take on our way – I'll grant them that – and this meant we could keep travelling a while more. Drifting from place to place. We tried to lie low, as our money trickled away on train tickets, shabby hotel rooms and bribes.

We'd achieved nothing. Everything was meaningless. Nothing good had come from our travels. And we'd stopped thinking about our parents long ago. Back, when we were with the circus – before things had gone to pot – Betty and I had tried to memorise all the faces in the audience. We'd even look into their eyes when we could. Then we'd sit at night and speculate about the ones we could remember, and imagine the various lives we might have lived if our parents had taken care of us. Or the life that might still be ours, if we had the good luck to find them one day.

At first I'd been convinced of the possibility of recognising our parents. Those shadowy figures from the hotel room. But I soon had to give up. And once I've given up on something,

I really *have* given up on it. Not so, Betty. She just kept at it forever. Driving me insane.

"But are you quite sure you didn't see them?" she'd ask, night after night.

"Can't you please just drop it?! Christ Almighty." I'd bang my fist into the table, or, when I got really mad, smash my head into the wall. And try as I might to stay on the wagon, I couldn't. I had to have something to get away from her constant whingeing.

"Oh, they looked so kind tonight..."

"Huh?"

"Those two."

"Who? Ah, right."

On and on she went. Until even she had to give up. Exhausted. We never found our family, and whatever people we did find, didn't want us. So we sailed back to Bigtown, with no other hope than to tread the same soil on which we'd entered this world. With no other desire than to be allowed to live, eat and take whatever came our way. We'd travelled the world in search of something that wasn't to be found. Now we'd be grateful for whatever we got. If only just a room and a crust. We'd not ask for more.

It was on our way back over the Pond, that we got the notion we were only half-siblings, that our parents had sewn us together in an attempt to make one child – one child that belonged to them both equally. But that when this failed, they'd abandoned us in the hotel room. This all made Betty so miserable she wanted to fling herself into the sea. I had to talk her out of it. Out of the idea that anybody other than God himself had sewn us together...and out of drowning herself too.

But sometimes I can't help thinking how different we are.

Uglybugly

There's so little that binds us…and yet, that's *all* we have to cling to in this world. The way I see it, we never left that hotel room. Leastways, I didn't. Betty's seen Heaven and everything, of course, but the way I see it, I'm still sitting in that darkened hotel room holding a mute little girl who cries. A cry-baby I'll never understand. And there's nobody I can talk to in there. Nobody who speaks my tongue. Nobody who'll ever understand me. Betty's my kid sister and I'm her big brother. And as the world passes by like shadows outside the windows, I go on sitting here, alone in this huge, darkened hotel room, with a baby in my arms. The way I see it, the whole world, Littletown and Bigtown included, has come into this hotel room with me, squeezed itself in, bringing hell at its heels. The entire world had moved into this hotel room and settled around us, inside us. And still, we are totally alone. She barely has me, and I barely have her.

The Safe

So, with some solid seafaring and miles of travel behind us, we were finally in Bigtown again. We returned home to a Mr King who sat waiting for us. Home? Well, we'd landed up in Bigtown at least, and, as fate would have it, the cripple sat waiting for us with a newspaper, a bouquet and what looked like a gift from Heaven. Instead it was the darkest, most fearful trap we'd walked into so far. As if we deserved anything else. The spoiled Merrik twins. The spoiled, ungrateful Merrik twins, who didn't have an honest fibre in their bodies. Who tried to cheat Nature, God and all mankind. A man and a woman woven together. As if that were possible! Mr King thought he'd made a good catch, but in the end – with the help of Frehley, Cougher and Uncle Rust – we'd be the ones to seal his fate.

Still, my job at Mr King's was, and is to this day, the best I ever had. You might even say I owe him a big "thank you" all things considered. And who knows, if it hadn't been for Betty, he and I might still be on speaking terms. But things didn't turn out well.

On the morning after we'd been taken in by Mr King, the black man knocked on our door. It was the first time in ages that I'd enjoyed a good night's sleep, and I'd have preferred to sleep longer if he hadn't taken it into his head to hammer the door down.

I'd been dreaming. Dreaming about the two Chinese girls who'd taken us up to our room the night before. One of them had helped me find my own clothes, then they'd led us into the bathroom across the hallway and filled a large bathtub. When I turned round they were standing there stripped to their underwear. Then, smiling, they'd started taking Betty's clothes off too. If I hadn't felt obliged to stop them, out of concern for Betty's modesty, they'd have stripped us both naked. They were laughing and giggling at first, but I managed to shake the champagne off for a moment.

"If you two don't lay off, you can forget this whole bath."

Not that it bothered me, but if Betty had woken up in her birthday suit, together with me and two scantily clad females, I'd never have heard the last of it. I certainly wasn't the least averse to being waited on by two beautiful girls. Finally, they brought in two big towels and a screen, so with my head buzzing with champagne, I wrapped us up in the towels.

With a bit of a to-do they got us up into the bath. Truth be told, the towel fell off Betty as we sank into the bubble-filled tub. But if she'd ever thought to ask, I could at least say I'd tried to protect her modesty. Once we were settled in the tub, one of the girls went for more champagne, while the other proceeded to wash us with a soap and sponge. Although as soon as she started on our privates, I made it very clear that that wasn't on. Reluctantly she handed me the sponge and lit herself a cigarette while I scrubbed Betty's pussy and organised myself inside my underpants.

"Misser King…velly wu-llied abou' hy-giene," she said, as she pulled her negligee up and sat on the toilet with her cigarette – legs smooth, their golden colour almost shimmering, tight arse against the seat.

"Look Misser! Champaing," she smiled as she dropped the cigarette between her thighs, down into the bowl, and went over to join her sister who was busy with the champagne. They were chatting so excitedly now, it was impossible to catch a word they said. But Christ, they were lovely. And looked after us so well. Sadly, they left the bordello soon after Betty and I were taken in. And maybe they were a bit on the young side.

After our bath we stretched out on the enormous bed. Wedged in between big, soft pillows as the girls served hot food. Betty was still asleep as they rolled reefers of hemp and put out a dish of the most divine chocolates. The sweet smell filled the room. I tried to prop myself up in the bed, my head growing increasingly heavy. The girls rolled about on top of each other at my feet, gossiping and giggling they slithered under and over each other. Not once forgetting to keep me supplied with chocolate and drags of the fabulous hemp. One lay on her back, the soles of her feet gliding back and forth over the luxurious coverlet. With my head getting dizzier and heavier, I contented myself with watching, as their bodies slid shamelessly from their negligees, and they writhed about laughing, fondling themselves and playing with their strings of pearls, as they opened and closed their legs for me.

"You must tell Mr King, I'm sorry my sister pissed on his carpet," I mumbled, with my mouth full of chocolate. "I'm... ever...so...ever...so...sorry..." was the last thing I remember saying. They nodded though I wasn't sure they'd understood. Then the world slipped away, and I surrendered to a blissful dream of two beautiful girls and a big bed and a bathtub.

Now, woken by the black guy's determined hammering on our door, I found my big pillow flecked with chocolate. My mouth was still filled with rich sticky goo. I must have dropped off with a chocolate in my mouth, and now I felt nauseous. Betty peered up at me over her shoulder and stretched. Then shuddered.

"The snake!" she gasped. "Did you see the snake?"

"Calm down, Betty. There ain't no snake 'ere now. That was yesterday. Calm down. We're in good 'ands now."

I tried to tempt her with something from the breakfast tray that had been brought in, not forgetting the few left-over chocolates. But as I turned to her with the dish, she let out a

29

scream.

"You've got blood round your mouth!"

"Calm down, Betty," I repeated, "it's only chocolate. 'Ere, take one…take two!"

Just at that moment, the black man walked in through the door, and Betty started shrieking again, this time with the bedcover pulled over her head.

"Mr King wants to see you both, sir," he said, fighting to be heard over Betty's racket.

"I see. But could you give me a moment with my sister? She ain't used to bein' waited on like this, you see. It ain't easy for 'er to express 'er gratitude."

"Did you hear that, Betty?" I said laughing, as he closed the door behind him. "He called me *sir*. It can't be that bad round 'ere, can it? They wouldn't call me sir, if this weren't a place of quality. C'mon Betty…Betty, you've got to come out now. Things ain't so bad. You'll see."

But however much I tried to reassure her, Betty went on sobbing under the bedcover, until she eventually poked her head out and helped herself cautiously to some breakfast. After which I got us out of bed and into the clothes that had been laid out for us.

"Now listen, Betty, you've gotta be polite to Mr King. He's gone to a lot of bother lookin' after us like this. This could be the chance of a lifetime. D'you get me? The chance of a lifetime!" I said before we left the room. "You've gotta get your manners out. I don't want no more whingeing!"

Never mind fainting or pissing, I thought to myself. Betty nodded quietly. And as soon we were reasonably presentable, we let ourselves be led down to Mr King's office. He was sitting behind his big desk. In the wall behind him was a safe – half-open – almost as if he wanted us to notice it. He waved us over to the couch that he'd clearly brought out just for us, since we could both sit on it without much trouble.

"So, how are you both? Did you sleep well? Have you eaten?" he said.

"It was heavenly, Mr King, totally and utterly heavenly. Though my sister slept through the heavenliest bit…" I winked. "If you get my drift. But I can say, with confidence, sir, that she's 'ad as fabulous a time as me. Fabulous, weren't it, Betty?" I prompted.

Betty nodded.

"Excellent! Sadly, both of you missed out on some *fabulous* times at last night's reception. But I can understand you both being tired after your journey. Did you sleep well, Betty dear?"

Betty nodded again.

"Thank you for putting us up last night, mister. Thank you…" she whispered.

Mr King leaned closer, with a confused smile.

"She says it was a shame we didn't manage to come back down yesterday evening, but she's very thankful for the lodgin's, Mr King."

"Excellent, excellent. But please, call me Biff."

"Well, thank you very much, *Mr King*…And we must apologise for our conduct last night, but perhaps things got a bit much for Betty. We ain't used to such luxury, you understand."

"You mustn't give another thought to last night's mishap, Earl," said Mr King with a smile. "Champagne has sprung the odd surprise on me too…since I lost these."

Mr King indicated the stumps hidden under his big desk.

"One of the tragic consequences of being like this, is that you drink like an elephant, but hold as much as a hen," laughed Mr King. "You're certainly not the only ones to have pissed themselves in this house. Though it's probably the first time anyone's dared to do it all over my Persian rug. But maybe not the *last*…I love champagne myself," smiled Mr King. "Love it!"

I peeped over at Betty, who clearly had no idea what we were talking about.

"Yeah, right," I answered, "I love it too…really love it, yeah."

"But I understand you're of a rather more careful disposition, Betty?" Mr King shifted on his chair and leaned across the table.

I suddenly felt a weight tug at me, just as I had last night. Betty had collapsed again. I could only hope she'd hold everything in this time.

"Tell me, Mr Merrik, does this happen often?"

"Well, now'n'then. Specially if things gets too much for 'er. My sister's a bit on the religious side, you see."

"Religious? Well, we've got nothing against religious people here, have we?" Mr King looked over at the negro.

"No, sir. Not at all, sir."

"Many of our clients are extremely religious,"

"She'll be glad to 'ear it. You 'ear that, Betty?" I elbowed her, but with no response.

"Just let your sister get the rest she so obviously needs. It's probably just as well – I need to talk to you. May I offer you a drink? Are you comfortable there? Excellent. I'll come to the point."

The negro went over to the bar and dropped some ice cubes into glasses with a pair of elegant tongs. They might even have been silver for all I knew. Smart, anyway. And the ice clinked luxuriously against the glass.

"Earl, let me explain what kind of business I run here. I assume that a man of the world, such as yourself, has seen most things so it surely doesn't need a great deal of clarification?"

"I think I have some idea…yes."

"Excellent." Mr King leaned back in his chair. "This is, I

can assure you, one of the most exclusive houses of pleasure in this town. Not to say the entire continent. This house is also one of the oldest in Bigtown – if not *the* oldest – and we enjoy a certain reputation not granted to everybody. It's no lie when I assert that our girls are among the healthiest and most beautiful in town. And we have the finest doctors to prove the one, and the finest clientele to prove the other."

"That's most reassurin' to hear, Mr King. But when it comes to payment for our lodgin's, I'm sorry to say we don't have that much to offer."

"Earl, Earl you mustn't worry yourself on that account. I'm sure we can come to some arrangement...that's why we're sitting here now..."

I laughed nervously.

"I don't think you know my sister very well yet." I said. "She ain't a great talker sometimes, but once she's set 'er mind against somethin', only God can make 'er think otherwise."

The ice cubes gave an empty rattle in my glass, and in an instant the black man whisked it out of my hand and replaced it with a full one.

"Earl, Earl, I shan't hear another word. Now listen! I can see it would be difficult to ask the pair of you to participate in the house's business...and I don't expect it. I'm not even sure it would be at all desirable. No, no. I wouldn't even consider it. All I ask from you, is your presence. Perhaps, for you to run me the odd errand...sit in the cloakroom maybe...greet our guests. Little tasks of that sort. Just to pique our clients' curiosity. And I'd like you both, of course, to escort me to the wrestling matches."

"Wrestling?!"

"Yes, absolutely. Apart from running this house, I still have a bunch of the finest wrestlers in the country. I'm sure you recognise Tim over there from earlier...but in the ring he's known as Tim Burley."

I was stunned.

"What...*the* Tim Burley?!" I burst out.

"None other." Mr King grinned and leaned further back in his chair. The black man – the great Tim Burley no less – nodded at me from behind the bar.

"But, but...ain't he your...your...man servant?!"

"Well yes, all my wrestlers work for me...one way or another."

And true enough, I would soon see Tim Burley in action both in the ring and the bordello. But right now, thrilled as I was to hear Mr King's plans for us, I just felt like a black hat had been rammed over my head...why couldn't I be alone now? I stared into my glass and sighed. Not that Mr King seemed to notice...

"I had my time in the ring too," he continued. "But those days are over, as you can imagine." Mr King cocked his head towards the missing legs.

"Sure," I whispered.

"Not that I ever really made it big...although in the beginning perhaps. But no, the highlight of my career was the day I lost these in front of hundreds of spectators, who got rather more than they'd paid for."

"Oh?"

"Stood on top of one of the posts in the corner of the ring. But then I took a tumble backwards, you see. And stupid as I was, I pushed off extra hard before taking flight. Crashed straight into the judges' table, and when the tabletop cracked, the veneer sliced into my thighs and ripped both my legs open."

I stared in stunned silence.

"And what the veneer didn't cut through, the table's steel frame got, before my bones snapped as I landed on the concrete. Nothing like that had ever happened before...and

Hell will freeze over before it ever happens again."

"Ouff, that's a dreadful story."

"Oh, I shouldn't trouble yourself over it. Life's been more than fair to me, Earl. No point sitting about complaining. I pulled a good lump of cash in that night. The association stepped up and raised a solid amount in compensation. And an optimist like myself knew how to put the money to good use. So, though I might not have accomplished any great feats, at least I got a seat of honour at Olympen which I use as often as I can. And just as I was helped then...I'm trying to help you now. You understand?"

I nodded.

"And if you think this is bad – what with my legs gone and face reorganised – you should have seen the guy I nearly finished off." Mr King winked. "Oh, and you should have seen me fly..." His eyes followed an arc across the room. "Fan-ta-stique!"

He laughed. I tried to look impressed, while not looking too excited – I couldn't exactly sit there with a big grin on my face.

"I dunno if I can promise anythin' 'till I've conferred with my sister," I said quietly.

"And Earl, let me tell you...I don't care whether you've got anything between your legs or not."

Mr King waved his hands.

"No, Earl, don't answer me...I don't care a jot. For me, you're a *man*, from top to toe. For me, the two of you are – even with this melted-together business – a man and a woman. You understand? Top notch, *top notch*...you hear what I'm saying?! Genuine or not...and you mustn't worry what anyone else says to the contrary."

Flushed and smacking his lips, he took the glass that had been placed in front of him.

"Cheers, Earl. Here's to the work of creation – and to fate – and to everything that's brought us together today."

I lifted my glass hesitantly. He smiled.

"But, just for the record…if the two of you ever *do* consider doing business here…" he said rocking his head from side to side with a sly smile, and tapping the table thoughtfully. "If the two of you do ever decide that that's what you *want*… well, you're heartily welcome. The door's open. All you have to do is knock. As long as everything's done above board, of course."

"Of course… But that's unlikely," I mumbled.

"Well, in the meantime, I'm just happy to have you both here. You'll make this house utterly extravagant, just by being here. You've no idea how long I've waited for this opportunity." Mr King gave the tabletop a final, enthusiastic little slap. "All your papers, the travel chest at the harbour, the authorities… we'll take them all in hand…and you'll have a regular salary like everybody else. Your worries are over."

"Mr King, that's too much really, thank you, thank you."

I fought back my tears.

"Earl," said Mr King, humping himself into his wheelchair with the help of Tim, "I'm the one asking too much. Maybe I'm just a vain old man…but I like the idea of showing the same generosity to others that has been shown me. It's not always easy to get by in this line of business, however much respect you've built up."

Tim wheeled Mr King over to me. I wasn't far off bursting into tears.

"You're both extremely welcome here, Earl. You've travelled long enough now. Welcome home."

He took my hand and squeezed it hard. He was a big man, despite having no legs. Handsome, even if that scarred face bore witness to his time in the ring. He squeezed my hand

36

firmly and gave me a hearty, red-cheeked, smile.
Then Betty woke up with a jolt.

And life was set to go on like a wonderful dream for some time.

Now, Betty came to again and Mr King offered her a glass of water.

"There, there," he said comfortingly. "There, there, sweetie pie."

Mr King showed us to the door. He knew Betty and I had some talking to do following our meeting.

When we came back up to our room, food and drink had been laid out for us, a large fruit platter. Betty ate hesitantly, her mouth still puffy from crying. Then I spent the rest of the day and half the night trying to make her see that this was the best thing that had ever happened to us. Reluctantly she agreed to stay. But only on certain conditions...

I must never leave her alone with Mr King. That may sound ridiculous, but I had to swear not to *abandon* her – as we do, from time to time, manage to forget each other's presence. A skill you get over the years when you live like us. She didn't want to have to sit alone with him in conversation. Next I had to promise that she'd never be forced to offer herself like the other girls in the house...and that if there was the least suggestion of it, we'd pack our things and leave. Additionally, that we'd go to church every Sunday, and I'd pray with her every evening. And in our prayers we'd ask Our Lord if he couldn't offer us another way out, than this. And, I had to promise to drink less. And, as far as possible, I had to resist using the house's services. But only as far as possible – Betty knew me better than to put her foot down completely on this point. Finally I had to promise that if the opportunity came along, we'd leave Bigtown. Meanwhile, she wanted to be able to take work when we had time to ourselves. *And* I had to make sure Mr King sorted our papers as soon as possible.

I agreed, and we stayed.

To Betty's astonishment, Mr King ordered a beautiful bible to be sent to our room. Exquisitely bound, it was a gift she accepted only on the understanding that she could pay for it over time. But for which, to my surprise, she gave Mr King a hearty big thanks, loud and clear, the next time we met him. Apart from that, they didn't really talk. She made it completely clear that any agreements Mr King and I reached, were his and my business, as long as they didn't affect her more than necessary.

Betty let him give her details of a suitable church. All friendly enough. She nodded politely and thanked him again. And, as a remarkable gesture, he even attended on one of those first Sundays. Making no more fuss over it than to give us a polite nod as we walked down the aisle after the service. He had an exquisite voice. I turned round during the hymns, as did others, and saw him sitting right at the back of the chapel, his hymn-book carefully rested on one of his stumps. Escorted by one of the girls from the house, who sat there with his hat in her hands.

Now and then he'd turn up like that in church, unannounced. And although their relationship wasn't markedly improved – and Betty only ever mentioned it tentatively and with some surprise – it seemed this gesture gave her some reassurance. If he could make sacrifices, perhaps she could too. And come Christmas, she gave him a piece of embroidery that she'd managed – with some difficulty – to stitch with her only hand. He gave her a hymn-book which was as beautiful, if not more, than the bible. Mr King permitted her to say grace.

And after a magnificent Christmas dinner, with Tim at the table and whatnot, they sang together from the new hymnbook. But then the usual silence fell. And pink cheeked, Betty carefully closed the book on her lap and gazed distantly into the fireplace.

"Excellent, excellent," said Mr King.

"We're ever-so grateful, Mr King," I whispered. "And Betty too, even if she isn't that great at puttin' it into words."

"Oh, don't give it a thought, Earl. You do your job here on earth and I do mine. And if we share a bit of the profits, nothing makes me happier." Mr King slapped a stumpy thigh.

"Thanks a lot."

"I might be the big guy and you might be the little guy here, but we're all equal before God," whispered Mr King. And we sat by the fireside while Betty took her afternoon nap, her belly filled with fine Christmas fare.

We're all equal before God – I'd heard him say that before, but in rather different circumstances...

Besides his countless sidelines – the wrestling, the cannery and various other enterprises, which I thankfully knew less about – Mr King's was the only bordello on the continent to offer the occasional freak. An additional attraction to the house's regular – although already exotic – selection. Betty should of course have been the biggest attraction of all in Mr King's house. But even excluding her, he had plenty of speciality acts dropping by to offer their services.

"And if there's anything at all, from God's glorious house of pleasure that my clientele desires, I shall endeavour – here in this humble shack – to give you everything Our Lord can offer. Call me God's go-between if you like. They've all been through these doors," I heard Mr King declare to his guests, laughing: "Eskimos...hermaphrodites...oiled Nubians...twins of every size and colour you could dream of...snake people...

dancers whose bodies will bend every which way...negroes who'll take her for you if you just want to watch...Chinese girls with dainty bound feet...Geishas...fat women who can barely get out of bed...and believe me ladies and gentlemen, a couple of them really don't...they lie in their rooms and wait, *bursting* with insatiable desire! We can provide women with any shape or length of leg...short, long, fat, smooth, hairy, knobbly kneed...just tell us how you want them! Whether you want young girls with full breasts, dwarf girls, dwarf boys, or Mexican wolf-women with the softest, blackest beards... women with hands and feet like lobsters ready to squeeze and claw...or men and women with frog-bodies to make your mouth water as they leap around...or women with waists as slim as the stem of the champagne glass you're holding now. Or visit Mr King's casino, and pit yourself against his armless and legless card players. Everything you could possibly imagine turns up in this house of pleasure at sometime. Some to just pleasure your eyes perhaps. Others to pleasure the flesh. If nothing else, just come to engage in an enthralling conversation over a great meal in the company of our fabulous guests. All you have to do is come! Come! Come!"

Most of it bullshit. But when Mr King was through with his spiel he'd sit there pink cheeked and with his glass raised, looking like he almost believed it himself.

Mr King's rhapsodies were something Betty and I never discussed.

THE KEY

"Everything they want. And a little bit more…"

Mr King smiled to himself as he dozed by the fireside. Then yawning, he winked at us both and squeezed my hand with a final *"Happy Christmas"*, before letting himself be wheeled to his bedroom.

What else can I say about Mr King? Except that I liked him.

Liked him a lot.

Not that I really have that much bad to say about him. And I enjoyed working in this line of business alright. It was like a dream, a fabulous dream. To begin with, we were paid just for *being around*. In the evening when the house was at it's busiest. We'd talk to the punters as a part of the entertainment. Occasionally, someone would pay to dine with us. But since Betty talked so little, and Earl Merrik a little too much, I was eventually put in charge of the cloakroom. Only very rarely did we experience any rudeness. Most of the guests were generous in their tips. And our wages were satisfactory and regular. So, that was how we spent our evenings in those early days – taking coats and handing out cloakroom tickets.

I was soon on good terms with nearly all the ladies in the house. Who'd throw me the occasional morsel, much to Betty's rarely vented despair. And in our free time, or when one of the girls took over in the cloakroom, I only had to take a stroll about the establishment, to feast my eyes – or sometimes more – on all sorts of exotic delicacies. Besides, Mr King had made it clear we mustn't be on permanent display in the cloakroom. The punters were to be kept on their toes, hungry for more, curious enough to return. So, as the orchestra played in the ballroom, I'd sit, mouth watering, groaning at the sight of the negresses in their soft silk dresses, winking and waving at me, and the oriental girls, dancing to the music, legs and more legs and long strings of pearls, soft feather boas and glistening lips. Kisses blown in the air. Milk-white young girls with soft, chubby cheeks and lustful, drunken eyes.

The excuse I usually gave my sister for a trip to the bar, was a cold glass of soda. On a good day I didn't hear a squeak out of her. But on bad days she could kick up a fuss, and demand we spend our break in our room. It was, she said, less noisy, less stressful, and we could make our own refreshments up there. Besides, if Mr King was as generous as he boasted, we could get them sent up. But usually, so long as she didn't have to see the snake or the monkey, she put surprisingly few obstacles in my way. In fact, she generally refused to acknowledge what was going on at all…this was somehow *my* work. And we had to have food. Clothes on our backs. A roof over our heads.

Mr King was rarely more offensive than you'd expect, or than was necessary for a man in his trade. He'd roll out the same old stories and chuck in a few well-rehearsed jokes – "Whores, whisky and straw," I'd hear him shout, in an attempt to titillate a hesitant guest. "All you need is a house filled with whores, whisky and straw!"

In reply to which somebody from the house – usually the barman, as he zealously polished the bar, or sometimes Tim Burley – would always yell out: "What d'you need straw for, Mr King?" Once, when I tried to chip in, I ended up covered in scratches from Betty jabbing her fingernails into my forearm.

"It's like this, you see," Mr King would answer, "when we've finished with the whores and we've drunk all the whisky, we'll set fire to the straw and the whores will run. And then we can start all over again!"

With that he'd slap the arse of a passing girl, who'd have

stuck it out for him with an expectant smile. That was usually enough to get the punters on track. And if, against all odds, they failed to laugh, Mr King would supply the laughter himself and pull a toothpick out from his pocket. Mr King was obsessed with his teeth, which he frequently cleaned with toothpicks, and he liked to hand these out to anybody and everybody, particularly his girls. Because if there was one thing more important than knockers and pussies in Mr King's opinion, it was good teeth. *"Lifesavers,"* Mr King called them. These toothpicks.

"Here, Earl, take a lifesaver," he'd say. "And give one to your sister!"

I soon knew the bordello like the back of my hand. And since our work in the cloakroom had been beyond criticism, I was eventually given the key to the house. Which meant my duties now included taking payment for the girls' services. The only hitch was that Betty would often put her hand over her ears to escape all the lurid details that the clients reeled off. Which might have been fine, if she hadn't tickled my neck so much by humming as well, to drown everything out. Later she received a polite request not to read from the Holy Book when there were punters in the cloakroom.

And when the shift was over I'd carry the cash dutifully up to the office and hand it over to Mr King who'd put it in his safe. Earl the money bearer. Earl with the key. I was the man of the house. The man of the house himself!

"Just remember one thing, Earl," Mr King said on the day he handed me the key. "I don't ask much of you. In fact, there's only one thing I ask…and that's that you're honest and straightforward."

Honest and straightforward…he'd repeat those words endlessly, as though they were greatest virtues in the world.

"You must be honest and straightforward. If there's one thing I can't tolerate, it's betrayal. Anyone who betrays me turns to dust in my hands. I loathe deserters. Do you understand, Earl? Are you with me?"

I nodded.

"Yes," I answered. "Yes, sir–r!" Then he placed the key in my hand. Like in a dream.

Initially Betty was less than thrilled about escorting Mr King to the wrestling matches at Olympen. But this changed when Olympen proved to be the place we'd meet the men who'd become our friends. We made friends in Bigtown. Real friends. For the first time in a long time. For as long as we could remember, if truth be told. And among these new friends, Cougher would be the man to win her heart.

It happened in a flash. I couldn't have been more surprised. And of all the dozens of men that fell in love with Betty, Cougher would be the one who'd finally have his way with her. Cougher, the freestyle wrestler on Christmas night, of all nights. All the men fell for Betty, and look where it got her. Now she's dead. My poor sister.

Mr King rolled into Olympen with us in tow, waving and smiling to the left and right. Delighted to be displaying his generous side. The Olympen was packed. Expectations were sky-high for this fight. Clifton "Cougher" Kaufman regularly ended up coughing blood, both during and after the toughest fights, and he was to face "Snakeman Jacob". And this was only one of the many championship belts up for grabs tonight. But however much tension there was in the room, something said Jacob would lose. All the odds and the public's sympathies were stacked against Jacob whose star turn was to drape a boa constrictor around the necks of his defeated opponents. Still, you couldn't help admire Jacob – he was brilliantly inventive and always delivered the goods. And even when he was almost too rat-arsed to stand, you knew you'd still get a show out of him. A show, and some supreme wrestling.

But Cougher's recent growing popularity, was putting

Jacob in an impossible situation. All the pre-match intrigues and storylines had been heavily biased towards him – Cougher was the hero who suffered endless betrayals, who fell victim to the other wrestlers' dirty tricks. And as his health deteriorated, he seemed to be defying death itself. He'd leave the ring at the end of most fights with a mouth full of blood. The more evil-minded punters even put bets on whether each appearance would be his last alive. Outside the ring too, Cougher was known for his good deeds, he and Frehley regularly raised money for charity. And there was something about his face that made you feel warm inside. So round and friendly, and always with a big smile. Sparkling white teeth in a bloodied mouth. Earlier in his career Cougher had gone by the name of Butterbean, a title inspired by his smiling countenance and physique. As a young man he'd been particularly large and the heat of the lamps over the ring made his skin gleam when he was in action. He was six foot eight and weighed in at thirty-two stone. But more than anything, Cougher looked like an overgrown baby – chubby thighs, cannon-ball body and short, chunky arms.

There was every reason to expect a fight of legendary proportion between these two. One was the king of dirty tricks. The other wasn't going to let any kind of dirty trick take him by surprise. Yet the crowd still couldn't decide who to cheer for. Cougher was the man they wanted to see victorious, while Jacob was the man they loved to hate. Nobody was better at whipping up a crowd and getting them to their feet than Jacob. He may not have been the *greatest* wrestler, or even the fittest, but he was one of the most charismatic.

Despite our lateness, we found our seats in all the commotion. Cougher was already standing in the ring waiting when Jacob came running in. Gleaming with perspiration, the snake in a sack over his shoulder. But when the umpire blew the whistle, Jacob didn't square up with Cougher as expected. Instead, he settled himself comfortably in his corner of the ring, and goaded Cougher, eyeing him up and down and squirming gleefully on his stool. Then he beckoned Cougher over with a mocking laugh, spitting out the occasional comment. And Cougher, sweltering and glistening under the hot lamps, wiped the sweat incredulously from his eyes, roared with anger and flung his arms wide in exasperation.

"Cummon, Fatty," Jacob roared, before rubbing his knuckles into his eyeballs, in imitation of a cry-baby.

"You see Jacob, there…?" said Mr King.

I nodded.

"I taught him everything he knows," the cripple lied.

Otherwise, we didn't say much. Angry mutterings and name-calling spread along the rows of benches. Mr King sat in tense silence, his fingers kneading the tyres of his wheelchair. And, as usual, Betty went into her shell. This was my time. I let it flow through me, like I was in a dream, while my carton of popcorn crumpled in my hand.

"Is Betty alright?" asked Mr King, without turning his gaze from the ring.

"Sure…sure…" I mumbled, my body rigid with anticipation. I didn't give a toss how Betty was, and Mr King didn't pursue the question. I was busy pouring popcorn down my throat with one hand, and waving the other, covering my suit with little white bits as they ran past my chin and down to the floor.

But then, as another hoarse roar rose from Cougher in the ring, Betty suddenly lifted her gaze. On our previous visits to Olympen, she'd always killed time by staring at the floor, or covering her eyes with her hand, while the clamour of the crowd sent shock waves through her body. She'd writhe on her chair, shudder nervously and gasp. She was not happy. I however, savoured every moment. Since I was a kid, there was nothing I'd wanted more than to step into a ring and vanquish them all. *Earl the Crusher. Merrik the Unbeatable*. But since I've neither a talent for acrobatics, nor fast with my punches, I wasn't cut out for it. But just being at the Olympen was the fulfilment of a dream. Until now Betty's anxiety had always stood in the way of a visit. So instead of worrying about her wellbeing, I was busy digging my fist into my carton of popcorn, and stuffing its salty butter-taste into me with a big grin.

"Enjoying yourself Earl?" said Mr King.

"You bet," I answered, my mouth full.

"Excellent, excellent. Anything else I can get for you?"

"Nah. I've got everythin' I need. Thank you, Mr King. This is totally and utterly fantastic. And I can see everythin' from 'ere! Everythin'!"

"Are you a bit thirsty maybe?"

I peered down into my half empty carton.

"Hmm. Well, now you mention it. A touch."

Instantly a large cup of soda appeared in front of me. Meanwhile, almost against her own will, Betty's gaze grudgingly followed the man who was about to win her heart. She clenched her fist as Cougher lifted Jacob into the air and smashed him to the floor. She gasped and whispered *poor man* when the blood gushed from Cougher's mouth in sharp bursts. And now it was streaming from a gash in his head too. Jacob threw Cougher against the ropes, sending him back and forth across the ring on shaky legs, before shooting an arm out straight so his fist met Cougher's blood-spattered Adam's apple. The giant went down on his back with a thud, and a column of blood spurted from his mouth. And as he lay there, Jacob strutted round the ring, rubbing his knuckles, gloating over his own magnificence and surveying the audience through narrowed eyes. He flung his arms wide towards the stands so the public could feed their eyes on his powerful – if not so muscular – torso. Smeared with sweat and Cougher's blood.

The moment had come for Jacob's star turn. Leaping between the ropes he fetched his sack, unwound its strap and tipped the boa constrictor into the ring. It glistened against the mat. It slithered around on the soft, blood-spattered underlay, searching for an exit. Its tongue flicked in and out of its mouth, in and out. It was time to choose sides. And now the indecisive public divided in two. One flank booed, pandemonium nearly breaking out in one stand. The other half, cheered the snake on, even though everybody knew what was coming. As for me…I was more than ready to see the snake. My sympathies may have been inclined towards Cougher…but I wanted it all…wanted to see the lot.

Cougher stirred. Everything went still. He lifted his right arm, then one leg, then almost rolled into a seated position. But his body immediately sank back lifelessly onto the mat. Then the public began to chant for the snake.

"Jo-nas, Jo-nas, Jo-nas."

Jacob lifted the snake. It glinted in the lamplight and coiled itself around his forearm.

This was all too much for Betty now, and she passed out.

"The snake, Earl, look at the snake…" she gasped.

Before letting the climax slip past her. Jacob kissed it and laid it on Cougher's blood-spattered throat. At which point Cougher revived, quaking and writhing as the snake squeezed his throat until the blood stopped flowing, and the applause threatened to lift the roof. In a gesture of triumph, Jacob wiped the sweat from his hair and strolled majestically round the ring, a haughty look on his face.

Cougher had fallen victim to the king of dirty tricks.

But we'd be grateful for Betty's fainting fit. Concerned

at his escort passing out, Mr King suggested I revive my comatose sister with a trip to the changing rooms. Hoping to get a look behind the scenes I wasn't slow to comply, and got swiftly to my feet with a little help from Tim.

Which was how we met our new friends.

Tim took us down to the changing rooms. The air hung heavily with sweat, and I gasped as the door opened. In the light of the ceiling lamp, Cougher sat surrounded by a band of anxious, and awesomely tall, friends. He was bleeding profusely from a cut in the back of his head. In the heat of the fight, Jacob had left the ring for a moment to steal a folding chair from one of the spectators, and getting back in the ring he'd wasted no time smashing it into Cougher's skull. Now the doctor was standing over Cougher's round, hunched body, jabbing a needle determinedly through the layers of skin and then tugging. Expressionless, Cougher lifted a white handkerchief to his mouth occasionally and coughed. Meanwhile, Jacob stood in a corner in the background, his face etched with guilt. He was doing his necessaries into a barrel. His newly inherited championship belt lifted above his waist. The sack with the snake lay on the lap of a man, who I took to be an old wino sleeping things off on the changing-room bench. The room certainly reeked of spirits.

Frehley got up, unsteady on his legs, and his back stooped under what was – at least for *him* – a low ceiling. "The Giant" Frehley measured seven foot two inches in his socks and weighed in at nearly forty stone. His breath lay heavy in the room. And it was as if you could hear his enormous lungs open and close with each breath. It smelled of a distillery in there. With one raised eyebrow and his mouth – lips thick as fingers – hanging slightly open, he watched with irritation as the doctor's rough stitches went in and out of Cougher's red and white wound.

"Jacob," bellowed Frehley. The voice of the man known

as the eighth wonder of the world, rang out in the tiled room. "Jacob," said the giant, "I'm very disappointed in you, and if you just dared drag that cowardly arse of yours into the ring with me, you'd know a thing or two."

Cougher looked up. "Leave the kid alone, Frehley," he spluttered. "If I'd got my hands on that chair he'd have been sat here, not me."

Frehley growled angrily and shook his head. When he spoke, the sound reverberated in your body – it tickled and tingled through our bellies and ribcages.

"Jacob puts food on our table. And if more people were as generous with chairs, we'd have less to worry about."

Frehley lifted his hand as if to say something, but staggered forwards instead, and got an irritated gesture from the doctor. With an angry snort, Frehley lifted his bottle back to his mouth. It was unusual to see him in a bad mood – he generally enjoyed life to the full, only too aware that his days were numbered. The way things were, Frehley was growing towards his own extinction. He was in danger of being crushed by his own weight, and had already lived way beyond his doctors' expectations. So he lived each day as his last. And with the same extraordinary appetite. Besides being the largest man on earth in his time, and definitely the largest *freestyle wrestler* the world had ever seen, Frehley drank a case of beer – if not more – every day. On an average weekday he'd eat a two-pound steak as though it was the most natural thing in the world. Often after devouring a whole chicken for starters. Washed down with a bottle of wine or two. Then for desert he'd knock back a bottle of cognac. And if Frehley passed out after emptying this down him there was nothing to do but wrap him up warm right where he lay. I, for one, barely reached his waist, and when the doctor got up, who I reckoned to be of more normal stature, he only just reached his chest.

Cougher looked up at Frehley. "Perhaps you should save some of that beer for tomorrow?" he said, coughing again.

Frehley turned his back on him and squinted at the fight plan in the dim light of the ceiling lamp.

Frehley had been one of Mr King's discoveries too. Already as a teenager he was eating his way into penury. His body refused to stop growing, and any attempt to find a cure was in vain. The growing just continued, and however hard he worked, there was never enough money or hours in the day. He was eating enough for a whole family before he hit adulthood. A solution had finally presented itself when Mr King – who'd just lost his legs in his awful accident – offered to be his manager. Mr King trained him up as a freestyle wrestler, of all things. Not that Frehley would go down in history as the fastest or smartest wrestler – or even the most daring – but he was indisputably the *biggest*. Everything about Frehley was big. He could have clamped his hand round my head and squashed it like a tomato, if he'd wanted. And as if he didn't defy nature enough already, he chose a life as an acrobat and bodybuilder. Without perhaps ever really being either.

At the height of his career, Frehley even got his own rail wagon so he could travel the country in comfort. With its own furniture and beds in the biggest sizes out. At other times he drove around in an old milk truck, with its original seats taken out and replaced with a long bench. And as a rule Cougher, and Cougher's loyal partner, the dwarf Spinks, would travel along with Frehley in his wagon or truck. And whenever he arrived in a new town he'd get a royal welcome. With garlands of flowers and banners at the station. Although when Cougher, the only guy who came anywhere near to matching Frehley size-wise, came along, he'd have to hide in the bathroom of the wagon. Or at the back of the milk truck. Because, though he and Frehley were the best of buddies in real life, up on the billboards they were bitter enemies.

But those days were over. Frehley had retired. Though he'd occasionally step back in the ring to raise money for charitable causes. He'd started the wrestling school with his own savings. In collaboration with Cougher, who was also getting on in years now. Together they organised most of the wrestling events in Bigtown and the surrounding areas. But even if Frehley's days as a touring wrestler were over, he still used his wagon when occasion presented – filling it with kids from an orphanage or a hospital maybe, and taking them for a ride.

But this early retirement had not been to Mr King's liking. Not only was Frehley a lost goldmine to him, but he was suddenly a worthy opponent. Still, they must have reached some kind of agreement – Frehley wasn't exactly a guy you'd want to fall out with, and however disgruntled Mr King was, he allowed several of his own wrestlers to train at the new school. For free, it must be said, so that Frehley did balance the accounts a little with the old amputee. It was an arrangement that seemed to suit them both. So although they weren't exactly buddies any more, they seemed to have no qualms about letting their names appear side by side on the relevant contracts or advertising for any jointly arranged events.

And now, there he stood. Massive in that cramped room. With Betty and I slumped on the changing-room bench, as Tim went off to fetch some cold water to liven her up. At last Jacob shuffled out from his corner. The doctor tidied the contents of his bag, in preparation for the next man, as the roar of the crowd indicated the end of the fight that was taking place above our heads.

Suddenly Jacob took the belt off and offered it to Cougher. "Here," he mumbled. Cougher looked up. "Here, take it.

I'll lose it next time we meet anyway."

Cougher shook his head and laughed. Another large red stain appeared on his white handkerchief as he wiped his mouth.

"No," he answered. "You did no more than was expected of you. Keep the belt." He got up and his body threw the room into darkness. Beneath the dangling ceiling lamp the two men embraced. Then Cougher gave him a friendly slap on the shoulder, and Jacob padded over to Frehley's beer crate. Uncapping two bottles he handed one over to Cougher, before his sly gaze suddenly fell on Betty and me, over on the bench.

"So, what have we got here?" he asked, putting the bottle to his lips. Jacob squinted at us in the dark.

"My sister passed out durin' the fight. So Mr King's nigger brought us down 'ere," I hastened to explain.

"What was that? Mr King's *nigger*, you say? Well, well, well, what d'you know…Have you seen…" Jacob turned to the rest of the gang. "Have you seen what Mr King's *nigger* has brought for us here, boys?"

"Yup. Tim came down here, dumped them, and left again," said the doctor. He washed his hands quickly and came and joined the others who were gathering round us.

The changing room was chock-full with bodies and sweat. It was hard to breathe and made your eyes sting. Like sal ammoniac up your nose. Frehley squinted at us in bemusement and placed a heavy foot in front of us. He was wiping the sweat off his broad brow, and lost in his enormous fist the beer bottle looked almost miniature.

"I think you should take a look at the girl, Doctor Irving," Frehley mumbled. The doctor immediately started examining Betty, shining a light in her eyes from a little torch.

"I know who they are." Cougher's voice filtered gently in through the crowd. "They're the Merrik twins…"

"That's right." I said, adding: "Earl and Betty Merrik."

The big men scrutinised us over their bottles. Cougher said no more. With a smile, and eyes glued on Betty, he dried himself meditatively with his towel before letting his gaze drop shyly to the floor. Then he peered back up at her hesitantly, and slumped back onto his stool, exhausted.

While the doctor was examining Betty, I observed Frehley. He was swearing over the fight lists under the light of the ceiling lamp, a piddling little pencil in his hand. Aggravated and a bit pissed – probably from knocking back a crate or more – he swayed to and fro in the dim light.

Frehley's body was big, but the price he paid was bigger. He was a prisoner in that huge body. It was as if impediments clung about this giant in an attempt to bring him to his knees... you might even have thought the problems themselves were responsible for his enormous growth, as they piled up. Life was like one long painful rap on the knuckles – in the form of book pages that refused to separate, tangled threads and flexes, gramophone records that crumbled like cookies before his eyes, or just refused to play, boxes of tiny drawing pins or screws and bolts that practically exploded around him as he tried to open them. And then these screws, bolts, drawing pins – or coins – might as well have been *glued* to the floor. A machine that worked without testing his patience had yet to be invented...the dials on the telephone, the knobs on the wireless set...they all resisted his fat fingertips. And once a thing was broken, there wasn't a chance in hell he could take out a toolbox and fix it himself. When he was on tour, and the hotels weren't forewarned, his bed would reach to his knees, and the shower head to his waist. He hadn't sat in a bathtub since he was a kid. Wherever he went everybody felt compelled to touch him and press him for an autograph... always on miniscule scraps of paper with miniscule pens. Even adults turned into kids when they met Frehley, climbing all over him. But more than anything, it was the everyday stuff

58

that drove him wild…the details that other people didn't give a thought to…apart from the telephones and wireless sets, there were the pencils that vanished in his hands, the typewriter keys that stuck together, the wooden beams his head bashed into when he was distracted, lifts that went on strike and stairs that threatened to give way…and then the clothes and shoes that not only cost a fortune, but had to be ordered weeks in advance. He was big and amazingly strong, but the price for this was that he was forced to move through life so slowly… since just about nothing in the world was made to suit a man like him.

And this was where Uncle Rust had come into the picture. Cougher wasn't much help – seeing as he was the one guy who matched Frehley size-wise, and struggled in much the same way – but Uncle Rust was light on his feet. He could run up and down the stairs for little things…and what was more, he was able to *hold* these dainty objects. Uncle Rust's fingers fitted telephone dials…he could even use a typewriter without looking at the keys…he could pick up pencils when they fell to the floor…bend down to pick up small change and count the takings…and his numbers fitted all those tiny little boxes in the ledger.

It had all started when Uncle Rust had been thrown out onto the street after getting on the wrong side of the law, and Frehley had offered to put him up for a night or two. It had been a favour to begin with, but Uncle Rust soon proved so indispensable to Frehley that he immediately appointed him as his assistant. So, Uncle Rust worked for Frehley as his factotum. And I worked for Mr King. In that sense, the two of us were alike…both of us being little men…although Uncle Rust stood head and shoulders above most.

Right now though, Frehley wasn't giving his assistant the friendliest of glances. He was still cursing over the fight lists, and wiping his brow with the back of his hand. Meanwhile, next to Betty, who was still being examined by the doctor, somebody stirred on the bench. It was Uncle Rust. He tipped his hat back and looked down in surprise – if not irritation – at Jacob's sack that lay draped across his lap. The bundle began to stir. Jacob laughed and winked at me.

Uncle Rust cleared his throat. "I'm not sure I quite appreciate your sense of humour," he said drily. His voice sounded like a cranky door opening. But without batting an eyelid he lifted up the sack containing the snake and placed it carefully on the bench beside him, before calmly sitting up as though he'd calculated every move. His gangly body was so thin and bony his trousers would have slipped down, without the extra holes in his belt.

"Well, well, well. What have we here?" said Uncle Rust.

"You'd better ask Cougher. He knows who they are," said Jacob. "The Merrik twins. Seems like they belong to Mr King. Tim dumped them in here before he went off. And that squirt there called Tim a *nigger*..."

"Merrik, what-was-it?" asked Uncle Rust, puffy eyed and craning his neck towards us. "Well, well, well. What d'yeh know." He shoved his hands in his pockets and his tongue searched lazily for something under his top lip.

Uncle Rust wasn't the easiest man to get close to. But once you got past the first scepticism, there was no limit to what he'd do for you. Despite his affliction he was – still is – a man of the best qualities. The only hitch with Uncle Rust was that he was on and off the needle. Mostly on. Though this didn't stop him being hard working, punctual and disciplined. As long as he got his necessary medicine, he kept on track. It was easy to think of him as old – he *looked* like an old man – but it was hard to tell whether it was age or the constant flow of morphine in his veins. But no matter if he was on the needle or not, Uncle Rust was always smartly turned out in a suit, tie and hat. So if you didn't look too closely, you'd assume he was just an ordinary guy on his way to or from the office – hat on, and reading matter tucked under his arm. Not that Uncle Rust was the least bit ordinary…here was a man incapable of doing the dirty on anyone. And although he needed a bit of help himself from time to time, his main talent was probably taking care of others. If Uncle Rust hadn't moved into the garret over the wrestling school, it was doubtful whether Frehley and Cougher's project would have stayed afloat.

Uncle Rust might not have been the man we saw most of, but in the end – when the shit hit the fan with Mr King and us – it was thanks to him we got out of Bigtown alive. And Uncle Rust was the one who took the rap for us when the time came. But right now, Frehley walked over to him, passed him the fight list and let the pencil roll out of his big palm and into his hand. Uncle Rust turned his expressionless face up towards his big friend, before giving him a faint, dull smile.

"Hey," said Frehley, "if you're done sleeping, maybe you could make yourself useful."

"Sure, sure," said Uncle Rust, squinting at the list through puffy eyes. "Let's see now…we're…Jesus, we're nearly done for the night. Can you credit it? That went fast!"

"Yeah, of course it goes fast, when you sleep through it all!" Frehley growled, grabbing another beer.

Frehley might be irritated now, but he rarely complained about Uncle Rust's work. *"Uncle Rust never rests,"* he'd say. And Frehley tried to keep him on the rails. But once in a while when things did go adrift, he always made sure he was alright. Fixed his groceries, his clothes and bills before things fell apart. And if it got too bad, Uncle Rust would take matters into his own hands, pack his things and move into Frehley's wagon, instead of the garret over the school. Mainly so as not to be a bother. But usually – when he wasn't working or away sick – you'd find him in the cafeteria just a block away from Mr King's bordello.

The stench of the giant's breath wafted towards the bench where we were sitting. He belched and then helped himself to another bottle, which seemed once again to disappear in his big hand. From his pocket the doctor produced some smelling salts, generally used to perk up wrestlers, and snapped the cartridge under Betty's nose.

"You oughter go easy with that stuff, doc. Whatever goes through 'er, goes through me sooner or..." I got no further before my nose exploded. I leapt up from the bench with a jolt that could have snapped Betty's neck in two.

"Holy shit! What the fuck's that?" I bellowed, bringing my hand to my nose, before it exploded into another sneeze. It burned.

"Steady there," said Frehley. "Steady, littl'un,"

"Huh?" I snarled, rubbing my face.

"Careful with this one," Cougher said to Frehley, laughing.

The doctor went to put his arm around Betty, probably just to help her sit back down, and I don't really know what came over me, but I swung round as swiftly as we'd got up. My head was buzzing like it was full of angry wasps.

"Just get your fuckin' paws off 'er, doc. And now we've got her back on 'er feet, I want that fuckin' snake gone before she sees it...or she'll pass out again."

"Bumpety-bum-bum," Frehley mimicked, smacking his thick lips. "He's got some mouth on him, this whippersnapper."

Betty was standing beside me now, stiff as a poker, glaring in terror at these huge men. And the instant she heard the word *snake* and spotted Jacob prowling in the background, grinning stupidly and with his beard covered in beer froth, she threatened to collapse again…the smelling salts were clearly the only thing keeping her upright. Frehley eased us gently back down onto the bench, and stepped back.

"You…you're alive," she whispered, looking over at Cougher with big eyes. Cougher answered with a gaze filled with tenderness.

But almost as fast as we were pushed down on the bench, we were back up again. Almost as though we'd been yanked up by the left hand. There it was quivering in front of us. For the first time since our arrival at the bordello, *the thing* had manifested itself again. And now, in a manner totally unfamiliar, the hand guided me straight over to Frehley and reached up towards him like an eager dog. Completely numb. Fingers and palm. And going of its own accord.

"Steady now, littlun," said Frehley, laughing.

I couldn't think what to say, at first.

"Eh…eh…I reckon it wants you ter say 'ello to it," I mumbled.

"Oh, really? It wants me to say hello? Crikey!" Frehley laughed. His teeth seemed small compared to the rest of his face. As though there was a smaller man concealed behind his face, and a smaller mouth behind the thick lips and prominent nose. The hand twisted itself round so as to slip, upside-down, into Frehley's right hand. Baffled, he gave a bow and squeezed it gently.

Then the hand swung decisively to the left to greet Uncle Rust with equal eagerness. He peered down at it quizzically, one eyebrow raised and hands buried in his pockets.

"Oh boy," he gasped, before finally stretching a hesitant hand out. "Well, well, well. I'll be damned!" He took the hand and shook it. "William Aukrust."

"Earl and Betty," I said, trying to smooth things over. "Earl and Betty Merrik."

But when it came to Jacob's turn, he just eyed us coldly up and down and snuck himself another beer. Then he ran his fingers through his curly black hair, dripping with sweat.

"I ain't shakin' that thing," he said, lifting the bottle to his lips.

Betty pulled away from him. The others probably assumed she was offended. But I could feel how hard her heart was pumping in her ribcage – so hard I thought it was going to leap out onto the floor. No. Betty wasn't offended – she was terrified. This, for her, was like greeting evil personified.

"Oh, come on Jacob," came Cougher's hoarse voice. "Show some manners."

Jacob grunted. He might be used to snakes, but he was more sceptical about taking this quivering object in his hand.

"Alright! I'm *Jacob*," he gave a brief handshake. "Satisfied?"

He pulled on a jacket and began stuffing its lining with beers. With his championship belt round his waist and his jacket bursting with bottles, he grabbed the sack with the snake and announced moodily that he was off to the wrestling school to sleep. And as one bottle after another crashed to the floor all the way out to the backyard, we heard Jacob holler and curse until the fire door finally slammed behind him. It would be a long time before we met him again, and then the mood would be very different. Meanwhile, Cougher would be content to let revenge wait. Besides, Jacob looked like he somehow needed that belt.

When it came to Cougher's turn to greet the hand, he misunderstood. Still dazed from his fight and with blood trickling into his eyes, he mistook the hand for Betty's and leaned forward to give it a kiss.

The other men laughed. But the sight of Cougher kissing *the thing* sent shivers up my spine. Cougher smiled, and without letting go of the hand, he fixed his eyes lovingly on Betty. And as they stood like that, and Betty finally dared to meet his gaze, I felt the sensation slowly return to the hand. I might even have been able to move my fingers, if they'd not been locked in Cougher's big, calloused fist.

"I'm Betty," whispered Betty.

"Cougher," came the gruff reply. "And you?"

"Earl," I answered, "Earl Merrik."

"Well, I'm Cougher. And if you've no objection, I'd like to invite your sister out to eat one day. You are, of course, welcome to keep us company..." he said with a wink.

"Well, well, well. What d'you know..." said Uncle Rust. "Looks like our Cougher's found himself a sweetheart."

"Yup, sure does," said Frehley.

Within minutes, Cougher, Uncle Rust and Frehley were ranged around us, and Betty was in floods telling them about the dreadful predicament she was sure we'd landed ourselves in.

The only person who seemed to register my existence at all, was Uncle Rust, who grabbed one of the bottles and slipped it – lovely and cold – into my hand.

"Ok, my friend, tell me..."

Uncle Rust dumped himself down on the bench. I took a deep breath and a large swig, before taking the plunge.

MUMBO JUMBO

I'd be exaggerating if I said I enjoyed the situation. The way Betty jumped in there and poured out her heart to these men in the changing room. It was way too sudden. And besides, I actually liked it where we were. But though I certainly didn't have any plans to move, I was as excited as Betty, if not more, that Bigtown was bringing us *friends*. Proper friends. A rare commodity. After all, real friends can be very difficult to get your paws on. Particularly when you've been dealt a fate like ours. Although there are some friends, like Mr King, that come almost for free. To begin with at least.

The atmosphere was a bit prickly in the car going home. Mr King seemed irritable and withdrawn when he realised where Tim had taken us. It had been his suggestion that we visit the changing room, but he hadn't meant *that* changing room. Mr King had wanted us to get to know *his* wrestlers... not Frehley's...and he certainly hadn't intended us to enjoy their company alone and without supervision. But although I overheard him yelling at Tim later that night, he bit his tongue when it came to us. He asked a few guarded questions about what it had been like in the changing room but beyond that he didn't say much. Just *one* thing...

"Remember who took you in, Earl, and gave you a roof over your head."

Despite Mr King's displeasure, we soon made it a daily routine to stroll down to the cafeteria where Cougher, Frehley and Uncle Rust were regulars. Besides, it was close – only a block away from the bordello – so we could make these little excursions, without it being a thorn in Mr King's side, or my needing a change of shirt.

And I was sitting there one day, rather chuffed with myself, wearing a new outfit and poking my teeth with one of Mr King's lifesavers. Trying to ignore the religious drivel my sister was occupying herself with, while deep down she was tripping with excitement at the thought of Cougher turning up. Uncle Rust was sitting opposite us. I was usually the one who'd end up chatting with him, or playing him in a round of cards without saying much. But whenever the big guys took time coming, Betty would monopolise the conversation completely. Then I'd just have to wait and hope that God would hurry up and turn her tap off. But today, to my horror, I noticed that Uncle Rust was playing along with her. And although I hinted for him to stop while the going was good, he continued to pour petrol on the flames.

"Oh, c'mon, damn it…" I sighed, when Uncle Rust ignored my suggestion again of bringing the cards out.

"Cool down, Earl…all in good time," he said, smacking his lips. "Or is it too much for an old bugger to get a bit of elbow-room to finish his soup?"

"Go on, eat your soup. But do you really 'ave to fire my sister up like this?"

Uncle Rust wiped his mouth and laughed.

"Yeah, you can laugh," I said. "You ain't the one who's gotta spend the rest of the day tryin' to get her back down-to-earth. She'll end up fuckin' sleepin' bolt upright if you carry on like that…Ain't no good for a night's sleep…nor the digestion, I can tell you."

"The digestion?"

"Yeah, have *you* ever sat on the bog with people preachin' over yer?"

Uncle Rust shook his head.

"Well, the last thing yer need, I can promise yer, is a born-again fluffbrain preachin' holes in yer 'ead…"

67

Uncle Rust bowed his head for a moment, letting his food go down.

"Earl," he said eventually, in a quiet voice, "if you can't put up with hearing your sister talk a bit, I suggest you take a stroll round the block, and we can take that deck of cards out when you get back..."

"But, but I can't just..." I began.

"You can't what?" asked Uncle Rust, grinning. "What can't you do, eh?"

"Oh, forget it!" I groaned, my sister sniggering idiotically next to me.

For reasons best known to himself, the old sod had clearly decided to aggravate the shit out of me that day. Exactly what he wanted to achieve – it wasn't easy to say. Perhaps he couldn't bear my self-satisfied grin. Because before Betty's religious speculations had taken off, everything had pointed to this being an exceptionally good day. First I'd been bathed and scrubbed by one of the girls of the house, and then she'd given me a going over with scissors and comb – it had turned out, that not only did the house offer the healthiest and liveliest girls, but some of Bigtown's best hairdressers. Even Betty let them pamper her like a doll when she was in the mood. But there was a big turnover of girls, so we had to grab the opportunity, as and when. Not all the girls were equally keen to associate with the freaks.

And when my new suit had arrived back from the laundry that morning, and I sat there freshly barbered and my chin smelling nice, I pulled out my wallet.

"Earl," Betty hissed, obviously feeling that the girl had already been more than accommodating enough with me. "Have you got no shame?"

"Calm down, Betty," I whispered, with my eyes fixed on the girl. "Well? Are we in business?"

"Don't worry, Mr Merrik," she'd said, shrugging her shoulders and getting down on her knees.

Now, I was sitting here feeling hacked off, with a soup spoon as a mirror, and comforting myself with the smell of the girl still clinging to my fingers and throat, while Uncle Rust took the rise out of me. Probably intending no harm. But I had a sense of where this could end. As soon as Betty was done with all her religious prattle, it wasn't impossible that she'd start talking about *the thing*...now she was on a roll. Even though she was usually so reluctant to say a word on the subject to anyone. And, for all I knew, that might be precisely what the old sod was angling after.

Still, I brushed the thought away as fast as it came...Uncle Rust was hardly known for nosing in people's affairs...nor for poking about unnecessarily in their souls. Which is why it took me time to see where we were headed. Preoccupied as I was with my new haircut and the fabulous aroma.

When it came to *the thing* and its conduct in the changing room, it was obvious that Uncle Rust had been the only one to really take note. After Cougher had kissed it, and certainly after my sister had begun pouring out all her fears and sufferings, it seemed the hand had been erased from the memories of the rest of the gang. But despite the fact Uncle Rust had on occasion steered the conversation, very delicately, onto the subject, I'd always managed to sidestep it. Now, the idea that he might finally give Betty the chance to bring out her favourite party-piece, made me nauseous. True, she generally had the good sense to avoid mentioning *the thing*, but as soon she got on good terms with anybody she'd always drag out the story of *the heart*...how she loved to talk about the heart!

And in the light of this new situation it was hard to know what to expect.

Perhaps she'd say with barely concealed excitement: "Earl

doesn't have a heart." And then, worse still, lower her voice and say with an involuntary shudder: "What keeps Earl alive is the...*the thing*."

Yes, right, and with Earl and *the thing* preying like some parasite on Betty and her precious heart it was hardly surprising her life was pure hell. And guess how much she'd have loved it, when everybody's eyes turned on that vile brother of hers. Now that she finally felt secure enough to let everything out of the bag, everything that scared her most. So our new friends would see what a scumbag they were dealing with. But then, after she'd scared herself to death with her own drivel, who'd have to sit up with her...after the sun had gone down and her friends had gone home?

Yes, too right. *Earl*. Earl would have to sit there and listen to it all. And apply every last brain cell to keep his cry-baby sister safe and warm.

Watching the situation unfold, with my back to the wall and grinding my teeth, that was exactly what I saw coming...and before I could stop her, my sister was in feet first.

"You know something, Uncle Rust," she said, taking a delicate sip from her teacup.

"No..."

"Some days I actually think it's *the thing* that keeps Earl alive."

Cool as a cucumber. Holding her teacup like the town's first lady without an anxious fibre in her body, she talked about her brother, as though he was sitting ten miles away.

"Christ Almighty, Betty!" I groaned. "D'you really have to wave your arse in Uncle Rust's face like that?'

Uncle Rust coughed, then laughed, spluttering soup over his trousers.

"Sorry, Earl, sorry," he said, taking a swig of water.

Just then, my knee started going up and down like a piston.

Calmly Betty put her cup down and rested her hand gently on my leg.

"Steady, Earl, we're among friends now…"

As if that would make it better. More than anything I was tempted to give my sister a clip round the ear. But I held my peace, for fear of making things worse. And sat there like some sort of maniac, hoping it would all pass quickly. My only prayer was that Cougher would turn up to distract her before things went too far. The prospects of any sensible conversation, or even a game of cards, had long since vanished. Eyeing the potential fallout of the day, I was more than prepared to lower my expectations.

But instead Cougher kept us waiting. And Betty used the time for all it was worth, putting Uncle Rust firmly in the picture. And when at last she was done, and her insane jabber had finally come to an end, Uncle Rust wiped the corners of his mouth with his napkin and leaned back with a freshly lit cigarette.

"Betty my dear, I don't think it's so bad. There's bound to be a natural explanation, you'll see."

After all this time I'm used to people talking over my head. One way or another. And even if that day took the biscuit, Uncle Rust's response could have been worse. And looking at him closer, his eyes did look extra glazed, so perhaps it was the fucking needle poking about where the sun don't shine.

"Look, just remember," sighed Uncle Rust. "All of us carry a little lump of hell inside us."

"Oh?" whispered the lady.

"And for anybody with even a modicum of soul, it's a daily battle to keep it contained…this little lump of hell they perpetually have to carry about inside them. And that's what it sounds like to me…this *thing* you're describing…that you and Earl have."

71

"Really?"

"And this lump of hell…it can cause people to do the strangest things. But what matters most is how you choose to attack it…because if you don't, it'll attack *you first*…you can be sure of that, my dear girl."

I couldn't hold back much longer.

"Uncle Rust, I don't suppose you could finish off with a story with softer edges, eh? Betty ain't gonna sleep for weeks, if this ends how I think…"

"Finish? I've barely begun!"

"Oh, be my guest…" I sighed.

"What matters," continued Uncle Rust, "is how you launch your defence. Because if this lump of hell develops a taste for the antidote of your choice, it's hard to say where it'll all end. You might be six foot under before it's gorged its fill, this creepy crawly in your soul, this *Uglybugly*," he muttered through clenched teeth.

"Thugbugly?" Betty whispered cautiously.

"Yes, *Uglybugly*…" That was the name Uncle Rust called it, and the word rose from deep in his throat with a gurgle.

"And this bug finds nourishment in all the things human beings can't let go of…or come to terms with…the things they refuse to forgive…things that rankle with them…the bitterness in the world…the despicable actions of one human being to another…that pop back up again and again like jack-in-the-boxes…however hard we try put a lid on them. And the two of you are so closely bound, so this bug has to gnaw on something. But if you've got off as lightly as I think you have – not that I intend to drone on about it – then I think perhaps you should be grateful."

You'd have thought Uncle Rust breathed with his ears, the way he went on. But I was getting seriously worried now, that my sister was about to reveal a whole raft of things that might put the matter in a whole new light. Things that have cost us dear. Things that would keep Uncle Rust awake at nights, if I didn't stop her in her tracks.

"Thankful?" I said, gawping. "Look at us! Would you like to be bundled together with your sister like this?"

"You both have your health, so perhaps it's just a matter of how you perceive it. Or how you *attack* it, as I said…because the hell that's burning inside this shirt of mine, has certainly developed a taste for its medicine. And no matter how much I feed it, Earl, it always wants more. So if you're proposing a swap, I'm all ears."

He had me there for a moment.

"Perhaps you've been given a twofold blessing and a twofold curse…perhaps Betty's got the ace of hearts…and you've got the bug in your soul…and this low-life bug might occasionally take the controls and muck about…but you should take the good with the bad, if you ask me."

Uncle Rust tipped his hat back.

"It might even be God's way of keeping you on your toes… of keeping things in balance. Who knows, perhaps you'd be dead if it weren't for a touch of *Uglybugly*. After all, the two of you are sitting here, all spruced up and pucker, while other people are lying in the gutter, weeping."

Right. So, I might be sitting there with my sister wedged into my side, but what did that matter when we looked *pucker?* Yes, Uncle Rust really had picked his day to take the piss.

"You know what, Earl," he went on, "this is something most people struggle with…so I wouldn't take it so personally, if I was you."

"Well," I said. "I don't think you've understood my sister."

I didn't agree with him – I'm not so sure now – but back then I just thought the old boy was too full of himself.

"I think we're carryin' a third man about inside us. No

kiddin', it's like I practically know 'im for real. And this devil can't talk for itself and can't run off. So it sits 'ere…right between us…doin' its best to fuck things up for us. D'you understand?" I spat out my toothpick, and pointed to where our ribcages met.

"A *parasite*, Earl?"

"Call it what you will…but *the thing* is right 'ere…and I reckon that if we could just get to look inside, you'd see what I'm talkin' about."

"Well, that's your way of seeing it. And maybe it's not so different to mine when it comes to it. But just ignore my blathering, Earl. What do I know – you're probably right."

He leaned forwards and gave me a slap on the knee.

"No problem, Uncle Rust."

"All living things attract parasites. People are born with the weirdest things in their bodies, so why not…There's sure to be a natural explanation."

"Yeah, that's right," I said, smiling.

"But if you *are* wrong – I think this *thing* you're both describing would die of its own accord if you gave each other some elbow-room. Give it a bit of light, and it'll lose its hold, you'll see. If something can't tolerate the daylight, it falls apart, when we have the courage to take it out and look at it. And if it *can* tolerate a little light, then at least we can find some comfort in knowing what it is."

"That's it exactly! I'm gonna give it light. If I can just get my sister to come into one of them machines…it'll get all the light it can take!"

"But everything's created by Our Lord…" said Betty, with a sarcastic smile, in an awkward attempt at closing the conversation or bringing it back to her favourite subject.

I'd noticed her anxiety spreading through her body. She had goose bumps all over, and now and then the odd shudder went through her. And if I hadn't been daft enough to get involved in this idiotic debate, she'd have started on about the gold-paved streets of Heaven and so on ages ago. At least that would have been preferable to this.

"What I'm tryin' to say is that *the thing* has either been with us forever, or someone's cut a space for it and then sewed us back together. You realise we're unexplainable? We're a medical impossibility, for God's sake!"

I rapped the table with my spoon and started on my cold onion soup.

"I ain't much of a believer in either the Devil or God, but there's just somethin' about it...natural or manmade...this *thing* 'as a mind of its own."

"You might be right, Earl," said Uncle Rust, scraping his spoon round his bowl. "But I still think that this *thing*, whatever it is, might be better at getting you *out* of trouble, than the two of you are at getting *into* trouble..."

"Yer what!?" I croaked. "Christ, there's a lot o' mumbo-jumbo pourin' out of you today! What are you on?" I said, but instantly bit my tongue – I wasn't about to give this smart arse reason to take offence. Besides, I wanted to show him that Earl could be equally smart, and shake a trick out of his sleeve when he wanted.

"Sure, sure Uncle Rust...you might be right...what do I know..." I echoed, wiping my chin thoughtfully. "Yup...you might just be right..." I said vaguely, stirring my spoon meditatively around in my soup, while simultaneously sneaking my left hand under my shirt and up to my throat.

Then, as Uncle Rust leaned over and lifted his bowl to his mouth to get the last slurp, and Betty sighed and looked about for her suitor, I clamped the hand around my throat and squeezed hard.

"Look out! *The thing!*" I cried, flinging myself back so the bench nearly disappeared under us.

Two women at the next table screamed. And Uncle Rust leapt up so that onion rings and soup flew all around him. I laughed with satisfaction. And the fact that Betty was spitting mad did nothing to dampen my glee.

"Ear-r-r-l," she hissed.

She looked around the cafeteria apologetically, before plumping her behind down firmly with a furious jolt. But I was doubled up laughing. I reckoned it was only fair to give the old bugger a bit of a scare. After so much bullshit. But Betty always cringed with embarrassment when I laughed.

"Earl, please…" she begged, red in the face.

She didn't think my laugh was at all appropriate for a grown man. It reminded her of a little boy being tickled, shrill and jerky. But that was her problem. She'd have to put it on the bill and lodge her complaint with the Big Guy.

Still, I hadn't laughed like that in ages.

Anyway, back at the cafeteria, Uncle Rust pushed his hat back from his forehead, and, after he'd wiped himself dry, his usually expressionless face broke into a broad smile. He chuckled and leaned back, arms crossed and tongue probing after bits of food.

We were even again. Friends again.

The Saboteur

But there's not much fun to be had with *the thing* usually. On the contrary. And although it doesn't make itself really obvious all the time, it manifests itself somehow almost every day. Whether in a moment's clumsiness, or in a prickling all over our bodies. It descends like a sudden rap on the knuckles. As a rule in the morning, before the sleep's even left us, but then it can stay all day...itching bodies...things falling to the floor... wasps stinging...doors squashing fingers...things slipping through them. Or our bodies getting tangled in things...tangled in things that are meant to be useful or give us pleasure. But more than anything, it reveals itself in clumsiness, in the loss of control from the left hand that sticks out of the intersection between us. At first I thought perhaps it was Betty, but she protested so hard, I realised it had to be something else. And when these things just continue, sometimes for days, it gets so intolerable that only liquor or hemp can carry us through.

Just before Betty and I got up from the cafeteria table, to walk back to the bordello, Uncle Rust came up with an observation that put everything in a whole new light – perhaps we really weren't so alone with these things after all.

"Bugs," mumbled Uncle Rust, almost talking to himself. "*Bugs*...all of us have some kinda creepy-crawlies inside us. And whenever I run out of my poison, I get it just the same as you. It's like the delicate blanket of bugs that's always in our bodies starts to grow and scrabble about, before gathering into one big ball, a ball of creepy-crawly bugs. Perhaps we are talking the same language after all, Earl. *Perhaps* we are..."

This made me wonder whether maybe we should try to smoke this evil out with the same poison that Uncle Rust used.

If it helped Uncle Rust get by, I reckoned it might not be so dumb. It couldn't hurt to try. But Betty wouldn't hear a word of it. And Uncle Rust leaned forward, with a stern expression…

"I don't think you've been listening, Earl. You don't want to arouse that appetite – you take my word for it. The moment *Uglybugly* gets a taste for it, it just wants more and more. And once you indulge it, it'll invite more of its greedy little playmates to the banquet. And before you know it, you'll be sitting there, empty as a shell, and your arse advertising the vacant space where your brain used to be."

"My arse?" I squealed.

"Believe me, Earl, I've seen stuff happen…so choose your poison with care!"

"Have you no pride, Earl?" Betty barked, for the second time that day, as we strolled home.

Uncle Rust knew what he was talking about. And since *the thing* seemed generally content to restrain itself, that idea went down in history as one of my worst. But although this creep might pretend to go into hibernation, that didn't stop it playing the odd prank on me. If only to remind us it was still on our case.

When we'd started settling in at the bordello, Mr King organised another party for us. After all, the previous one had ended in scandal. But as the pimp knocked back the champagne, he wanted to show off some of the house's wares.

"We should have a little initiation ritual, don't you think, Betty? We need to make sure Earl can handle himself when he's on the job!"

"By all means," the little lady snapped.

Mr King slapped one of his girls on the butt to get her into gear, then opened his wallet and shoved me a bunch of banknotes.

"Shan't cost you a penny, Earl. There! Take this…"

She began to dance, swaying seductively and dropping her clothing piece by piece to the floor. My legs almost started to go of their own accord, as I backed nervously across the room. She was getting sort of close. It was almost too much at once. With everybody's eyes on us, at least. Her exquisite oiled body, a wonderful citrus aroma from her golden skin, long black tresses that swept through the air. And everything moving, filling my vision. Closer and closer. Before I knew it, we had our backs against the wall of the ballroom. Pressed between the wall and the dancing girl – who was now stark naked – I wanted to show off a bit. Prove I was man enough for the job.

So I puffed on my cigar, cheeks burning. And tried to maintain my cool. While I looked the girl up and down, taking her assets in as best I could. Then, trying to look casual, I leaned out with my arm to the side, at the same time as swinging one leg elegantly behind the other.

But as my hand met the empty air, Betty came tumbling over me. In our fall I grabbed one of the long, heavy curtains, pulling the curtain rail and everything else down after them. With the fabric twisted around us, we lay there in a heap on the floor. The music died. The naked girl stopped dancing and set about disentangling us, while I whimpered with cigar burns on my face and hand.

"Damn and blast!!" I hissed, thrashing about on the floor with my sister on top of me. "I could've bloody sworn there was a shelf there! It was *the thing*…the fuckin' *thing* made me lean out…but there weren't nothin' there but a curtain! A soddin' curtain. Fuck!"

And there lay Betty, with that sneer of hers, while everybody else roared with laughter.

Mr King quietened the crowd.

"Look! Don't stand there gawping. Go and make yourselves

79

useful. Hush!"

Betty was jubilant, and laughed harder than she'd laughed for years...all the way up to our room. And even after we'd gone to bed the laughter continued to bubble out of her. Unstoppably. I lifted my hand to give her a clip her round the ear, but held back.

"Earl, you wouldn't dare!"

I looked at the hand and then burst into floods.

"There, there, Earl..." she whispered with a smile, as my tears subsided. "But you did get what you deserved."

However upsetting it was, she didn't think I had anyone, or *anything* to blame, but myself. In fact, this was a warning from God of the misfortune that might have awaited us, if that wicked Earl had taken us down that path. That was *her* view on it all.

"But don't you understand?" I sobbed. "I've got a saboteur!! Inside me! Inside *us*!"

Some days I'd just scream if it got too much: "I can't take any more!" As I thumped my chest to see if it shifted. But as a rule it would lie there calmly, doubtless plotting more devilry...more prickling...more cackhandedness...more torment. More evil.

I think the first time *the thing* really, really freaked me out, was when we first decided to leave Bigtown. It had already been manifesting itself more and more frequently. At first, I asked Betty to stop mucking about. We'd just endured a whole week of torment. But now we were standing in front of the mirror in our berth, on our way over the Pond, while I was shaving. Betty was putting her hair up beside me, when I froze.

Hanging beside the mirror was a little cabinet we kept our stuff in. Out of the corner of my eye I saw the hand sneak up and open the cabinet door. But in an instant it withdrew like it had been caught red handed. All without me doing a thing.

"Betty…" I whispered, "did you open that cabinet door?!"

"No," she answered. Betty hadn't noticed anything, not even that the door had opened.

"The hand…" I screamed. "It opened the cabinet door!" I stared down at the arm now hanging motionless between us. I shook it, opened and closed the fist.

"The hand…it opened the cabinet and I didn't do nothin'!"

Betty hadn't seen or felt anything, but she found it all really disturbing.

I began having trouble sleeping. I had recurring nightmares – my body would be powerless, and it would float up to the ceiling of the darkened room, sprawling and without anything to hold onto, anchorless. While a fearsome, ear-splitting noise would fill my head and come gushing out of my mouth. As though Hell itself had opened and was rushing through my head. I began to lie awake at nights – staring at the hand – waiting for its next move.

"Impossible to say what'll happen next," was all I could say when Betty expressed her anxiety too.

I began drinking more and more heavily, just so as to sleep. But what really struck me as strange, was that a cough would follow, on the days after *the thing* had manifest itself. A cough. Black lumps. Like oil. Coating my tongue. Ridges of black between my teeth.

FLEAS AND LICE IN FREHLEY'S HOUSE

Weeks passed without our seeing or hearing from Uncle Rust. It was like the earth had swallowed him up. And when we tried to get anything out of Frehley and Cougher, they just smiled and exchanged knowing glances until finally, Cougher told us that Uncle Rust was trying to quit his habit for good.

But as Frehley started laughing – not that we understood how that could be so funny – Cougher said that we'd have to see if Uncle Rust's efforts paid off first. But that there was nothing to worry about.

The next time we saw Uncle Rust at the cafeteria, our first thought was that it must have been his appearance that had put that smile on the old codgers' faces – the last few weeks had knocked ten years off him.

"Uncle Rust?!" I shouted in amazement towards his table.

I was very happy to see him, since my expectations for the day had been pretty low. We'd only really been meant to meet up with Cougher. That is...*Betty* was meeting up with Cougher...not *we*. I'd have had plenty of time on my hands to do whatever I wanted, if I hadn't had to tag along. But all I had to look forward to now, was a couple of hours of romantic drivel, not to mention the horny little whinge-bag's involuntary heart-thumping, before we wandered back home. And after surviving this agonising torment, my work would be the only thing that could put me in a good mood again. Work was – for once in my life – my only pleasure.

But today, Uncle Rust looked unusually lively and fired up. He could barely keep still, with his eyes like tin plates, as he thwacked his newspaper repeatedly against his palm. By contrast, Cougher sat there, big and heavy, and unmoving before he saw Betty and smiled. And when her heart started going I almost thought we'd faint. It was nauseating. Not only had her juices finally started percolating through her, but it was a clear reminder of who had the pump.

Cougher smiled and pushed a couple of chairs up for us. But as he did so, Uncle Rust was instantly on his feet, tapping his toes and fidgeting with his newspaper, before sitting back down.

"Can I get you something, Betty?" asked Cougher.

"A glass of water and a toothpick, thank you," I said quickly. Uncle Rust slapped his newspaper down on the table.

"Oh come on now, Cougher...is it really necessary to drag this out?"

"You gotta steady up a bit now, Bill. We shouldn't forget our manners surely, *even* if you have got a little surprise for us!" Cougher smiled.

"Little?! Yeah, yeah, whatever you say." Uncle Rust leaned back sulkily, with his arms crossed.

"Look, Betty. I'd like nothing better than to spend the rest of the day with you alone, really and truly I would but Bill has something he wants to show us. Something he wants to show *both of you.*"

"Huh? What? What?" I screamed, almost ecstatic.

"Shut up, Cougher," interrupted Uncle Rust. "You bloody old gossip, you...don't go spoiling everything!"

Uncle Rust was tapping and clattering his feet impatiently and fidgeting with his newspaper again.

"Alright, alright. Now listen – Betty – Earl – would it suit you both to come back to our place, so Bill can show you *something* up in his room?"

"Sure would! Let's go! Let's go now!" I said, nagging like a kid, euphoric at the idea of escaping their romantic jabber.

Betty nodded, a fraction disappointed, as she sat there in

her best frock. Still, she was curious enough not to kick up a fuss. We all left the cafeteria and we were soon sitting in Frehley's milk truck with Cougher behind the wheel.

"So, what's cookin'?" I asked.

"Wait and see," Uncle Rust said, smiling at us from where he sat, leaning halfway out of the truck window. "Wait and see."

On our arrival he took the stairs up to his room with long strides. But when Cougher's turn came to follow, the stairs creaked ominously under his weight. And with every step he took, and each stair that groaned, it dawned on me more starkly, that Betty's frail body would one day lie under – or, more revolting, *straddle* – that heavy sweaty body. Glistening with anticipation and lust, with my sister lying there with a wet juicy fanny. The thought was *sickening!* I'd have pushed it away with a smile before – but what might have once seemed like an amusing idea, had suddenly gotten heavy – literally! With no clue how I'd tackle it.

But if she had to…she had to. Betty could live her life, as long as I could live mine. My only hope was that Cougher wouldn't take too much time over it…and it would be no loss if he turned out not to like it much. Gentleman or no, the thought of having to spend hours in the sack with the Butterbean humping my sister, wasn't exactly music to my soul. Who knew what embarrassments might result?

"Whoops. Awful sorry, Earl! Didn't mean to slink in on you like that."

"That's quite alright, Cougher. But it'd be nice if you could keep your paws on your side of the bed from now on."

"Of course, Earl, of course. My fault, I'm sorry…"

"And keep an eye on the time please – I've got work to go too!"

"Just a little longer, Earl, and then I'll warm up the truck for us!"

It was bad enough putting up with all their coffee mornings – positively hectic in frequency lately – and the intolerable chitchat that accompanied them. Not to mention all the romantic frippery that Cougher showered on Betty, which threatened to take our room over completely. Mr King commented wryly, that if the bordello ever went bust, we'd always be able to open a chocolate shop or run a flower stall.

But, truth was, I'd never have stood in the way of these two turtledoves having each other. *Once,* at least, if only for the sheer entertainment value.

On reaching the final landing, in front of Uncle Rust's room, we suddenly heard Frehley's voice from the floor below.

"Are you lot up there?"

"Yup," Cougher shouted back.

"So are the twins there?" he shouted up again. A moment later we heard him put his foot on the first step. Breathing heavily. Again it creaked, as ominously as before.

"Hmm, I'm not sure about this," muttered Frehley, cautiously setting his next foot down.

The step shrieked back.

I was beginning to get curious about what kind of secret awaited us. It had to be something very out of the ordinary, if Frehley and Cougher were both prepared to risk their lives to get up here. But what? Was Uncle Rust sitting on the Ark of the Covenant? A state secret? Some new discovery to turn the world on its head? Or freshly-popped popcorn and a screen with moving pictures of a giant gorilla cavorting among the tops of skyscrapers and roaring at flying machines? If so, we'd be out of that door as fast as we'd come in, since Betty couldn't stand either the wireless or movies. No, no, no! The poor little thing couldn't stand ghosties in boxes, or ghosties on walls.

We could already hear Frehley's breathing getting heavier

below us as, trembling with uneasy concentration he worked his way up. Step by step. A hand clinging resolutely to the banister. As if that would be of any help if he suddenly plunged through the stairs.

"I think we ought to go in," said Cougher. "The staircase won't take the weight of all four of us at once."

Uncle Rust's room was crammed with papers and books of all kinds. Most were stacked on shelves or in neat piles, some thrown in cases. As far as I could see most of the books were filled with pictures of bugs. Insects. Of every species, shape and colour. But it was the big, black ones that sent shivers down my spine. The room was otherwise as impeccably turned out as Uncle Rust himself. And in the middle – behind one of the bookcases – stood Uncle Rust's bed and a washstand at which he now stood with his sleeves rolled up, washing his hands. In the centre of the room a long table was covered with a white cloth.

"Great place you've got," I said.

Uncle Rust didn't answer. Finally, after a lot of fuss, Frehley managed to squeeze himself in through the tiny attic door and stood, head bowed, under the roof. Followed closely by the dwarf Spinks, Cougher's partner.

"Well, has the performance begun?" asked Frehley, lungs squeaking.

Uncle Rust shook his head.

"Everybody here? Right! Let the performance begin!" Uncle Rust turned off the lights.

"This better be good – I ain't had nothin' all day, food or drink," I muttered in the dark.

Frehley put a finger to his lips and told me to shush. And before I'd managed to ask where the film projector was, Uncle Rust turned the ceiling lamp on over the table.

"Roll up! Roll up! Ladies and gentlemen! There's no reason

to be afraid!" he announced, pulling the large white tablecloth away.

And that was it...or so I thought.

"What? Not even any grub? What kind of rubbish is this?"

With his face like a dark-eyed angel under the ceiling lamp, Uncle Rust flashed me a murderous look.

Frehley chuckled and pushed me towards the table. Looking closer I saw it had a hollow top, covered with a sheet of glass. I was peering down into a display case. And there, spread across the bottom, were tiny miniature houses. Little houses, little streets, little cars. And tiny little gardens.

"Ah, so lovely!" sighed Betty.

"Hmm, brilliant," I snorted. "A matchbox city. So what else you got? Toy trains? Tin soldiers?"

"Shhhh!" everybody chorused:

Frehley pushed me even closer to the display case.

"Oi, talk about shovin' us around." I mumbled. "...yeah, yeah, all very nice, Uncle Rust...all them tiny things and that, but..."

"But look..." said the dwarf Spinks, standing on tiptoe and leaning over the edge with a finger on the glass. Uncle Rust lifted the glass plate off and began lifting the roofs off the tiny houses. Here and there he dripped something carefully from a pipette before he started poking at things with a pair of long tweezers.

"Right, that should do the trick," he whispered with satisfaction.

Then I saw it. Slowly at first, but then faster and faster, the display case was coming to life. As though the sun was rising over this miniature town. The little cars started driving carefully around the streets, diminutive rocking chairs rocked to and fro in the houses.

"Jesus," I whispered. It was then I noticed all the little bugs working or going about their business. It was a flea circus. A gigantic flea circus! Or, more correctly, a flea city although there seemed to be a little visiting circus too.

Some fleas were pulling carts, others sat like grandmothers knitting in their houses. Carefully Uncle Rust placed a large magnifying glass over the town, and I could see that all these little creatures were dressed in minute outfits – tiny little clothes, in all colours. Some fleas were sitting in cars, in their hats and coats. Occasionally cars crashed into each other, before driving on as though in a panic. All the fleas walking along the sidewalk or in the road, had little weights to stop them hopping out of the display case, fastened to their bodies by Uncle Rust's dextrous hands. And with every house he opened and every roof that disappeared, we watched more life unfold – little tattoo shops, motor repair garages, "Uncle Rust's Butchers and Fishmongers", a greengrocer, a cobbler, and a cinema. On the corner a masked robber was on the lookout for easy pickings. Fire engines and firemen in shiny chocolate-wrapper helmets. And when Uncle Rust finally lifted the top off the circus tent, we saw a tightrope walker and a juggler lying on his back kicking balls in the air. Outside the ring a flea wearing a leotard lifted weights. On a banner behind him were the words, "Frehley: The Biggest Strongest Flea in the World!" In comparison to its body, the weights were enormous. And pirouetting in and among the other fleas were the tiniest little ballerinas, holding equally tiny parasols. All this and more.

"I hope you won't be offended, but I've made something specially for the occasion," whispered Uncle Rust. He pointed with the tweezers.

On a little podium two fleas stood next to each other, so close, that I suspected Uncle Rust of cutting them up and sewing them together. And next to them a little town crier with a loudhailer. I recognised the names fast enough.

"Earl and Betty. The Fan-ta-stic Twins…"

"Oh," sighed Betty, "how beautiful…"

Not far from the podium, another flea was shuffling along holding a huge bouquet. Nobody needed to say who it was, and Betty was soon shedding tears. While I did my best to hold mine in, as I felt the shame at my earlier rudeness spread through my body.

"It really is fantastic," I whispered, "totally amazing."

"You see here, the destiny of the world, Earl. There'll be nothing on this earth one day apart from these bugs perfected over millions and millions of years of evolution. The human race has only existed for some few thousands of years, but it's already starting to stretch things. We're nothing but a flicker. Great and small. The earth goes round in circles, and soon everything will be forgotten."

Uncle Rust was beginning to sound like Mr King, when he held forth about his bordello.

"But these bugs – they'll be around until the sun stops shining! Everywhere! In every nook and cranny. And ladies and gentlemen…There's not a thing anybody can do about it!"

Our little gathering applauded. Betty even clapped her one hand against her chest which she usually felt was below her. And when the applause stopped Uncle Rust produced a suitcase with the words *Uncle Rust's Fantastic Circus* written on the lid. Inside there was more of the same, this time just a simple circus. Now he took out a matchbox and began lowering one flea after the other into the case and setting them to new tasks…tightrope walking…high jump…weightlifting…two of them rolling around with each other in a tiny wrestling ring. And everything lovely and shiny. Decked in sparkly sweet wrappers and things that Uncle Rust had saved over the years.

"Bill?" asked Frehley quietly.

"Yes?"

"Are you keeping count of all your fleas, or what?"

"What d'you mean?"

"Well, it's just I suddenly feel itchy. I could swear something's crawling up my back."

Uncle Rust peered down into his matchbox, into the suitcase and the showcase. As though he could somehow keep track of all his fleas.

"You mustn't let yourselves be fooled completely, your imaginations might be playing tricks on you. Most of our little friends are long dead, there's a touch of fine mechanics going on here too. So don't discount the possibility that it's just in your head, Frehley."

"Ain't that a bit disgusting?" I asked.

"What d'you mean?" asked Uncle Rust.

"Would you like to walk in a city full of dead men?"

"Probably not, Earl, probably not…"

"But Bill, *some* of the fleas are alive, aren't they?"

"Yeah, sure. But they don't just hop onto people like that. They're mostly gathered from horses and dogs, have to be, or you wouldn't be able to see them. Human fleas are too small. So there's not much risk…"

Just then, Cougher slapped himself hard on the cheek, and Spinks started gyrating his shoulders although he said nothing.

"Gentlemen, gentlemen," said Uncle Rust, attempting to calm them.

But the two big men were soon delousing each other in the shadows outside the beam of the ceiling lamp – Cougher standing with his hands up Frehley's shirt. Meanwhile Spinks was gripping his hips hard and twisting his upper body in an attempt to reach round. Betty and I stood next to the display case, watching this whole performance in disbelief. It seemed almost impossible that Frehley could notice anything so small on that massive body.

The giant was wriggling like a little girl from Cougher's tickling.

"Alright, alright, just stand still," said Cougher laughing. Then, red faced, he closed his fingers very gently on the flea, and put it back into Uncle Rust's matchbox.

Meanwhile, Spinks was rocking his head gently from side to side, with his nose stuck in the air in an attempt to stem the blood streaming from his nostrils. (The tickling had provoked a series of violent sneezes and his nose had exploded in a spray of blood.) Trying to avoid his delicate nose, he crooked his shoulder in a futile attempt to smack his ear. Eventually, all the fleas were hunted down, and the gathering turned to the display case for the performance to resume.

It was just at that moment I saw my left arm shoot out and crush one of the fleas as it swaggered along the sidewalk, in its overcoat and hat, oblivious of any impending danger.

The room fell silent. The finger squashed the poor little creature with a screwing action into the surface of the table.

"I don't think that was very nice," whispered Uncle Rust.

And as if to add the final finishing touch, the finger concluded its action with a flick, sending the corpse in a gentle arc through the room.

"I think that'll do for today…" Uncle Rust's face was white with suppressed anger.

And before anyone could draw breath, he lifted the glass plate and put it back over the table.

"But – but, it wasn't *me,*" I stammered.

"That may be." Uncle Rust didn't meet my gaze; instead he closed the suitcase, put on the light, and threw the white sheet back over the flea city.

THE THING

Did you really have to squash that louse?" sobbed Betty, in the milk truck on our way back to the bordello.

Not a louse, a *flea*, I thought, saying nothing. What could I say exactly? And with Cougher sitting next to us, how could I explain things without adding to my sister's agony? Soon I was bawling like a kid too. Everything was spoiled. And all because of some pathetic little flea.

Cougher, who'd sat there saying nothing for ages, finally broke the silence with a gentle sigh, expelled through half-closed lips.

"I'll chop that bloody hand off," I sobbed.

"Stop talking nonsense," said Cougher calmly, his hand resting on the steering wheel. "Things will sort themselves out."

I really don't like to talk about *the thing* to all and sundry, so I only ever do it if I must. For example, when it's done something really awful – though not too awful either, then it's best to keep schtum if I can get away with it.

I was the first to discover it, not on the boat. No, long before that. It's impossible to be sure, but I think I got my first glimpse of it in the hotel room years ago. Like a shadow creeping up on us. At first we didn't call it anything in particular. Because we didn't notice it much, it wasn't there all the time. But then it seemed to grow as we got older. In the beginning we just thought things got clumsy now and then. And eventually we had lots of names for it: Humpetybumpety, Mr Topsyturvy, Spiller Man, Mad Muddler, then Humpetybumpety again. Until, we finally landed on *the thing*...

But if I were to say what I thought *the thing* was, then I think

I'd say it was a devil. Not the kind of devil you read about in books, or the kind Uncle Rust talks about that you can't touch or feel, but one of flesh and blood. A beast of prey enmeshed in your flesh, permeating your veins, where it scratches and prods, and twists and turns to get free, perpetually dissatisfied. Sometimes a drink will drive it away for one paltry moment. But at worst this just makes it nastier…so it twists and turns, and coils and hooks itself ever deeper into your flesh, sending its spawn racing into every corner of your body. Then there's nothing else to be done, but to drink more until you can't feel it any longer. But the next day, when the bottle is empty or you can't take any more, and you think it's given up again, it starts to ooze out in your sweat…scurrying out of every pore in your body…scrabbling and scratching over your skin. Just like the little bugs, Uncle Rust described…tiny beetles and mites spilling everywhere, scuttling away to hide from the light. One under the newspaper, so the newspaper tumbles to the floor… one under the plates, so the plates fall out of the cupboard… the cupboard loosens from the wall…the wall cracks…a chair skids…a spoon slips from your hand…a glass from the table… the table from the house. And doors lock…doors glide open… doors jam…a key wedges…clocks stop ticking…clothes get hitched up or lie scrambled at your feet…sugar turns to salt… salt spills over the table…milk sours overnight. There's grit in your food and shit in the well…the windows won't close… the catch won't budge…fingers glue together…drawers lock themselves…laces undo…the pillow goes hard and the sheets twist…your sores won't heal and your head can't forget…feet trip you up and shoes slip…A tangle of hair, cables and yarn… unravelling cardigans that get you in a tangle…bottles that spill…wallpaper blistering…stones in your shoes and mats in your hair…embers that leap from the wood burner…you bite the inside of your cheek…and pull on a thread with no end…

but go on drawing it in, until *it* spills all over you.

Like the sound you never hear of things as they give way…
those tiny, tiny beetles and bugs that press and squeeze, and
wedge themselves between anything and everything. And
that never let anything work out…or in. Or up or down. Or
to or fro. The wind that slams doors on fingers…a finger that
finds its way to the scab and picks, scratches and investigates,
twisting, turning. The world that takes little bites out of you,
first one, then another, until you're forced down on one knee.
You scarcely notice it to begin with, until it weighs you down
like a slow avalanche of sand and earth and water. It. It is
butterfingered. As you watch all those possibilities you're
so desperately grabbing after, slip between your fingers. *The
thing* is the price you pay to live. And it's all according. For
some the price is lower…for some much higher…yes a price.
Or, then again, just a shadow…a spirit. A hand creeping in the
night.

And even if I've no recall of it next morning, if everything
has just vanished and blurred into darkness, I still feel its
effects – not only in my sweat and in my flesh and on my skin
– but in the cough that comes with black, tarry clumps that
stain my mouth and tongue with a sweet and bitter taste. Like
death itself.

But whatever *the thing* might prove to be, and however blind a fury it might get into, it wasn't too stupid to find Uncle Rust's weakness in a twinkling, and to find the one little thing that could push him over the edge. And the instant it found a crack, a hairline fault in Uncle Rust's casting, it struck. With terrifying precision. It located Uncle Rust's sorrow, the whole world's sorrow, in a single flea. And with that, he was back on the needle. It didn't take more to knock him off his perch. To knock him back, so to speak.

That day, when Uncle Rust showed us his flea city, was maybe the only day we ever saw him really happy. For a moment. A little flash. Before everything died with the flick of a finger. And I felt helpless to do anything except take every opportunity to apologise for this flea-murder. Even though, in truth, *the thing* had been behind it all.

"Earl, you gotta stop this now, it isn't your fault." Uncle Rust smiled faintly, his veins full of medicine. "Look, maybe this can't be put down to whether one little flea dies or not. I am who I am. And I need what I need to live. Especially if it takes so little to knock my legs from under me."

Not that this was much comfort. I'd seen the disappointment in his face when it happened. In his fight against the needle Uncle Rust had invested weeks in intricate and painstaking preparation to get everything up and running. To escape the hell he told us burned inside his shirt.

He had, in the moment it happened, been living completely and utterly for his little universe. And now everything lay abandoned under the sheet. Stone dead to a man, and all

95

fastened to their miniscule mechanical devices. The flea city had become a city of the dead. And if it wasn't the flea itself that mattered, it was the action, the shabby demonstration of spite, that had come as such a blow to Uncle Rust. The calculatedness of it. It had taken so much to make him happy and get him clean. And so incredibly little to disappoint him.

Poor Uncle Rust, who only ever gave and never took. And who would soon sacrifice himself on Christmas Night no less, so we could escape Mr King's clutches. Christmas. A day that must be the saddest day of all for him. Betty and I had each other at least.

With the passing of every year Uncle Rust lost something, instead of receiving anything – he had no food on the table, no parcels under the tree. That was the way things were before he'd met Frehley and become his factotum. And that was the way things would be again. All because I couldn't keep my fingers out of the till and finished up in a blazing row with Mr King...

Uncle Rust's misery began when the law rolled up one Christmas Night many years ago, demanding he come down to the station. They were hard times, and with no other means of earning a living in the run up to Christmas, Uncle Rust had been turning up every morning at various markets about town. Carrying his suitcase with the words *Uncle Rust's Fantastic Flea Circus* written in smart, shiny letters on the lid. And to begin with, despite the hard times, things went pretty well – Bigtown hadn't seen a flea circus for years. In fact, they'd been outlawed, since recurrent epidemics had triggered hygiene fears. And although such fears were unfounded – since it was rarely a case of having live fleas or the kind that lived on human beings – the council had to appear efficient.

Now the law had got wind that Uncle Rust was selling medicine under the counter or, to be more precise, the *suitcase*.

And that the flea circus, which in the light of the on-going epidemic might have been enough for the authorities, was nothing less than a cover.

So right in the middle of Christmas Night Dinner they barged in – Pest Control and the law – with their snarling dogs, flea powder, and whatnot, and ransacked Uncle Rust's apartment in search of fleas, lice and Uncle Rust's medicine.

"That's quite a dinner you've treated yourselves to this Christmas, innit?" sneered one of the police officers, dumping himself down on a kitchen chair. "Tell me, how's it possible… that people of *your* sort have the dosh for such a fine spread?"

"What were you expecting?" answered Uncle Rust quietly. "That we'd be sat here in the dark eating bugs and creepy crawlies? That our Christmas entertainment would be one big round of delousing? *Fuckin' creep,"* he whispered to himself.

"Hmm, I couldn't rightly say," sneered the policeman again, poking at the sole of his shoe with Uncle Rust's fork.

"Alright, alright. Lets get this over with…" Uncle Rust pushed his dinner plate away from him and crossed his arms.

The policeman looked up from his shoe and at Uncle Rust, who was still sitting at the end of the table with his napkin stuffed in his collar.

"You'll have to come down to the station with us, Mr Aukrust."

Soon Uncle Rust's wife and kids were out on the street, while the men got to work peppering the apartment with flea powder. And despite not finding much – Uncle Rust's medicine (for his own use, it should be noted), and a case full of dead, but *neatly* dressed fleas – they didn't let him out for three days. Sick and exhausted he walked all the way home in a freezing blizzard, only to discover he no longer had either a home or family to come back to. And that he'd been palmed off with a few possessions, flung into a box outside the door.

They hadn't even let him keep the hemp that he drank as tea for his asthma and took for his sore eyes. Furious, but still shaky and ill, Uncle Rust walked all the way back to the station to demand the return of his suitcase. So he'd at least have something to put his clothes in.

But he was informed at the station that his suitcase had been burned in the interests of hygiene.

"So you've *burned* my suitcase, well that takes the biscuit...Tell me," said Uncle Rust trembling, "do you realise this whole business has cost me my home?'

The officer shook his head and told him he had only himself to blame.

"Why? I didn't invite you over, did I? You didn't even bother to give me a fine!"

"Hmm, you've got the Christmas spirit to thank for that."

"Christmas spirit? But you found nothing. Just a few inconsequential trifles," snarled Uncle Rust.

"Well some of them *inconsequential trifles,* Mr Aukrust, is like a pact with the Devil, what'll carry you straight down to Hell."

"Well, I was managing to live with those trifles...and my family were getting along alright too, until you turned up."

The policeman shrugged his shoulders, a newspaper in front him.

"Well, maybe I *am* destined for Hell. But one thing's for sure, I'm not the only one who's made a pact with the Devil," sighed Uncle Rust. "And if the pact I've made costs me my soul...it's *your* pact that guarantees my little *inconsequential trifles* will lead me to Hell."

"Look, Mr. Aukrust! I ain't gonna say this again. You'd better get out of here, if you don't wanna spend another night inside."

"I'm just offering you my opinion, Mister, just my opinion.

But one thing to bear in mind when you want to make a pact with the Devil – however good your intentions to begin with, you can be sure things will turn out differently. If a guy gets a spark on his jacket, the last thing you can expect is thanks when you try to put it out with petrol!"

There was scarcely a breath left now in his sick body. He sank down in front of the counter.

The policeman folded his newspaper.

"Opinions from your sort don't count, so just shove off."

Even if Mr King wasn't too keen on Betty's romance, or the friendships we were cultivating outside the bordello, he managed to keep up the mask. Only dropping the occasional disparaging remark about our gang – mainly aimed at the flowers and chocolates that filled our room, or Uncle Rust's bad habits, or Frehley's voracious appetite.

"Amazing the school even stays afloat, with the amount that fat arse puts away...But as long as it's not my kitchen he's raiding, then...Oh! Forget it Earl! I don't mean it. Frehley's worth his weight in gold."

But it pleased him that my sister no longer pulled a long face every time Olympen was mentioned.

Now, after so many tough years, there was barely a moment without something to look forward to, without something to be happy about. Every single day the two of us woke up filled with expectation. And then I'd either accompany Betty to her rendezvous, or do whatever work Mr King had set me... without a grumble.

And though the rows of bottles were a temptation, I rarely succumbed, which reassured Betty. Surrounded by such sinfulness, she saw this as a ray of light. And when I allowed myself the odd reefer, she turned a blind eye, since I'd proved so persevering and dutiful. She wasn't too sure about the smell, but as long as it was just a question of one or two she didn't seem too bothered.

"Medicine for my eyes," I chuckled.

"Oh yes, I'll believe that!"

"And for my asthma too."

The downside was that the hemp sometimes affected her

too. All too often it put her into a state – so she thought – of ever increasing religious enlightenment. Then in rapt contentment she'd give lengthy descriptions of the Heavenly Kingdom she saw rising before her. At best, she'd declare simply that now… *NOW*…God was most definitely with us. He was present, and in the midst of such sin, that was a marvel. She convinced herself that we were a sign from the Lord. We were here for the girls. That was it. We were here for the girls, sent forth as a guiding light from God, a reminder to Mr King, and so forth.

Meanwhile, with the key in my pocket, I carried out my work in the house, carrying the cashbox up to Mr King's office every night. And we spent almost every free moment with Cougher, Frehley and Uncle Rust. In the cafeteria where Uncle Rust liked to read the newspaper to us. In his croaky voice, full of dust and agedness. About everything that was going on out there in the world. About a war that was brewing, and all sorts. Fabulous and gruesome.

Our trips to the church with Cougher, and their rendezvous at the cafeteria, were what made Betty happiest and filled her days with eager anticipation. But also the chance that she might meet her sweetheart at the wrestling.

And all this had brought about a change in her. I'd already begun to notice this change when we were getting dressed to accompany Mr King to Olympen, for the first time after Cougher's defeat against Jacob.

My kid sister had started to doll herself up a bit. Not a lot. Just a bit more than usual.

"Don't look at me like that, Earl," she whispered, peering at herself again in the mirror.

"Huh? I ain't doin' nothin'," I laughed, straightening my tie.

As time went by and their love grew, Betty found it harder and harder to conceal her desire for revenge, so long overdue.

Jacob was constantly on the road, probably on the other side of the continent, and it didn't seem that either Cougher or he were in any hurry for a return match. And, of course, she couldn't stop droning on at me about the thing with the snake...that terrible, scary snake.

"Do you think he'll win next time, Earl? Yes or no?"

"Yeah, sure. Of course he'll win. If he bothers to turn up. But listen, Betty, not everythin' that happens in the ring is for real. You got to understand that."

But just as when we'd looked for our parents, Betty was wrapped up in her own naïve hopes and expectations. It was useless to try to explain the workings of it all. She had no understanding of the game. Any explanations of how much Cougher and Jacob really cared for each other, were a total waste of time. Betty just sat there with cloth ears as she continued.

"But don't you think Cougher's stronger now? I'm sure he won't let himself be tricked again, when the chance comes..."

And this went on and on. All I could do was smile and try not to lose my rag. But then, at least she was on side for once, as she indulged in her wild speculations as to whether Cougher might be more cunning, better trained, and altogether less trusting when he fought that beast of a man again.

She'd been far too dazed to notice the kindness the two wrestlers had shown each other in the changing room that night. And now she was too worked up to register the concerns Cougher frequently shared with the rest of us about his friend. You could ask her a question and she'd just sit staring into space without answering. The fact that Cougher was actually Jacob's teacher, passed her by completely.

"Yes but, Betty, why don't you just ask Cougher yourself?" I said. "He'll explain everything."

If there was anybody in the whole world who could explain

things to her, I reckoned it had to be Cougher. But she wasn't having any of it.

"Ooh, no…I wouldn't want to interfere," this little featherbrain said quietly. "It'll have to wait."

So instead, Betty nursed her ever-increasing anger. An anger always directed towards Jacob. To her this was a battle between good and evil incarnate – Cougher was Our Lord's Man, her devoted churchgoer, while Jacob was none other than the Devil's own spawn. She'd clench her fist as she sat there fabricating her own reality. And each time we went to Olympen, disappointment would descend on her like a dark cloud, the minute she discovered that neither Cougher nor Jacob were up on the billboards again.

Yet she'd still be overjoyed every time Cougher came up to her at Olympen, and ask politely if he could join us. And since Mr King was in no position to say yay or nay, he'd sit there all evening, comforting her, while the old amputee eyed them suspiciously. Cougher would point out all the various wrestlers and tell her their histories, and try vainly to explain the plot-lines they played out in the ring.

"Besides," he'd add, "it's mostly for show. You mustn't believe everything you see down there. It's mostly for fun…it doesn't hurt half as much as it looks."

"But tell me, Cougher," she plucked up the courage to ask one evening, "aren't you going to give that horrid snake-man his comeuppance soon?"

"All in good time," laughed Cougher, who'd finally given up trying to clear Jacob's character. "All in good time."

" 'Cos he really needs to learn a lesson, the way he carries on. It's awful!"

Cougher laughed again. And coughed.

I tried my best not to get involved. Betty had her own life now. The two of them could get on with their own thing. I

was just happy my sister had found someone to love at last.
It wasn't my business what they talked about. Cougher was a
good man, a real gentleman with the best intentions. And so
long as they gave me enough elbow-room to get on with my
own thing, I wouldn't have had anything against the two of
them getting married, or having kids or what-have-you. Not
that I exactly had any worries about Betty getting up the duff
in the too near future.

Cougher hadn't exactly been breaking the door down with
amorous advances. Flowers and chocolates, sure, but *the flesh*
could wait. For a long time the two of them seemed content
to sit up close, whispering sweet nothings. Until one evening,
when things were getting really rough down in the ring, I
suddenly felt Cougher's hand close tight round Betty's. It felt
good and safe. Not a bit unpleasant. Betty turned away and hid
her face behind Cougher's shoulder. They rarely made such a
show of their affections. From time to time I'd feel Cougher
tracing little circles in Betty's palm with his ring finger. She
liked that.

Anyway, I made a tidy packet on it. Mr King and I had
made a wager ages ago, on when Cougher would try to get into
my sister's knickers.

"Give that horny bastard a couple of weeks without any
action, and he'll give up on your sister!"

But I knew better. And now that Cougher's hand had finally
come secretly sneaking over, Mr King had no choice but to
pay up. With my popcorn crunching between my teeth, I stuck
a crisp banknote in my pocket. It was almost as though Mr
King interpreted this whole thing as an omen.

"You know what, Earl?" he whispered. "Maybe I've been
at this game too long – maybe I should give up before I lose
my touch."

"Shhh," I whispered, "don't go givin' her more ideas now.

Before you know it, we'll be sittin' here, prayin' for mercy while she runs around town, tellin' the world she's single-handedly cleansed the whorehouse of sin."

"Whorehouse, Earl?" said Mr King, looking around him anxiously. "I run a respectable business, my friend…you just remember that."

Respectable or not. Even if she moaned less these days, waking up every morning filled with excitement, and rarely making herself difficult, Betty still hadn't given up the fight to leave this establishment. And when it came to Cougher, she always felt she had to hammer it in that never, under any circumstances, did she ever take part in the activities of the house. She was only there as Our Lord's Light. A prisoner of circumstance. And each time Cougher, would try to reassure us both, that he neither suspected her of such a thing, nor would he ever pry into the source of my income. As long as it didn't impinge on his life, he wouldn't meddle.

"Live and let live," said Cougher. "I know good people when I see them."

Mr King seemed happy enough for now, too. We added a certain lustre to his reputation, as living proof of his generosity – with all the good exposure that brought the bordello. People made the trip just to see for themselves if the rumours about these twins were true. We were the added spice. The welded-lovers (or however it was presented)…man and woman fused as one.

And every Sunday Cougher, who assured us he'd seen many far seedier businesses than the one we were involved in, would turn up dutifully at the bordello to accompany us to church. And who knows how things would have gone, without these church visits. Because when things finally turned nasty between Mr King and us, these trips would prove useful. If not our salvation. When, with the exclusion of these Sunday trips, Mr King put us under house arrest at the bordello, church offered us our only chance to contact our friends, our only chance to plan our escape.

But, as I've said, there was no hint yet of the challenges that awaited us. Mr King smiled at me, as I sat there in Olympen, without a care in the world. We were, for now at least, on the best of terms.

"He's got the taste for it now…" Mr King whispered, nodding towards the two turtledoves.

"Sure has. But it ain't nothin' to worry over," I whispered back. "She's primness itself. And if you fancy another bet, just say. 'Cos you'd have to pour boilin' water on them thighs to make 'em spread. She's been that way since birth, and I reckon she'll be that way til we're pushin' up the daisies. The Good Lord's savin' her, yer see, to pop her cherry himself."

Mr King gawped.

"So I wouldn't get your hopes up!"

He laughed heartily and slapped his stumps.

"Whereas me…I'm just the opposite…" I chuckled, stuffing my mouth with more buttered popcorn.

Mr King put his arm round my shoulder.

"But you know something Earl, what you can't have, you have to buy," whispered Mr King, his nose tickling my ear. And there we sat. Cougher holding Betty's hand on one side, and me with the cripple close, on the other.

All of us full of hopes and anticipation.

When we got back to the bordello later that night, he and I got completely hammered together. It got totally gross and embarrassing. Perhaps Mr King meant it as a gesture of humility when, with a row of pretty girls gawping before him, and Tim watching in horror from behind, he rounded off an otherwise perfect evening by pissing on the huge rug. With his knob out, shirttails to the side and arms thrashing, he pushed his way through on to the rug, and went for it.

"Because I can!" he declared, his eyes barely able to focus. "Because I can! We're alike you and I, Earl...more alike than you'd think!" He looked down, satisfied and pink-cheeked, at the stream that splashed out onto the rug.

Betty ended up completely out of it too that night. All the make-up she'd started to slap on these days was smeared across her face, and she barely knew her own name. She just laughed, or cried, I'm not sure which. Though it was probably for the best, because later Mr King let me indulge my every desire.

"Won't cost you a penny, Earl! What d'you fancy?"

He pointed around at all his girls, sitting there with their unbuttoned blouses and soft, glossy lips. Whether the alcohol had clouded his vision, I don't know, but he even pointed in the direction of the little monkey, and for a moment it chattered back nervously at the blustering old cripple.

"I think I'll pass on the monkey, Mr King, but with your permission, I'd like everything else. Everything!" I yelled. "But stay clear of my sister!"

And any girl I pointed to, I had.

One after the other, in any which way.

The next day Betty and I lay upstairs in our room, taking turns to puke in a bucket. If she'd lost the power of speech the night before, she'd certainly got it back now. And she was saying things I wouldn't have believed could pass her lips, if I hadn't been there to hear them. Betty was not best pleased. Not at all.

"To think you've managed to get us into this mess, Earl! Just think…!"

"Yeah, but isn't it thanks to Mr King we've got everythin' we could wish for, and a roof over our heads and grub on the table?"

"Oh, belt up Earl. You can be such a blockhead sometimes."

"Yeah, but it's almost too good to be true, innit? Well, innit?"

"Too right, it's too good to be true! He pissed on the floor, Earl! Just think! He *pissed* on the floor."

Truth was, that nobody had had the heart – not me, not Mr King, nor the rest of the house – to tell her what lay behind the cripple's vandalising of his own Persian rug. And if anybody had told her what had happened on that first day we came to the bordello, she'd have died on the spot. So I held my tongue.

It was around this time that Mr King hired a trapeze artist to spice things up in the house. They rigged a rope for her in the ballroom that stretched from the floor up to the ceiling, before coming back down to the floor through a hook. At the other end of the rope, Tim stood ready to hoist her up to the ceiling and set the rope in motion for her to perform her tricks.

For a few evenings everything went perfectly. Dangling upside down with her foot locked in the rope, she spun round faster and faster, as it swung in gigantic circles through the room above the tables and floor, higher and higher towards the ceiling, at breakneck speed as the music whipped up the tension. Then, as she removed her clothes, the garments seemed to fly from her, snatched by invisible hands to whiz through the air. It was dizzying, almost nauseating to watch her naked body spinning and spinning. Round and round, with the guests gawping. Faces turned up from the dining tables and from the dance floor. The girls of the house casting envious glances upwards, and at the climax of this crazy act, cash would rain down onto the floor beneath her.

This, Mr King counted as one of the greatest events in the history of the bordello.

But a few evenings later it would all come to an abrupt end.

The house was jam-packed, after rumour of this woman had spread so fast. The trapeze artist had just let her garments fall, and the floor had been showered with money from the spellbound guests, when her hair suddenly swept into a candelabra. Only for a moment. At first everybody thought the danger had passed, and we all breathed a sigh of relief. We even began to think it was a part of the act, that she'd intended to blow out the candles. But as Tim began to slacken the rope to bring her back up to the ceiling, the horror of the situation suddenly hit us with a terrible clarity. At first she just hung there, holding the same stiff pose. Smiling with outstretched arms and legs pointing out from the rope. Then suddenly her long tresses seemed to unfurl as though from inside, opening into a ball of flame. Arms thrashing, the woman began screaming. Mr King dropped his champagne glass and yelled.

With her hair a mass of flames, and her body growing increasingly limp, the trapeze artist swept through the room. Her head smashed into the various objects in her path, and with each object she slammed into, the rope spun in increasingly uneven circles. A palm tree fell over, its pot crashing into the floor. On the other side of the room a painting caught fire as she dashed into the wall. Flames started to flutter across the wallpaper, as her spiralling body continued to spit clusters of burning hair. Finally she whirred into the floor, setting the curtains alight as they fell on top of her. Tim ran to her, putting out the flames with his hands. While Mr King wheeled himself out into the centre of the ballroom.

"Gentlemen! Gentlemen!" He shouted. "No need to panic! You hear! No need to panic..."

Mr King wanted to offer free drinks downstairs, but nobody seemed to hear. The straw had caught fire at last, and all the whisky in the world wouldn't prevent the guests and whores from fleeing the house in a furore. Though Tim succeeded in extinguishing the flames, and preventing the whole house, the entire dung-heap, from burning to the ground. But the room reeked of burned hair. And before I could even catch sight of her again, the woman was carried out in the scorched curtains.

This episode cost Mr King dear. The entire room had to be restored and the odour of the burned woman lingered for ages. Besides, he had to pay good money for the whole thing to be forgotten too.

Some time later, when the rumpus had finally died down, I heard Mr King talking to Tim in the office.

"Tell me Tim, did you ever get such a *hard-on?*"

Eventually Mr King let me start at the wrestling school. Although only a couple of times a week. And on condition that my training took place early in the day, and that I let Tim teach me a few moves.

"I hardly ever see the two of you these days," Mr King complained gently.

But what he really wanted, probably, was for Tim to keep an eye on us. He wanted to keep tabs on us. For fear he might lose us completely to Cougher and Frehley. He was pretty sure where he had me, but it wasn't so easy to tell with my sister. And if there were plans afoot of our leaving the bordello in search of a new and better life, he wanted advance warning. And his concern was hardly baseless, considering Betty still complained bitterly at times. It can't have passed him by – Mr King was anything but stupid.

"Just remember who took you in Earl," he repeated. "Just don't forget that, and we'll stay on good terms...you and I."

"Of course Mr King."

"But just to be on the safe side, we'll send Tim along with you."

"Oh, really?"

"Just to keep a lookout. You never know what can happen when the boys get going. A pair like you are an easy target. Trust me. I know what I'm talking about. Blood lust. Blood lust." And with these reassuring words, he sent me on my way.

I still managed to sneak off from Tim once in a while. I'd career around the streets of Bigtown with Betty in tow...blood pounding round my body. And they'd surge through me...all the names I'd have had up in the ring...*Earl the Warrior...Earl*

111

the Bloodthirsty...Earl the Avenger...another place...another life.

Most of the men at the school were a size (or three) too big for me, so Spinks was appointed as my instructor and sparring partner. But with Betty only agreeing to this very reluctantly, and exclusively so as to spend more time with Cougher, our progress was pretty slow at the start. I was itching for the day I'd finally get a fight. And Spinks's endless repetition of details wasn't what I'd had in mind. Most of our training went on him finding techniques so I could grab him and lift him. It wasn't just tedious, it was exhausting. Besides, Spinks smelled vile, like sour milk. And every time I threw him down onto the mat, I hoped and believed that he'd finally stay down. So we could get on with some proper training. So we could fight.

But no matter how often I threw him to the ground, he'd be back on his feet just as fast. Why he didn't just end up falling apart was a mystery, the number of times he'd thumped onto the mat. But Spinks proved to be a robust little devil. Insatiable. With flashing eyes and a massive grin. And he insisted on adding smart little moves too, nifty little steps to entertain Betty. While I just lifted and threw, lifted and threw, until I thought my arms would drop off.

What with my giggly kid sister and this grinning dwarf arsing about, it was a relief when Cougher stepped in now and then, to offer some serious support and encouragement. Little flirtations aside.

Of the old boys, Spinks was the only one who still earned his living from wrestling. Cougher and Frehley were both pretty much retired now, and besides, the wrestling school was a demanding enough business. So, now and then, Spinks still pulled on a costume that looked like an old suit of armour, and toured the continent under his stage name Iron Nugget. And as the Iron Nugget, he'd demonstrate his mind-blowing muscular control by getting people to smash all kinds of things against his body. After which he'd pick up the bits, crack a grin revealing his strong, white teeth, and gobble them down. To the public's ecstatic delight. And he swallowed swords and ate fire too. As his star turn, he'd blow huge columns of fire, over his defeated opponents. You could feel the heat spread through the venue, almost to the top of the stands. And given half a chance, he'd go on to smash bottles and light bulbs on his opponents, and then crunch up the shards.

Whenever Spinks came across anything he'd not tasted, he always had to try a bit, out of curiosity. It didn't matter what – electric cables, cups, beetles, curtains, or even Uncle Rust's potato soup. Yet, truth be told, he was very fussy in the food department. He preferred to make his own food, so unsurprisingly he became the wrestling school's cook. But if he did on rare occasions get grouchy, it was because he had bellyache.

"It rattles when he sits on the bog," Frehley joked.

As well as swallowing swords and other things, Spinks had – in his relentless quest to expand his repertoire – taught himself to stick a variety of objects up his nose. Spoons, nails and worse, all found their way up his nostrils. But even though his determination was as great as his curiosity, this was a failure. Spinks's over-sensitive nose – an explanation perhaps for his finicky tastes – would start bleeding if he so much as sneezed or even picked it. A talent he'd long tried to capitalise on in an attempt at being Cougher's diminutive opposite, he'd sometimes blow clouds of blood over defeated opponents. Some spectators felt this act of mockery went beyond the pale. Like when he'd started swallowing live goldfish. Spinks would stand in the middle of ring, triumphant, only to be pelted with paper cups and other trash.

"Somebody fucking get that dwarf off," they'd scream.

Uglybugly

The show would be over and Spinks would shuffle out of the ring, shoulders bowed and blood streaming from his nose, or carrying an empty goldfish bowl.

Spinks dug out one of his discarded wrestling outfits for me one day, a black leotard with a single strap across the shoulder. I went straight over to the mirror, put it on, flexed my hard muscles, and grinned at my reflection. Then I picked up the dumb-bells. I'd done a lot of weight training recently – anything to get out of doing all that thankless throwing.

But now Betty had started to complain about her figure, because my increased appetite meant she was putting weight on her arse.

"You're getting bigger and stronger Earl, but I won't be able to get into my clothes soon."

"Ha! We can buy new ones," I said lifting the weights in front of the mirror. "With all the wages I've saved, we can treat ourselves to some new clothes."

I was getting strong, and looked good. I wasn't hitting the bottle so often, and was even eating fruit and vegetables. She should have been grateful instead of moaning. After all, I was in better shape now to protect her. But if it was going to cost me a new wardrobe to keep this Little Miss happy, she was well aware that I stashed a bit away each night. From Mr King's till. Not a lot. Not so much that he'd notice. But enough to cover a few running costs. And his till was always stuffed, so it shouldn't really have been a problem. One night, when I'd allowed myself a rare drop or two, I did admittedly cram my pockets very full. But then there she was, straight on my case, giving me an earful.

"Earl!" she whispered fiercely. "Ear-rl!"

Reluctantly, I pulled the banknotes from my trouser pocket.

"Whoops! Seems like the hand's been at it again." I joked,

115

laughing.

But Betty refused to take it as a joke or to be fooled.

"More like, Earl Merrik's been at it again." She cocked her head and eyed me sternly.

"Alright, alright," I muttered, putting most of it back. "Look, there's hardly space for more in the till and the night isn't even over."

"That's not the point, Earl. Put it all back."

"There won't be no new clothes for you tomorrow, then," I said, taking a defiant swig from my glass. If she was so determined to be difficult, I could be uncooperative too.

"Considering how hard I work and how much I push myself for the two of us."

"That really isn't the point. I don't want to steal from Mr King."

"When did you start gettin' such friendly feelin's for the old cripple? Didn't think you gave a toss about him?"

"I just don't want to get into trouble again with all your nonsense, Earl."

"But you want clothes...you want food. You're a great expense to me, Betty. You owe your brother a bit, don't you think? Still, that's no problem...I'll just have to take a trip up to Mr King's and ask for a pay rise. Tell him how spoiled and expensive to run my little sister's gettin'."

"Yes, you do that, Earl," said Betty, offended, and returning to her book.

The next day we went out. I bought myself some new clothes. A jacket, a waistcoat and a new hat. And if that wasn't enough, we splashed out on a new frock for Betty. And she wasn't too high-principled to accept it. The problem came when we got back home, and she tried to hide behind me when Mr King came rolling towards us.

"Ah, Betty," he called out, "what a lovely dress!"

"Yes, isn't it!" I answered for her.

"Earl...Earl...bought it," she whispered, her head bowed.

"Well...I must say...you're very kind to your sister...and how did you get the money for that?"

"Well, I've scrimped and saved since we got 'ere...an' we 'ad a bit of cash from before too...not that the clothes you've bought for us aren't smart...but it feels good to be able to buy something with our own money...if you get my meaning."

"But of course...there's nothing compares!" smiled Mr King. "Nice hat, Earl!"

"Yes, isn't it," I answered, and handed it to him.

Mr King took the hat, held it up and ran his fingers along the brim, nodding in admiration.

"What d'you say Tim? I think I might buy a hat like that myself..."

Tim nodded.

Then he handed the hat back to me and let himself be wheeled off again, whistling. Betty breathed a sigh of relief.

"There, you see!" I said. "Everything's just fine."

TIM

I stood in front of the mirror at the wrestling school, lifting the dumb-bells rhythmically in front of me, my imagination racing. Even though I'd promised it would never go that far. Betty had made it clear it wasn't on the cards, and that I shouldn't go getting ideas. Under no circumstances would she climb into that ring with all those big men going berserk.

"No way am I going to risk having that snake put around my neck," she said.

But the idea was too alluring to let it rest. Surely I had to be allowed to dream. A little. I tried finding a suitable name: *Earl 'The Prince' Merrik. Earl the Crusher. Earl the Mighty. Earl the Master Wrestler. The Miracle.* I pictured Frehley and Miracle Merrik, waiting in the corner, sweaty and ready, as the man in his short-armed black and white stripy cotton shirt walked into the centre of the ring with the megaphone.

"Ladies and Gentlemen! It is with great pleasure that Olympen presents the eighth and ninth wonders of the world... Wrestler Frehley and the gruesome...the spectacular...the merciless...sewn by the Devil himself...Earl the Crusher!... Earl the Merciless...Earl the Miracle...the greatest...the *greatest,* I tell you."

An evening for bloody retribution. And the public are going mad, clattering chairs and roaring. In the opposite corner I can see Jacob with his snake, and Tim Burley wearing a gruesome mask on his face. Restless and impatient. In the wings, Cougher and Spinks are standing by, ready to run to the rescue if the match gets dirty. Which is guaranteed to happen, with two such amazingly unbeatable and fear-inducing wonders like ourselves. Who wouldn't be driven to dirty tricks?

And behind me Betty. Poor terrified Betty. Virtuous prudish Betty. With scorn in her eyes.

"Just dream on, Earl…It's not gonna happen."

I peered at her in the mirror. She was standing there smiling.

"You know somethin', I reckon that's exactly what you should let me do. What's it come to if you can't let me dream in peace sometimes?" I asked, lifting the dumb-bell.

A moment later Tim came in from the changing room and walked over to me.

"Hi, Mr Merrik," he said.

"Hi there," I said, forcing myself to lift the dumb-bell one more time, as he stood watching.

"You're getting the hang of those weights, sir," he said slowly.

"Yeah, I am!" I pressed myself forward and forced myself to lift it yet again.

"He's got so strong!" Betty chirped.

Now I really was desperate to make one last lift.

"Yup, I can see that." Tim didn't move. I was beginning to get irritated. The weights were heavy enough without this black guy standing there, stiff as a poker, staring at me. As I rested my arm, Betty exchanged a few words with him before he turned to me again.

"Well, now," he said eventually. "What d'you wanna do today sir?"

"How d'you mean?"

"Well, Mr King sent me over to instruct you…so we can assess the possibilities."

"Really?" I wiped away the sweat. "But I'm comin' on fine. Besides I've got Spinks, so I'm sure things will work out. But thanks."

I lifted the dumb-bell again.

"I dunno if you remember what you and Mr King agreed?

He laid down some conditions, sir? You made a deal, and that's why I'm here today."

"Mr King says this and Mr King says that," I muttered.

"Besides, Spinks has gone for the day."

"He has?" I looked at myself in the mirror.

"I'm afraid you must excuse my brother," Betty suddenly chimed in.

"Oh, really?" Tim peered at us, and smiled quizzically.

"Yes, he's not very good with strangers."

"With strangers? But we've known each other a while now, haven't we Betty?"

"Well, yes. It's not that," Betty ventured.

"What is it then? There's not much can compare with my credentials, I can assure you both."

"I don't doubt your credentials as a *wrestler*," I said. "I've seen you in action. You're good…better than most."

"So, what is it then, sir?"

"Well, I don't know…but Spinks has kinda got the knack… me and my sister are delicate…you see…and what with her bein' so scared…I don't want her gettin' more anxious than necessary."

"Oh, I've got no problem with Tim spending some time with us, Earl," Betty added hastily.

Tim peered at me.

"Alright, alright…it isn't that you haven't got the knack…I can see you're more than smart enough to *learn* how to be a good wrestler…but I can't see how your kind could have much to *teach*…if you understand? It just isn't in the black man's nature to *teach*. A nigger might *learn* to drive a car…but he can't *invent* a car…if you ask me…"

"I understand, Earl," said Tim. With that he walked out.

I stopped to catch my breath. Betty and I drank some water before going back to the weights. Uncle Rust came over to us.

He leaned with one shoulder to the wall, some lists in front of him and a pencil behind his ear. His eyes glazed.

"Mornin'," he said.

"Hi," we answered in chorus.

"So, how's the training going Earl? You're putting on weight."

"Yup."

"But have you got everything you need? Everything alright? Are the boys being good to you?"

"Yup, yup. Everything's perfect. The nigger's naggin' a bit...but apart from that everything's perfect!"

Uncle Rust settled back against the wall and took his pencil out from behind his ear.

"You don't say? Well, I think the *nigger* is a bit offended by you at the moment."

"Oh. Why's that?" I asked.

"Earl, couldn't you stop calling Tim a *nigger?* A man like you should know better."

"Yes but, but...you just called him a nigger yourself a minute ago."

The room went silent. The other men stopped their training. They glared in our direction. Betty pinched my arm and shook her head.

"Earl," sighed Uncle Rust, tucking the lists under his arm. "D'you really think I meant it?" He looked up at me again.

"He may as well call me a nigger...Mr Aukrust," said Tim behind me.

"There you see!" I cut in.

"It's obvious that's how Earl views me... But we've got an agreement with Mr King...and I'd rather not take payment for a job I haven't done."

"You're getting *paid?*" My jaw dropped.

He nodded.

"Just so you know, Earl," said Uncle Rust, clearing his throat. "The majority and, I have to say, the best of the wrestlers you see behind you have learned a great deal from Tim. So perhaps you're the numbskull, since you can't take his guidance."

"Helluva lot of chat pouring out of you today," I grunted. "You still bitter about that flea, eh?"

Uncle Rust sighed. "No, I'm not bitter *about that flea*. And if it hadn't been for a bit of chat, the human race would never have got beyond its infancy, Earl."

The dumb-bell was getting heavier. With everybody staring at me, what I wanted more than anything was to lift it up defiantly, glare back at them all, and carry on until they all got bored and got back to their own business. It was then I felt the hand go numb. I stood there, getting increasingly red in the face, trying my hardest to lift the weight. But it wasn't going to happen. Finally, with everybody still staring at me, my left fist opened of its own accord, and almost threw the weight to the floor with what I expected to be a crash, but with what proved to be a miserable dull thud, like somebody tenderising a steak.

"My foot," I screamed, "my foot."

But when I looked down I realised it wasn't my foot, it was Betty's.

"Hmm, very interesting..." said Uncle Rust caustically. "Is there a doctor here?" he shouted. Nobody answered.

"My sister!" I yelled. "My sister!"

Betty looked down at her foot in astonishment, then back up at me. I felt like my head was about to blow off with the pain. We'd suffered quite a bit back in the institution where they'd done all those tests...the icy water and nails and allsorts...but this was in a league of its own.

"Oy," said Betty.

We managed to manoeuvre ourselves over to the wall.

Oddly enough, Betty was walking almost normally, while I was limping. And with every step she took, the pain shot through my foot.

"Uncle Rust," I whimpered.

"Do I look like a doctor? But *Tim,* on the other hand, he's dealt with all sorts over the years."

"Well, I'm not exactly a doctor, but I can certainly take a look at that foot," said Tim calmly. "*If* Earl permits it, that is?"

I nodded, my eyes closed. Tim crouched down in front of Betty. Gently he unlaced her shoe and then, just as gently, pulled her stocking off. He took her little foot in his big hand. And now she started wailing. And I felt Tim's cool fingers on her hot, swollen foot.

"If you think Tim doesn't somehow have the right to exist," said Uncle Rust, "I can assure you that goes for all of us. God's no more bothered about you, than Tim here. So grit your teeth Earl, life's too short, sooner or later you'll snuff it. Meanwhile I think you'd do better to take every friend you can get. And without wishing to cause offence...I think you lack the instinct for finding the *best* friends. If you get my drift...sorry Tim, but that's how I see it."

"No worries, Uncle Rust. We all have a right to an opinion. But I think we might need an ice bag." Tim stroked Betty's foot softly, and – with the exception of Cougher's comforting hand during wrestling matches – this was the closest anybody had been allowed to get to her in ages.

Afterwards Frehley drove us home in the milk truck, and we spent the next few days in bed with Betty's foot rested on a cushion. Very soon the pain disappeared from my body, and settled fully into hers. But I'd started sleeping badly. Slowly but surely, it sank in. I didn't dare move for fear of disturbing Betty, and sleep only came when I finally decided I'd never call Tim a *nigger* again. And that the next time I saw him I'd tell him just that. Not that I thought I'd ever be completely comfortable with it. We are what we are. But my life would never be quite the same again.

The hand, it seemed, had made its point. But I decided that from now on, I'd only train my right arm. If it was going to come up with any more antics, I wanted to be prepared. It was time to show that bug some muscle.

JACOB

One evening at Olympen, Betty would finally get an outlet for all that anger she'd been carrying around. She gasped as we walked into the arena. Because at last, without Cougher having breathed a word, Jacob and he were billed as the night's big attraction.

But to the public's great disappointment, and Betty's even greater joy, not so much as one drop of blood was spilled from Cougher's mouth that night. At first, it looked as though Jacob had the upper hand. He came at it hard, and soon Cougher lay stretched out in the ring belly up, as the snake writhed in the corner. Jacob clambered up onto one of the posts. Ready to fling his full weight down on Cougher's chest. Betty's face went chalk-white and she clutched her handkerchief with equally white knuckles, as she held back the anger and tears that were ready to explode.

But just as Jacob threw himself from the post, and everybody was convinced that now, now Cougher would be crippled for life under his knees, Cougher rolled elegantly to the side. Jacob crashed into the underlay so hard that the mat almost threw him back onto his feet. And from that moment, the fight was Cougher's. And as Betty screamed *yes! yes!* Jacob got a thorough beating. On paper at least.

Finally Cougher lifted the snake and held it up before him. Betty shrank at my side. "No, Cougher," she whispered. "No, don't do it."

But instead of putting the snake round Jacob's neck – which would hardly have served any purpose – Cougher put it gently back in the sack. Then, with a smile of satisfaction, he pulled the drawstrings. In one decisive movement, he let the weight of the snake's body drop so that the bag snapped shut and hung, as though from a gallows from his outstretched hand. Then he slapped it down onto Jacob's belly. *Finito*. The End. The Fight was over. To mixed reactions from the crowd…but Betty's obvious delight.

"There," she said smiling, cheeks flushed. "There you see a true gentleman, Earl."

Mr King, however, shook his head and threw his hands up in dismay. Words couldn't express the disappointment he felt about Cougher not giving Jacob a taste of his own medicine. And when I asked if Betty and I couldn't take a trip to the changing rooms, his answer was terse.

"Sure, by all means. You just run along down to your friends. But you can show me out first at least, so everybody can see who you arrived with."

We did. And the instant he was installed in his car, we rushed down to the changing rooms. Betty's heart thumping. But no sooner had we entered the steamy semi-darkened room, than Betty turned on her heels to run out again.

There, on the bench, sitting next to Cougher, was Jacob. With a bottle in his hand and a towel over his shoulder. And if that wasn't enough, the two of them were talking and laughing together. Cougher was actually sitting there *praising* Jacob for his performance.

This must, of course, have come as a bit of a shock to this little featherbrain.

"Well I never. Hi there…if it's not the fantastical twins!" Jacob said, smiling, as though he'd been looking forward to seeing us again.

"But…but…" stammered Betty.

"Betty, I want you to meet an old and very good friend of mine," grinned Cougher, glistening with sweat. Not one single fleck of blood on him.

Terrified, Betty let herself be led over to the bench where Jacob took her hand and bowed politely, almost grandly.

And before the evening was done, Betty finally heard the whole story with her own ears. Though some of it had to be explained several times before it sank in. But when she did at last see how it had all hung together – how the game worked and what went on behind the scenes – her anger gradually subsided. Sighing, she started to laugh – at herself and at everything.

"So, you see, Betty," said Jacob "we couldn't exactly be enemies. Not with all the preparations that go into a fight like that."

"How could I be so stupid?" she said over and over. She laughed then shed a tear. Until laughing and crying, she dabbed a handkerchief to her eyes.

And as the two men talked on excitedly, she heard the tragic circumstances under which Jacob had entered the world. And reminiscing about Cougher and all the wonderful things they'd done together, Jacob started to get sentimental.

Maudlin even.

Leaning forwards, with his elbows on his knees and picking at the label on a bottle restlessly, until there was nothing left but flakes of paper and glue, he started blubbing to my sister.

Imagine that…*Jacob*…the world's most cunning and evil wrestler. My hero – if it hadn't been for his being pitched against Cougher that night – was sitting there blubbing, with his belly spilling over his tight leotard, unable to pull himself together.

"Cougher was like a father to me," Jacob whispered, wiping his nose with Betty's handkerchief. "And d'you know why?"

Betty shook her head.

"Because my father ought really to have been my grandfather – can you imagine? Not that he could even manage that. And when I finally got the chance to meet him in the ring, it wasn't just for show, I can tell you. And if it hadn't been for Cougher that night I wouldn't be sitting here today...that much I promise."

Jacob sighed.

"My life's pretty damned awful when you think about it. It stinks. But being up in that ring...well...it's not just the only thing I *can* do, it's the only thing that makes me *happy*. I couldn't stop now and become...a school teacher, say."

Betty nodded quietly, then shook her head at the sadness of it all.

"And everything I ever learned, I learned from Cougher here."

He winked at us, as he put the stripped bottle to his lips.

"You see, Betty!" I chimed in.

"But not the thing with the snake?" she asked. "The snake's really horrible."

Jacob laughed hoarsely and wiped the underside of his nose delicately, before folding the handkerchief.

"What, my mate here? What the fuck have you got against my mate?" he said.

Betty recoiled. But Jacob's voice was gentle – it was – a manner of speech, nothing more.

"He's my best mate," he explained, running his fingers through sweaty black curls. "There's not a wife who'd put up with me and the life I live. Forever on the move and battered and bruised every night. I carry everything I own in that sack. And there's no more evil in him than in any of Our Lord's creations – not a grain. And you mustn't go thinking my opponents come to any harm from him either. He's well trained, and it's all just for entertainment...you got to understand that."

Betty nodded sceptically, before he added:

"He doesn't squeeze *that* hard...so long as he's had his

dinner…" Jacob laughed hoarsely again, and drained his bottle. He limited his consumption that night, saving his heavier drinking for life on the road.

When Jacob had gone off to take a wash, Frehley padded over to us.

"Can you two come on a trip tomorrow?" he asked with a gleeful smile.

"A trip?"

"A little excursion. We're going out in my wagon, and you're heartily welcome."

Cougher came over and stood next to the giant, smiling with equal excitement.

"I don't know," answered Betty sadly.

"You don't know?" I asked disbelievingly. "Of course we'll come."

Cougher shuffled uneasily.

"Don't you want to?" he asked.

"Of course I want to come," whispered Betty, "but I don't know if we'll be allowed."

"Huh?" I asked.

"By Mr King, I mean," she said, starting to cry again.

"Betty, Betty, Betty" said the giant gently. "It'll be fine. I'll ring Biff and we'll sort it out."

"Are you friends with *him* too now?" wailed Betty, feeling that nothing made sense any longer.

"Well, not friends exactly. But d'you think he'd pick a quarrel with me?" Frehley placed a big index finger gently under Betty's chin and lifted her tear-stained face. "Betty, look at me. I win any argument! Any! D'you think I'm frightened of a weedy little man in a wheelchair?"

Betty shook her head and smiled.

"Uncle Rust! Come on! We've got a telephone call to make!" said Frehley, as he thundered out.

"Yeah, alright, alright," mumbled Uncle Rust, stretching himself out on the bench.

Frehley ducked his head back under the doorframe and yelled into the changing room.

"Now, Uncle Rust! Not tomorrow!"

Cougher sat down on the bench and put his arm round Betty.

Alone at last.

I sighed.

A drip from the shower echoed in the abandoned room.

Doubtless Mr King was pretty bad-tempered and uncooperative with Frehley on the phone at first, but now that he'd agreed to the trip, he insisted on packing us off with a whole case of champagne.

"Here, take this."

"A *whole* case, Mr King?"

"Frehley'll probably drink the lion's share, if I know him right."

Mr King wasn't mistaken.

Early that morning I stood looking over his broad shoulders, as he wheeled himself around the kitchen, with a large basket on his lap that he was filling with every kind of provision. Perhaps because he wanted to prove he wasn't offended or jealous, it was impossible to dissuade him from turning his kitchen upside down in his search for goodies – chocolates, pâté, new baked bread, soft-boiled eggs – that he insisted on boiling himself, despite the bother involved, and more. Even though this was quite unnecessary – Frehley had already organised food and drink in plenty.

"Perhaps you could come too?" I asked. "You know each other, don't you?"

"No…I don't think so." Mr King hesitated. "Things are a bit complicated with Frehley."

"Complicated?'

"Well. Not exactly complicated…but he keeps himself to himself…and I keep to myself…and the two don't mix."

"Oh?"

Mr King stopped. He pressed the brakes on his chair, and stared out of the window as though his mind was somewhere else for a moment. Then he re-released the wheels and went back to filling the basket.

"I was the one who took Frehley in…gave him food and a roof over his head…I even got him medicines so he wouldn't grow to Hell and back. But the minute wonder-boy got his head above water, he betrayed me. You understand?"

I just looked at him.

"Frehley started this wrestling school. Without me. And I, well I started *this*." Mr King gazed up at the ceiling, then shrugged his shoulders.

"He gave me a tidy sum – and the investment paid for itself it's not that – but that was all. I'm only too glad to help people, but I don't like being betrayed. You understand? I don't tolerate that."

I nodded my head.

"Not that I'm complaining." Mr King waved the idea aside. "It pays to be positive!"

He smiled before sticking an apple in his mouth and taking down another ham.

"There, that should do! You must send my greetings to the giant, and we'll see each other on your return."

When we arrived at the train station with the big hamper and the case of champagne, carried for us by Tim, everything was ready and waiting. Frehley was sitting in the middle of the wagon at the end of a long, fully laid table, a broad smile on his face and a napkin already tucked into his collar. Since the wagon was joined to the back of a train it rocked like we were in a little ship, though Frehley had taken care of this with all his nifty fittings. Anything loose was bolted down or put behind heavy cupboard doors. Nothing was left to chance.

"Welcome to my table!" The giant opened his arms out wide, so they practically reached from one side of the wagon to the other.

And there we sat – Cougher, Spinks, Uncle Rust, Tim, Jacob and ourselves. And a couple of Frehley's and Jacob's lady friends. Jacob sat there, smart and freshly groomed, with his sack ready-packed, since he was planning to jump off towards the end of the trip. A new championship, a new belt, awaited him. We ate and drank and cracked jokes as we enjoyed the fabulous view. Plains, tumbleweed, fields and countryside as far as the eye could see, and deer and racoons that bolted nervously as we passed. Spinks reckoned he'd seen a huge bear, but nobody believed him. Now and then it fell silent around the table, as we sat in the dark, thundering through a tunnel. Then Frehley would laugh to himself at the end of the table. Cougher and Betty enjoyed every second, and I felt his ring finger playfully circling her palm under the table.

Our journey lasted morning to evening. And we drove through Littletown twice that day – once on the way out, and once on the way back. Not that I paid much attention to it, the only thing that struck me about it was the sweet smell of confectionery and chocolate that hung in the air. Spinks stuck his head out of the window to smell it both times.

"Littletown," he sighed. "Littletown, Littletown. Nothing smells like Littletown."

It was twilight, and we were out in the middle of a plain, when the train started to slow on a bend and Jacob suddenly decided that this was his moment. Throwing his sack over his shoulder, he leaped from the train. To everybody's horror. The wagon tilted to one side as the big men all stormed across the wagon, in an attempt to hold him steady.

"Careful, careful!" bellowed Frehley, clinging to the table.

Cougher shook his head despairingly. And although Jacob's lady friend burst into tears, he couldn't hold back the laughter as he waved goodbye. Jacob had clearly planned his exit, because at the next station the wagon was turned and joined to another train that would pull us back home. Cougher scouted in vain for his friend, but a few days later he got a postcard from him saying everything was fine. We all had our doubts, of course, but we were somewhat reassured. It was a sign of life at least.

On the way home, exhausted, and with my belly full and my head heavy with champagne, I slept in Frehley's big bed, while next to me, Cougher and Betty lay in each other's arms. It was all a dream. A lovely rare dream.

And for the first time, and perhaps the last, I felt really sorry for Mr King.

Mr King looked almost surprised to see us again. The hotel was quiet when we got back. The ballroom was almost empty, the house almost without guests. Mr King had settled himself on one of the sofas and sat there with a cigar, looking dejected. We crept in, and he didn't see us before I put a hand on his shoulder.

"Earl!" he burst out, throwing his cigar into the ashtray. And then seeing us both – "Betty!"

Almost as if he'd expected me to get rid of her on the way back.

Mr King stretched his arms out to us and we gave him a big hug.

"Well, were they good to you?" he asked.

And so we told him about our trip.

"Can I offer you a bite?' he asked finally.

"Thanks, Mr King, but we're stuffed. Frehley had heaps of…"

I bit my tongue. His face twitched involuntarily.

"Your hamper came in very useful!" Betty chimed in.

"Yes, we're stuffed with it all," I added.

Not that I was sure we'd even opened his basket during the entire trip. In fact it was still in the wagon, not that I dared mention that.

"But luckily Frehley was responsible for downing most of the champagne," smiled Betty.

"Excellent, excellent," smiled Mr King

But though he smiled, I had a niggling fear that he'd cry himself to sleep with the thought of what he'd missed. Even Betty remarked on it as we went to bed… that Mr King seemed sad.

Sad or not – the fact that we'd come back seemed to have a reassuring effect on Mr King. He stopped making veiled comments every time we went to meet our friends. He and Betty stopped their whingeing. We came and went as we pleased, without having to worry what he thought.

Better still, I stepped up my training. Which was less taken up with Spinks' boring attention to detail, now that we had Tim helping us too. Tim continually invented new grips for me to use on Spinks. Obvious impediments taken into account, things started to look rather impressive. Tim would give me the wink just before I had to go for a throw, so when Spinks came hurtling towards me, I'd grab him and fling him round. With Spinks on the mat, Tim would throw himself off the corner post and crash into him so hard, the mat would curl like a whip under our feet. After which we'd rush in and fling ourselves on top of the heap of bodies.

"Earl the King!" I'd scream, Betty covering one ear.

After training we'd eat together. We followed a diet Tim set up. It satisfied my appetite, while letting Betty keep her figure.

And every Sunday Betty would let Cougher take her to church. We'd meet at the cafeteria where he still gave her a regular bouquet of flowers, which she'd put in water in our room and not throw away until he gave her another the next Sunday.

But although Betty had stopped moaning quite so much, she still hadn't given up her campaign to find somewhere else to live.

As a rule the subject would come up after the service, when the three of us were sitting on a park bench or in the cafeteria. With my arms crossed and a toothpick to gnaw my frustration out on, I'd twist myself as far away from her as possible as she prattled on. She was entitled to her opinion and I mine.

"Cougher, I want to leave…and I want to live with all of you," she'd whisper, the bouquet lying in her lap.

"I know, Betty, I know."

If I tried so much as to hum a little tune to myself, or maybe whistle – mostly at the pretty girls that passed us on the street – she was instantly back on my case. She was incapable of giving me any bloody time to myself. She'd probably have preferred us to sit and whinge in chorus. And I wasn't about to do that. Why should I? On the whole I was quite content with how things were, so what was there to moan about? We'd gone through worse. And rarely better. I let my gaze wander over Bigtown's street life; the newspaper boys, the trams, town sparrows hopping about, fruit sellers and food stalls. Not forgetting the endless stream of girls passing by.

I took a toothpick out of my mouth, so as to whistle.

"Ear-rl!" Betty snarled. "Earrrrr–l."

"Now, now," said Cougher and laughed. "Now, now Betty."

For the first time ever, I felt healthy and strong. This not only increased my appetite, but increased my urge to help myself to the leggy delights that floated about us in the bordello.

The Girl

One evening, I was sitting there, with one of the bordello's
girls, after she'd already been more than kind. Betty had
protested for the first time in ages – she was getting almost
as prudish as before, again for fear of coming out badly with
Cougher. Still, I'd managed over time to have quite a few of
the girls.

But I told her straight now, that it was my money that went
on it. And since I'd generally managed to stay off the bottle,
and hadn't found the same happiness as Cougher and her, she
went reluctantly along with it.

"It's not like we've all got a sweetheart like you."

"Alright, Earl, just go ahead. See if I care!"

"Where's *my* love interest…that's all I'm asking?"

"Alright then, Earl. Get it over with. Quick!"

"Yeah, yeah…don't hassle me either!"

And afterwards the girl – who seemed almost as keen on
me, as I was on her – sat there with a flush in her cheek, and
wearing hardly more than shoes and a string of pearls, which
she passed now and then over rouged lips. Her long legs draped
over my lap. She tousled my hair, as I ran my hands over her
slender thighs. And since I wanted her to stay, I plied her with
chocolates and tried to keep the conversation going.

"Perhaps I could buy you some clothes?" I asked, as the
conversation threatened to dry up.

"Ear-rl…" sighed Betty.

"You just shush," I said, lifting my hand to her, then
lowering it again to rest against the delicate skin on the inside
of the girl's leg.

"Have you really got the cash for that, eh?' the girl asked.

"Course I have," I said. "The old cripple and I are on pretty good terms, let me tell you. We're like mates."

"Oh really? How comes?"

"How comes?" I asked. "How comes?! Well, he's only gone and given me the top job in this house."

"Stop it, Earl," whispered Betty.

"Stop what?! Tell me, has anyone else here got the keys to the house, eh?"

Betty said nothing.

"Have you really got the keys to the house?" the girl said, purring softly and still playing with her pearls. With a faintly teasing smile as though she was bored or didn't want to believe me.

"Of course!" I answered. "I have to have them, you see, when I take the cashbox up at night."

Earl, the idiot, was starting to lay it on too thick.

"Where?"

"Where what?"

"Where d'you take the cashbox?"

"Up to the *office* of course..."

"Have you got the key to the office, then?!" A tremor went through her, and she let go of her pearls. She leapt up from the sofa and started to flit back and forth in front of us, fumbling with a cigarette as she tried to fix it into her holder.

"Do you go up there often?"

I nodded.

"Really? *Honestly?*" She cocked her head, with narrow teasing eyes.

"Yeah, yeah," I said, reaching for her hips. I estimated I had enough money for another trick. The aim of my chatter certainly hadn't been for her to swan around like this. She perched reluctantly on the armrest, then flipping her shoes off she stuck her feet under my thigh.

139

"Can't you take me up there with you?" she asked, placing the cigarette holder between her teeth.

"Maybe…" I said hesitantly. "I'd have to ask Mr King first of course, but…"

"Not later. *Now! Pleeaase!*" she said, rocking her legs restlessly from side to side, so I lost sight of her pussy. She stroked me under the chin, and turned my face to hers. "Earl…I *really* want to see the office…and Mr King's safe…that would be so exciting…*pleeaase.*"

Betty told me later that she'd known it would all end in disaster, if I started to mess with the girls. Which I thought was pretty unfair – I just chose the wrong girl to make friends with. And my pride and curiosity made it impossible to resist the temptation of sneaking up there. Just to take a look. Nothing more. And to maybe get a trick up in the office. That was all. For the thrill. Plant it up her in those luxurious surroundings. I had the key. I'd never had the chance to try it in the office door, and I couldn't be certain…but it might just fit. If it didn't, it wouldn't be disastrous…it would just be a matter of tiptoeing off again…no harm done.

"OK, but it'll mean a trick more," I said.

"Of course!"

"For free…"

She considered this for moment. "Alright, but first I want to see the office *and* Mr King's safe."

"I don't think you should talk about things like that with my brother," Betty said sternly.

But the girl just laughed coldly, and picked up her clothes. I laughed too. And before I knew it, I'd let this leggy beauty lead me up to the office. Where reluctantly, with legs like rubber, I fished the key out of my pocket, listening all the while for any noises inside.

"Earl," hissed Betty.

She'd fought with me all the way. Here and there, her shoes had left black marks in the linoleum. But not a word had left her mouth, for fear we'd be found straying in the corridors.

"Come on, then," whispered the girl. "See if it fits. Come on."

I stuck the key in the lock.

It refused to go round.

I sighed with relief.

"Oh, well," I whispered, shrugging my shoulders.

"Doesn't it fit?" she asked scornfully.

"No, perhaps he's changed the lock," I whispered.

"Pff! Come on," said the girl. She grabbed my hand and yanked the key round so hard I thought her nails would come loose.

The door opened.

Mr Bugs

We were barely two minutes in this Aladdin's cave, before the shit hit the fan. In that brief moment I did little more than scratch my head and speculate on my next move which basically involved getting into the girl's knickers one more time. But when we'd finally got inside, all she did was to start prowling about. Without aim or purpose. She sniffed around like a little cat, rubbing herself up against Mr King's sofa one minute, and helping herself to his drinks in the next. Breathless with excitement, face flushed. Until she finally plopped into an armchair with a glass in one hand and cigar in the other. Comfortably planted in Mr King's chair now, she whacked one leg up on the desk. A pile of papers scrunched under her heel, as she swivelled slowly from side to side, legs spread, cheeks aflame. Stuffing the cigar in her mouth, she slowly drew her skirt up.

But just as I thought my moment had come, she was back on her feet again.

Betty was rigid with fear, trying to forget where she was. With tightly-shut eyes, she was trying to blot me, and my activities, out of her head. And the girl was doing nothing but flit about, I decided it best to show her the safe as quickly as possible, and get us out of here before she refurnished the whole room.

"This," I whispered, "is where the old duffer puts his savin's."

And that's how we were, when Mr King suddenly appeared from nowhere with Tim behind him. And there he sat in the doorway, shaking his head and sighing.

In his lap lay a document wallet.

"Earl, Earl..." he said, sighing again. He shrugged his shoulders and let himself be pushed into the room.

"Well, well, well," he whispered, turning the light on. "It had to come."

Mr King ordered the girl to leave.

"I'll deal with you later, alright?"

Not needing to be asked twice she was out of the door, which Tim closed behind her. I just stood there shaking my head and wiping my snot with the back of my hand.

Mr King spoke in a soft voice. Almost scarily soft. He seemed anything but surprised. Which made me wonder later if he'd set the whole thing up. Just whet Earl's appetite – the inquisitive fool – send a girl down to offer him a bit of nookie and ask a few dumb questions. Then all he had to do was wait. Like a spider for a fly. Wait to pocket his prize...my sister.

Who, of course, immediately started to howl.

"I'm so, so sorry, Mr King. We weren't going to do anything," she sobbed. "It was my brother. It was my brother. I couldn't do anything about it, nothing, you must realise..."

But Betty's excuses fell on deaf ears. It was me he had in his sights.

"So, you finally discovered that the key fitted the office door too. Well, well, well. I wasn't even sure if it fitted myself. But that means the whole house has been open to you all this time. So why haven't you tried before? Earl...why haven't you tried before?"

Surprise to say, he didn't lay a hand on either of us. Neither Betty nor me. He just sat there quietly, looking more and more disappointed. In fact, the thought didn't even seem to cross his mind.

"Look Earl, I'll be kind." Mr King stroked his hand over the document wallet. "I run a reputable business. And my girls don't have too bad a time. We maintain certain standards, and besides there's no need for unpleasantness. But as things stand…well…the two of you owe me a substantial wodge of money."

I didn't understand what the old scoundrel meant by us owing him money. We'd barely touched the safe, or anything else. Besides, I'd only been curious. After a drop too many, and that little whore pestering me to see what was behind that big door. When it boiled down to it, the main thing was that she'd promised me a trick.

"I think it's time you had a little chat with your sister," Mr King said, as though it was the most natural thing in the world, as though he was suggesting I take a walk round the block.

Betty looked up, her jaw dropped. She couldn't believe her own ears.

"Please, please, Mr King," she begged, sobbing so hard it was barely possible to make her out. "It was my brother…it was my brother…"

And with that, she started rattling off all the things that I'd apparently forced her into doing. Right from when we were little kids. Everything! As though she was standing before the Almighty on Judgement Day. It flooded out of her. Because nobody must think *she* was actually to blame for anything… oh no…it was her *brother*, who else, who'd lured her into it all. From start to finish, down to the smallest detail. She even mentioned the cocktail sticks and ashtrays that had gone from the bar.

Mr King hid his face in his hands as if this was all too much to take in. He shook his head solemnly, while, behind him, Tim coughed to hold back the laughter.

After her list of such petty trivialities, I almost believed we'd come through this alright after all. But then she started serving up a few bigger, and more uncomfortable confessions, that Mr King most certainly appreciated hearing. He could have taken some of them, straight down to the station, if he'd wanted, had extortion not been preferable. Without a thought for the cripple's motives, my sister now flung the sluice gates wide open. Although scattered in among her confessions, came the odd little prayer, prompting the Almighty to appeal to Mr King's conscience.

In other words, it was one long embarrassment from beginning to end. Betty and I had spent our entire lives together, we'd experienced exactly the same things, yet she could still be so bloody *gullible*. It felt like I was carrying the whole world's superstitious faith and confusion in one gigantic bundle on my back.

I wasn't getting a word in edgeways. So, I used my time to try to plan a plausible explanation for how we'd got into this mess. An explanation that would outweigh Betty's new confessions on the credibility front.

*In our eagerness to do the best job possible...*No-no-no! As we went past the office we saw...As we went past the office we *noticed* that the door was open. The door was open, and so we felt it was our plain, simple duty to investigate the matter more closely. It would have been bad if anyone had nicked anything from our boss...our *dear* boss. And since, in fact, Earl Merrik knows a thing or two about wall safes, and safes in general, it seemed as well to investigate the matter right away, before reporting back. *And so there we stood...It's a mystery, boss...an out-and-out mystery. You must forgive my sister... she's just scared...so scared she'd admit to murder. This isn't the first time either, so you mustn't believe half what she says. It's just the fear talking.*

After Betty's testimony, unnecessary as well as long-winded, Mr King motioned to Tim to pass her a handkerchief. I still hadn't opened my mouth. But when the opportunity did finally offer itself, it felt like my lips were sewn up.

"Boss," I began, "it was our duty…our plain duty."

"Duty?" Mr King smiled, an eyebrow raised in surprise.

"Yes. It's a mystery."

"A mystery?"

"And since Earl Merrik knows a thing or two about wall safes…and safes in general…it seemed just as well to investigate the matter right away."

"Christ, what do you know about safes? Are you in the *security safe business*, perhaps?"

"Well…no…"

"Have you ever been in the security safe business, Earl?"

"Not exactly."

With all the time in the world I wasn't going to find an excuse to get us out of this one. Besides, Betty had started snivelling again, and now the cripple turned to offer her a second, equally clean, handkerchief.

"My poor child, calm yourself. We'll sort this out, don't you worry."

Without warning, Betty curtsied, in gratitude for his words of comfort and the clean hanky. Not only did this knock me off balance (my knee was aching after a session with Spinks) but it also made me lose my cool.

"You mustn't listen to her, boss…she admits to all sorts. She's so full of guilt all kinds of lies come out of her…all the time. She'd admit to murder to get herself out of this fix."

I could have bitten my tongue.

"Oh? So what kind of fix is she in, Earl? I can't understand a word the poor child is saying. Can you understand what she's saying, Tim?"

Tim shook his head.

"I think perhaps you'll have explain to us what kind of fix Betty's in. *Is she in trouble?* Has somebody taken advantage of her? Not in my house, surely. Don't tell me Cougher's had his way with her, that old eunuch?"

Now Betty started to howl. Her sobs shook my body, and my voice trembled as I tried to explain myself. And when Betty cries, it's just a question of time before I start leaking too.

"No, boss, I…" I shrugged my shoulders, and was on the point of giving up, head bowed and staring down at our shoes. Betty with her fingers deep up her nostrils, before wiping her nose tidily with the handkerchief.

"So there is no fix?"

"No boss, I…"

"Good! Then I think we should sit down and have a little chat. I don't see any fix either…only opportunities!" Mr King gave his leather document wallet an enthusiastic slap.

"In fact, I see a great many opportunities for us. For you, me and Betty. So we need to sit down and talk. Talk business. *Proper* business, Earl."

For a moment I thought we were home and dry, when Betty blurted out the most damning confession of all.

"Earl…Earl's been stealing money from the cashbox…" she said, bursting into floods again.

"I know that," said Mr King. "I'm an experienced business-man, you know. I keep my accounts…that sort of thing."

"But it's been every evening, Mr King."

"I'm aware of that too, Betty, you needn't go on. I'm painfully aware of your brother's pilfering…to the last penny. And I can assure you, I am as shocked – not to mention *disappointed* – as you. But people are always looking for shortcuts in this line of business. It's hardly news."

Mr King peered over at me as he spoke. He didn't take his eyes off me for a second, before he beckoned to Tim, who wheeled him into place behind his big desk. Mr King ran his hand over the tabletop and straightened the papers that the girl had crumpled under her shoe.

"Take a seat, take a seat! Tim will find you some drinks and something to smoke."

Tim walked over to the drinks cabinet, while Mr King took out a pen and a piece of paper.

"I suggest a salary rise, Earl. How does that sound?"

I nodded and cleared my throat.

"Yeah, right, boss…that would be…well…"

"Or to be more precise, I suggest a change of employment for the two of you here in the house. You do understand the kind of employment I'm suggesting, don't you Earl?"

I nodded, and he resumed a milder tone. He leaned over one of his stumps, his forefinger picking at his thumb. But though his voice was mild, a bitter shadow had fallen across his face.

"It'll make it easier for you to pay off your debt too, won't it? You'll earn the money you owe me in no time, and I don't want to use force either, Earl. It wouldn't look good if anybody got the impression that I *forced* people into this business."

He was talking through clenched teeth.

"On the other hand, it would be a shame if I had to call the cops, and inform them of all the strange goings-on in my office. And with one of my most trusted employees."

With a glass of fine whisky in one hand, the cripple placed the pen – probably because he was in such a rage – in our third hand. My left. It has on occasion been mistaken for Betty's right of course. Although then it would be back to front.

But previous pranks aside, it had always seemed pretty

unusable for any precision tasks such as writing. We'd never tried to train it, or even considered it. The hand was clumsy and only ever brought us disaster. In my present state of fear, I hadn't even noticed it go to sleep.

But now, before either Betty or I could draw breath, the hand reached out and, twisting itself into position, it scribbled something on the contract. Then, with his eyes fixed steadily on me, Mr King rolled the document up. At first I thought we'd keel over in fright, but then, as it was being rolled up, I caught sight of what was scrawled on the page:

en og en er tre
Med hjul og bein
skal du og ditt
synke som en stein

— mr. Bugs

one plus one is three
with wheels and bones
you and yours will
sink like stones
mr. Bugs

The pen then flew back into Mr King's hand in one swift and precise gesture, like clockwork. With the exception of the murder of Uncle Rust's flea, I'd never seen the hand turn in such an immaculate performance.

Realising Mr King hadn't seen what was written, my

paralysis of fear suddenly turned to a chill in my soul. In a moment of clarity I got an idea…

"Can we have two weeks off on sanitary grounds?" I shot in.

Betty looked at me open mouthed. But I owed her this much, despite everything, so I gave it my best shot.

"Sanitary grounds?"

"Yeah, 'cos she'll be gettin' her monthly soon, and since I don't get them she gets them for two, y'see."

"Sounds mighty peculiar," said Mr King, astonished. "Tim, don't you think that sounds peculiar?"

Tim nodded.

"With all respect boss, are you in the twins business?"

The cripple drummed his fingers thoughtfully on the rolled contract.

"Well," he said, "I am now, in a way."

"But 'ave you been in the business *before*, I mean?"

He viewed me suspiciously.

"If nothin' else you 'ave to admit it's rare for you to come across a pair like us. As far as I know – and I've been in this business all my life – there ain't no other pair like us."

I was selling us, as so often before. Though it was hard to say whether he could see through my bullshit or not.

"We're a medical impossibility you know. A man and a woman. Some doctors don't even believe in us, they say the evidence ain't clear enough, and we must 'ave been sewn together but you and me know better. So of course there's lots of things with us what's different."

Mr King took a deep breath. He was rolling an invisible grain of sand between his thumb and forefinger, and poking something between his teeth with his tongue.

"Betty, is this true? D'you really get it that bad?"

Betty nodded.

And since she'd just sold herself as honesty personified, he took the bait.

"Tim, pass me the calendar please," he demanded after a long pause, during which his eyes almost seemed to light up. Tim passed him the calendar. Mr King traced his pen up the page, then down again. Finally he smiled and pushed his lower lip forward.

"You know what? I think we might perhaps give you a little leeway. How does the twenty-fourth sound? That gives you a few extra days. But only if it lasts that long, of course. If there's any change, we'll have to review the situation."

He dropped the calendar and looked at us sidelong. Then he lifted his glass.

"Tell me Earl, man to man...between us *men*...no more bullshit...have you been straight with me about her maidenhead?"

I nodded.

"There's been nobody?"

I looked at him, then over at Betty who was fumbling with the embroidery on his handkerchief. This was clearly "my time" now. Betty was in her own dream-world, determined not to hear the precise nature of our business – our negotiations over the price of her pussy. Betty was somewhere else, far away. I was on my own.

"One, two, three, or maybe five, or ten?" Mr King rattled a box of matches at me. Reluctantly I accepted a cigar from Tim.

"None, boss. No one at all. There was one who almost... but no, nobody."

"Not you either, I take it?"

"*Me?!* No, no. Christ, that would be somethin'."

"Perfect. *Perfect*," he repeated, lighting my cigar with a match. "I just had to check. Rumours are going round, but now that I've got it from you, my mind's been put at rest."

"Betty's a good girl," I blustered through my smoke.

He nodded and lit his own cigar. Then he leaned closer towards Betty.

"Excuse me?" he said.

Betty came to.

"Yes," she said, with a veiled look.

"Could I have my handkerchief back, please? It was a gift, you understand. It's important to me that I don't lose it. You can have a lifesaver instead." Mr King held out the box of toothpicks.

Betty nodded and folded the handkerchief, before placing it in his hand, initials up. He gazed down at it, puffing on his cigar.

"Excuse me, boss," I said.

He looked up at me, as though he'd lost track of where he was.

"Yes?" he said.

"The twenty-fourth...ain't that Christmas Night?"

His face broke into a grimace, like somebody had stuck a lemon in his mouth. He worked his tongue around his mouth, and pulled out a long strand of cigar tobacco, which he rubbed disdainfully off into the ashtray, before his face lit up again and he looked across at me.

"Yup, precisely. That was the idea." He smiled.

"I understand," I whispered, clearing my throat.

After that we sat in silence without a word. Apart from Betty's faint sobs and sniffs, and the fire crackling in the background. Mr King stared vacantly into the air as he puffed on his cigar. I thought that it was best just to sit tight and wait. That he might change his mind, tear the contract in two and say that it didn't matter…that he'd taught us a lesson, and since it had clearly sunk in, we'd never mention it again…or something of the sort. I hoped this nightmare would end, and that we'd return to the same blissful dream as before.

Instead time ticked, and it felt as though he was just waiting for us to get up and go. Or perhaps he was just revelling in the situation. Eventually, he stuck his cigar in his mouth, released the brakes on his wheelchair, and swivelled his back to us.

"A pleasure doing business with you, *Earl Merrik*. And a real pleasure meeting you. I assume you know who you're dealing with now…" Mr King slipped the contract into his document wallet, rolled out from the desk, and demanded I turn my back while he put the wallet in the safe.

"Not to be rude, Earl, but one can't trust anyone these days." Mr King let out a short, scornful laugh.

"You could probably come to some arrangement with a bank," I remarked.

He laughed scornfully again. I got up and we started towards the door. Passing the mirror I saw his back in front of the safe. Then I met Tim's gaze, over by the bar. He lifted his glass to me and gave me a little nod. Perhaps the battle wasn't lost yet. If nothing else, we'd won some time. And right now, time was something we couldn't get too much of.

"Earl?" said Mr King behind me.

"Yes?"

Uglybugly

"Have you heard the joke about the third hand?"
"Yes," I answered quietly, "several times."
"Funny isn't it?"
"Yes," I whispered and closed the door.
It was time to talk to our friends.

THE FIGHT BEFORE CHRISTMAS

The next day, seeing if he could catch me out in another lie, Mr King insisted that he'd have Betty's knickers for inspection from now on. Closer investigation could wait until nearer the time. At first we thought we'd use coloured syrup of the kind Frehley and Cougher used for special effects during fights. But we soon realised this would be sussed out immediately. So instead we took a bunch of knickers to church with us on the following Sunday. And after explaining the situation we let Cougher – who'd begun battling with his health more and more – cough into them during the hymn singing. We then passed these on to Mr King, who inspected them with great dissatisfaction.

"Christ, what is it with you people?!" he groaned.

Cougher hadn't held back exactly, and Spinks had helped out too. The cripple threw them back across the desk, screwing his nose up. So, we gained time and kept him at bay. And during the week that followed, our ever resourceful friends hatched a plan which would not only save us and leave Betty's pussy intact, but would get us out of Bigtown and to the safety of Littletown.

Not that it was going to be plain sailing. Early one morning, Mr King knocked on our door to get Betty's knickers as usual. As disgruntled as ever he handed them back and said:

"I think it's best you stay in the house from now on. There have been a few disturbances recently in this part of town. And, as with everything, I'd prefer to look after my investment until things calm down. Sorry, Earl…just business."

Neither Betty nor I had heard about any disturbances.

"Disturbances?"

"Yes, there have been some disturbances. The neighbour-hood isn't what it used to be."

"But what about church?" Betty asked.

"Ain't nobody gonna make that sorta trouble on a Sunday mornin', surely?" I added.

Mr King mulled it over.

"Alright. Go to your damned church…but Tim will accompany you."

"Cougher can come with us, boss. Nobody picks a fight with Cougher."

"Now listen, Earl. You either go with Tim, or you can forget going to church altogether."

So, apart from our trips to church, we were under house arrest. And living in one of the more disagreeable rooms in the garret too.

"I need this room for a more profitable purpose, than to accommodate two such ungrateful, spoiled brats," said the old cripple sourly, closing the door.

But the strangest of all was that he gave our room to the girl who'd lured me into the office, and to our downfall. And we didn't hear of her suffering any consequences either. On the contrary, he lavished his affections on her, just as he had once on us. He took the key from me, and reduced my duties to a minimum. It was a stroke of luck he chose Tim to watch over us. Communications were carried between our friends and us, via Tim, as we sat in the cloakroom greeting the guests. It was Tim now, not me, who carried the cashbox up from the cloakroom to Mr King's office. And in the evenings he'd inform us of the plans our friends were hatching for us.

And there was another ray of hope too – Mr King wanted us to continue escorting him to Olympen, so that everything would seem, on the surface at least, unchanged. To the outside world, Mr King looked as bountiful as ever, and continued to get nods of approval as he entered the stands.

"Just make sure you smile, Earl. You're here to make me look good. That should be a simple enough job, I'd have thought? Just remember those diminishing debts, and I'm sure you'll manage it."

And I tried my very hardest, till my jaws almost shook with the effort. Now and then Mr King might pass the carton of popcorn but the days when he'd splash out were clearly over. And although Mr King barely touched the popcorn himself, he'd always pass some sarcastic comment.

"Dear me, Earl, there'll be second helpings, you know. And you really must share with your sister."

He'd only ever put one single piece of popcorn in that scornful, grinning mouth. His stained teeth would grind the popcorn into pieces, as though he'd got something inedible in his mouth. Like an insect or little piece of paper.

"Disgusting…I don't even like popcorn," he said on one occasion, handing the carton to a little girl beside us.

We were sitting there one evening, when the spectators in front of us suddenly got up from their seats to make way for Frehley. He usually hovered in the wings and rarely showed himself, unless he was standing at the ringside for one of his wrestlers to add some spice to the show. But now he was pushing his way up towards us. Exactly to plan.

"Mr King…Betty…" Frehley nodded and smiled. "Earl…

it's been a while since I saw you at training."

I nodded.

"Yeah…I've had a lot on…I've had a lot to do down at the *house*, Frehley."

"Yeah, right. But guess what, Earl, the perfect opportunity's come up for you to have a go in the ring."

"Oh really?"

"Yeah, and I won't hear any objections. In fact we've made the poster and everything, so you've gotta get going if you're gonna get in shape."

"Oh, I ain't sure. Betty complains so much about 'er foot. And there's been so much to do. I've got a really important position in the 'ouse now, and I don't wanna shirk my responsibilities."

"But I'm sure Biff can give you one evening off. This fight'll be something else, you know. It'll be a mass brawl like the world's never seen, with wrestlers coming in from all over the country. And this one's for charity."

"Sorry, Frehley, but my new position…"

"Your new position? What could be so important that you'd wanna miss an opportunity like this for charity an' all?"

I felt myself going red. This wasn't what Tim had prepared us for, Frehley was going off script.

"Nah, I don't know. You'll have to ask Mr King."

"Well, Biff. What d'you reckon? Earl can participate, surely? You're not running a slave shop down there, are you?"

Mr King squirmed in his chair.

"Exactly when had you planned for this to take place, Frehley?"

"The twenty-third. There can't be that much to do on the

day before Christmas Night, surely? Even in your line of business?"

"Well, I don't know...with the Christmas rush...there's a lot of money to be had, even for us...there are plenty of lonely men out there, Frehley."

"But this is for *charity*, Biff. And it can't make that much difference if Betty and Earl aren't there. And you're invited, of course. We need your cash – can't pretend otherwise. You're known for your generosity!"

Frehley laughed as though he meant it.

"And all our contributors will get their names on the poster that's going up at the kid's home, down in Littletown."

"Really? So it's for a kids' home...I see..."

"Yeah...just think about those poor kids, Biff. Besides the whole thing's gonna be broadcast on the wireless live. And it'll be filmed. Imagine!"

"Hmm. I'll think about it. Trouble is I'm holding a party that night. Yes, hmm, for *charity*."

"Oh, come on Biff!" Frehley smiled. "You can serve champagne any time. We're talking big money here, Biff... *BIG* money...more than you can scrape in with some little tea party."

A clumsy thing to say perhaps, but it seemed to wash over Mr King.

"The poster's already been designed. Don't you even wanna know what's on it?"

Mr King stared at him.

"Earl 'The Little King'..." said Frehley, describing the layout of the words in the air before him: "The...Little... King. And we could put an advertisement on it for that canning factory I hear you've invested in. Or whatever suits you, Biff. It'll make you look good, whatever."

It wasn't long before a crowd of curious onlookers had gathered round us, mostly determined to touch and examine Frehley. And now they were all standing there waiting for Mr King's answer.

"Alright." He said, with an uneasy smile. "If it means that much to you, I'll send Earl over. But time's pretty tight at the moment, so if there's to be any training, Tim'll have to do it with them, in the cellar at the house. I'm not having the twins running around town...not with it being so unsafe now."

"Unsafe?"

"Yeah, unsafe."

"So it's a deal?" Frehley leaned forwards and stretched out an enormous hand.

Mr King stuck his hand in Frehley's, and although Mr King was a big man, his hand looked like a little boy's locked in Frehley's thick fingers.

"Deal?" said Frehley.

"Deal."

"And you're not a man to go back on his word, are you Biff?" Frehley still hadn't let go of Mr King's hand.

"Me? No." And with that Mr King gave a final, affirmative nod.

Then, with Mr King's hand still in his grip, Frehley turned his face up towards the row of benches behind us.

"Mr Mayor! So *you're* here, eh?!" he shouted up. "Fantastic, I hope you're enjoying the entertainment tonight. Guess what! I've just booked the Merrik twins...they're gonna have a go in the ring the day before Christmas Night...imagine that!"

And the Mayor – who wasn't exactly chums with Mr King, but good friends with Frehley – grinned back.

"Yeah, I was just sitting here listening. That's fabulous news...Good luck Earl!" He gave us the thumbs up.

Mr King ground his teeth. The carton of popcorn crumpled in his hand. Frehley flapped his arms and bellowed at all the curious bystanders so they leapt back with squeals of delight, before wandering back to their stands.

Driving home in the car Mr King didn't hold back.

"You tricked me good and proper there, Earl, I've gotta hand it to you. Though I doubt you're the brains behind it all. What are you brewing, eh? A little escape act, maybe?"

"Us? Nothin' Mr King. I just want the chance to fight, that's all. And a chance like this don't come along too often. And Mr King....thanks for helpin' us. I mean it...thanks a million."

"Bullshit, Earl, complete, utter bullshit. You two are up to something, I know it. Right in front of the Mayor and everything. Have you got no shame?"

Terrified of giving anything away, I said nothing more, and as a reward for my silence the scoundrel added: "And whatever Frehley offers you as a fee for the night...I'll send Tim with you to pick it up...you owe me every penny...guaranteed... however much that traitor scrapes together."

He didn't say another word. And however terrified Betty was, she wasn't giving anything away. For once, she managed to keep a mask. She did her best to keep her mind off it, but we both knew what was at stake.

And as Uncle Rust said – when we'd finally escaped and were almost out of Mr King's claws – "Even an idiot can be a genius, if he keeps his mouth shut. No offence Earl, but you're partly to blame for the mess you're in."

Posters were soon up all over town. With an advert for Mr King's new cannery. It promised to be the greatest spectacle ever. It was only the third event of its kind that Frehley had arranged. And Cougher had promised to take his final bow. But there was another trump card up on the billboards…the Invisible Wrestler was making a comeback….as Frehley's ally, no less.

This was a twist beyond most people's comprehension – Frehley and The Invisible Wrestler were billed to fight against Cougher and Spinks. In other words, Cougher and Spinks would not only have to beat one, but two lethal opponents. The public did not expect Cougher to survive his last fight in the ring.

And even behind the scenes people were concerned about Cougher's deteriorating health. He was coughing up more and more blood, and Frehley was out of his mind with worry. He monitored the situation hour by hour, and was even prepared to strike him from the poster. After training sessions, the spittoons were filled with red clots. But Frehley and Spinks were still out at nights, sticking up more posters with the heading "Christmas Ball at the Olympen". A poster that promised a…"Star Spangled Elfin Christmas Spectacular."

"A Speckled what?" I asked Tim as he handed me the poster one night, and the letters danced before my eyes.

I managed, with some effort, to make out some of the names on the poster – famous names from all over the continent. Like The Flying Cockroaches, Los Hermanos Desperados, Masha & Dasha Krivoshlyopova who were making the journey over the Pond for a double fight with the Schappel Sisters, Dr Funky

Dung Johnson, Mr Miracle, Long Lipped Jensen, Herod the False & Kimgun, the Convict, the Highwaymen, Cry Baby Boris, Shifty Sheik, and Spinks who was appearing as the Iron Nugget. And to top it all Dom Wilder, magician and king of escapology, was going to hold a magic show. (Unfortunately this was cut when Wilder cancelled. He was up to his neck some place else – Littletown, the place we'd soon be going to ourselves.) And last – but not least – Earl Merrik. Betty had asked not to be billed.

I scrunched the poster up and shoved it under Betty's skirts.

But of all the attractions, the one that excited most interest after so many years absence – more even than Frehley's comeback or Cougher's farewell – was the Invisible Wrestler or, as he was otherwise known, the Phantom Wrestler.

"Well, if he hasn't dug up the Phantom Wrestler again," muttered Mr King, as he drew the poster from under Betty's skirts. He unfolded it and held it out in front of him. All in all, he seemed impressed.

"This has *gotta* be good, Earl," he laughed. "I'll have this if I can get the creases out it'll look pretty smart in my office. *My office*, Earl. You'll have to take a trip up there one day… take a look…"

It was the Phantom Wrestler that was generally blamed by the wrestling community for Cougher's cough and wrecked lungs. Not because of anything he'd done in the ring – most people doubted he even existed – but because of the strain of keeping the Phantom alive.

When the Phantom Wrestler was first introduced to the world, it wasn't with big fanfares. "Butterbean vs. the Invisible Wrestler" the billboards had said. And Butterbean, later Cougher, had entered Olympen first. To great applause, as usual. But then he'd been left standing in the ring, waiting in vain for the Phantom to arrive...until the public's patience almost reached bursting point.

"Rubbish!" they yelled. "Rip off!".

With no fight to be had, and the public about to tear their seats out, Cougher shrugged his shoulders, put his dressing gown back on, and stooping between the ropes he'd put his foot onto the first step, intending to return to the changing room.

Then, and only then, did the Phantom Wrestler strike. Out of nowhere, Cougher was punched in the back. Bent double he sailed out of the ring and landed straight on the concrete. Then Cougher, who had a luxurious head of hair in those days, was hauled on to his feet by his fringe, and lifted into the middle of the ring. The audience couldn't believe their eyes. Cougher was suddenly fighting for his life against an invisible man. He was thrown into the air and spun about in a wild Flying Mare, his arms were twisted behind his back, several solid knuckle punches made his stomach cave in, and then he was flung through the ropes before thundering limply onto the floor, belly up.

The public was on its feet now, waiting for the next move. Everybody's eyes searched the posts round the ring. There was complete quiet in the Olympen...then a whistling sound came through the air, and something heavy slammed hard into Cougher's chest. Cougher lay there lifeless. The referee lifted Cougher's arm, once, twice, three times. Then he stopped the fight and declared the Phantom the new champion, before screaming for a doctor.

Meanwhile, in the confusion, the new champion had snuck out of Olympen. And, equally mysteriously, the champion's belt had vanished with him.

The feud between these two men was to be a lasting one – from time to time, as Cougher toured the continent, they'd come to blows. Meanwhile, the Phantom grew so cocksure of victory that he let Cougher invite whoever he wanted to fight alongside him. And he could invite however *many* he wanted too. But though the Phantom had to face them all single-handedly, he was masterful in setting Cougher's partners up against each other. They'd bump into each other inexplicably…a push would come from nowhere…a pinch…a kick up the arse. And in that tense atmosphere it didn't take much for the sparks to fly. Cougher, and his long time partners and friends, would suddenly let loose on each other until they all fell down, as good as dead. Time after time the Phantom Wrestler went off with the champion's belt, without a defeat.

But just when the Phantom Wrestler's popularity seemed to peak, the public began to question his existence. They started heckling from the stands, yelling out that Cougher was just wrestling against himself. That the whole thing was nothing but an infantile prank. It didn't matter what fantastical antics Cougher came up with. On a few unfortunate occasions Cougher invited these punters up into the ring, and what was more unfortunate was that some of them accepted the challenge. Whether this was prearranged or not, not everyone thought it was sportsmanlike – no matter what they might normally expect from an evening at Olympen – that family men in their Sunday best should get a hammering, as their children screamed in horror.

Out of fear for their reputation, and hoping to restore the Phantom's declining popularity, Frehley and Cougher sought help. Soon Cougher was initiated into the secrets of illusion by the magician Dom Wilder. With the aid of lights, cables, coloured syrups, hidden trapdoors, a little music and ventriloquism, the act reached new heights.

The new scenario began as before, with Cougher entering the ring and standing about waiting, while a spotlight scanned the room for the Phantom. Who was as tardy as ever. And in only a hair's breath of the audience's patience turning to dissatisfaction, a blue dressing gown and an equally blue turban would emerge in the spotlight. This blue figure would race down the central aisle and up towards the ring, but just as it arrived the robe would fall. Then the headdress would unravel, and the public, who had gasped in unison at the Phantom's entrance, would let out one long ecstatic roar that went on and on. Meanwhile Cougher would pace up and down in his corner, measuring his opponent. And since Cougher could, unlike any other mortal, actually *see* his invisible opponent, he'd stare right into the whites of his eyes without blinking. And the two of them would stand like that until the room filled with a deathly hush.

And then the Invisible Wrestler would speak.

"I'll crush every bone in your body and suck out your eyes!" The Phantom's voice was horrible, like darkness itself hissing and screeching. So frightening that the organisers had to advise children to leave the hall during fights.

The public crossed themselves. Then, despite Cougher's hard, unswerving stare, the Phantom would suddenly launch his attack from behind. A shabby move. But the fight had started and the public screamed. Otherworldly forces locked Cougher in a clinch, flung him in the air, made his belly cave in, wrenched his arms behind his back, and forced his legs into contortions. Cougher bellowed in agony. And when everything looked to be at its worst – when the fight was over, and Cougher lay there smeared with blood from top to toe – Spinks would come storming out of the changing room carrying a huge white cloth.

And although the fight was long lost, and Cougher lay stretched out, Spinks would throw this cloth out into what looked like an empty ring. And then, like a miracle, a huge body would be seen thrashing about under it. A body writhing in pain from the many punches and various throws that had been inflicted on it. Then together, Spinks and Cougher, would tighten the cords.

"Bring in some feathers and tar!" Cougher would shout, with a bloodied mouth.

The idea was to pour the tar over the invisible villain. And reveal his true form at last. But every time the Phantom was about to meet his end, the lights would go out, throughout the whole building, before eventually coming back on just moments before all pandemonium broke out.

But by then, the cloth would be empty and the villain gone. And Cougher and Spinks would be left standing there dejectedly, all their efforts wasted. Over and over again, he would slip through their fingers.

Although the Phantom would, on occasion, leave traces. Mysterious tracks of blood that led out of the ring and up towards the changing room. A dropped glove. A blue turban. Soon the newspapers were offering a reward for his photograph. Meanwhile pages and pages were filled with speculation about him…who was his fellow conspirator? …who could be behind this evil being, too cowardly to show its true face? An entire column was dedicated each week to listing the likeliest suspects. Generally this list consisted of actors who'd just laugh the whole thing off. The only person not to feel flattered, was probably a woman who explained that she had actually been at one of these fights but that she'd concluded the figure under the cloth was *extremely fat*.

Every fight was followed by a huge press gathering. The police sometimes even surrounded the arena in the hope of catching the Phantom Wrestler and claiming the reward and not least in an attempt to stop anybody sabotaging the electricity supply. But apart from the odd variation, it was always the same. The lights went out and the villain vanished.

And when Cougher did eventually beat the Phantom, who of course escaped, rumour had it that Cougher's cough was because of the exertions of this ventriloquist act.

Whether or not this was true, the big man's health was going downhill.

And Betty cried herself to sleep every night.

Every single night.

Mr King might seem ruthless and cold on the surface, but according to Tim it seemed the whole situation weighed heavily on his heart. He spent less and less time with the girl who'd taken our room, and for the most part he sat alone in his office, where he'd doze exhausted in his wheelchair, late into the night. According to Tim he often shed a tear by the fireside, before he straightened his back and said:

"What must be done, must be done."

Once someone had done him an injustice, they had to pay for it. There was no room for forgiveness in Mr King's regime. He didn't tolerate betrayal. This was his only law. And it was this law that would finally lead to his whole world caving in. Uncle Rust had a flea. Mr King had his law.

I wasn't feeling too great either. Not only was I fearful of the fate that awaited us if we stayed at the bordello, but the thought of the forthcoming fight kept me awake at nights. I could barely get any food down, my voracious appetite had gone like mist in the sun, and the little I did force down made my stomach uneasy and bloated.

And Betty, who still hadn't grasped what a vital role she was going to play in this big fight, tried to comfort me as best she could. Even though she was the one who cried herself to sleep each night. When I went to bed each evening she'd sing a song we learned as kids, and which she hadn't sung to me for years:

Sleepy sleepy-so
Sleep is all you know
Sleepy sleepy-so
Sleep is all you know
Sleepy sleepy so and so ...
Eyes are heavy, foot is slow
Hands are tired, heart is sore
Neither body nor soul can keep no more
Sleepy sleepy-so
Sleep is all you know
Sleepy sleepy-so
Your eyes are snuffing out the glow
Sleepy, sleepy sleepy so

LITTLETOWN

The Other Side

The church bells are ringing, I'm sleeping and dreaming that there's blood dripping from my hands, blood is dripping from my hands drop by drop as my sister sings, until I wake with a start. I look over at Betty, her body is hanging limply, head flopping. Not a sound when I lift her, not a sigh, not a groan. Nothing. She's gone to the other side, where everything is black. Betty with the beautiful face. Betty with the heart. All swallowed by darkness. So that I also stand halfway in the black shadow. Death is waiting outside. But I am ready. It won't be the first time we've met one another. Though there's little to meet. Death is just…black.

My feet tingle as I stretch my legs, then we drag down the aisle. Betty and I. Together towards Death.

The first time we met death, we must have been about nine or ten. Then I'd been the one to cross to the other side – alone – while Betty hung about on this side. I'd finally persuaded her that we should run away on an adventure. Up towards the lake not far from the orphanage. And as we sat on a bench overlooking the lake so she could take a rest, I killed time looking through my cigarette cards – pictures of wrestlers, with their names, what they weighed and so on – when one of the cards was suddenly caught by the wind. Without forewarning I jumped up after it.

"Ow!" screamed Betty, holding her side.

But I wasn't listening. I was following the flying card with my eyes, leaping now and then into the air, only for my sister's weight to pull me back down, until it landed in the shallows.

"Can't we just get someone to fetch it for us?" Betty whined, her arm resolutely at her side.

"No, we can't," I said, knowing that our escape wouldn't be looked upon kindly by the people at the orphanage. And since the card was about to sink or float out even further, I decided to get it myself.

The problem was, of course, Betty. But with a struggle, I managed to get us down to the water's edge. Now all I had to do was lean out and grab it. If I'd been alone now, without this hysterical load in tow, it would have been a different ball game. And that's a fact. Anyway, I got us down there, with Betty kicking and screaming at my side. I tried to hush her, and after a while it seemed to help. But then just as my fingertips touched the card, she lashed out again and yelled that she wanted to go back to the orphanage. It's hard to say what happened next, but there was a lot more kicking and screaming, and a moment later we were under the water.

And Betty couldn't swim. And Earl certainly couldn't swim.

So we sank.

Before floating up again just as quickly as we'd gone down. Which was strange because neither of us, as I've said, could swim. Later Betty told me that she'd thought I'd brought us up, but I hadn't. And for a while I thought she'd been the one to bring us up, for which I was very grateful. But neither had happened.

We were hanging there by *the hand*. My left hand, the third hand had locked itself around a root at the surface. We hung there for a long time. She above the surface, I below. What my sister was busy with, I've no idea, religious speculation perhaps, who knows. Anyway we hung there. For ages. And Betty, happy enough at being saved herself, took her time trying to get us both up out of the water. Even when she was found by two walkers, she was reluctant to let herself be pulled out, for fear we'd be punished back at the orphanage. Though she was probably quick enough to thank them afterwards, and equally quick to tell them whose fault it was that we'd landed ourselves in this mess.

Meanwhile I'd been lying under the surface. Completely helpless. Unable to move a finger. All I remember was that I was alone. In that clear, lukewarm water I lay completely alone. Warm. Sunlight. Pondweeds. Sand and roots. Clothes swaying. Everything swaying. I looked upwards and saw my own reflection, alone, mirrored in the sunlit surface of the water above...

Then it went black. Completely black.

It wasn't until we were back at the orphanage that I opened my eyes. We were too weak to get a thrashing, so all in all it turned out pretty satisfactorily. Extra rations at supper, plus I'd finally lost my belief in God. But somebody else would soon take over there. If I'd been purged of my faith, my sister had got herself a good double helping. She managed to hold out until the next evening, but then she was hell-bent that I tell her what it had been like on the other side. She wanted to hear about the Kingdom of Heaven and all the beautiful things she imagined there. Angels. Streets of gold. All so nice, so bright, so pure. And whether we were there together.

"And did you get to talk to God?" Betty asked.

"Yeah," I lied. "And you did too."

"What did he say?! What did he say?!"

"Oh," I began, "this and that...reckoned you should trust your big brother more, for example."

"And Mum and Dad?"

"And Mum and Dad..."

And so it went on. I believed Betty had saved the day and

dragged us out of the water, so she deserved that much at least. Betty pestered me for details about Our Lord's House, and I lied and embroidered. To make her feel safe maybe, who knows. Sometimes I didn't need to say a thing, Betty just carried on, on her own, inventing and fabricating. All I had to do was nod. Right until the day I finally just gave up and told her the truth. Besides, by then, Betty had admitted to how events had really panned out that day. That she'd been no more responsible for rescuing us than I had. So I owed her nothing less than the truth.

"It was just black, Betty. Nothing more. Just black… black…black."

Not the cosiest bedtime story. And Betty clutched at one ear with her hand and tried to block the other with her shoulder. When that didn't work she began to shout…not very loud, but with a droning noise to drown me out.

"You're lying, Earl. It isn't true. It isn't true. Why are you lying?!"

She refused point blank to accept that *this* was the truth, rather than the other garbage I'd been serving up.

I soon decided to take less notice of Betty's chatter. (Some advice along the way: never try to negotiate with religious people. Unless you've got it in writing, their word isn't worth shit. Especially when they have God on their side to advise them on how best to screw you.)

It didn't always make me kind, or gain me the most respect, but it made me the strongest. From then on I determined to try to grab the good things in life. Betty could get on with her own thing, of course, as long as it didn't stop me enjoying life. But from now on I made the decisions. Mostly anyway. She knows how to dig her heels in now and then. Often at the most critical moments. When there's most at stake. Like when we'd finally arrived in Littletown and found a doctor who might have unlocked the mystery of our condition, once and for all. When we got the chance to be put in a machine that could reveal how we were put together. She refused. Yelled and screamed. Of course. It was ungodly for a machine like that to go ogling inside our bodies.

"I don't want to, my dear sweet Earl, I don't want to. I don't dare. It wouldn't be right. Oh, please!"

Or:

"Listen you evil skunk. I don't want to go into that machine, hear? Besides, who knows what they'll find? Just imagine if they discover you've got no heart? Have you thought about that? You haven't got a heart, Earl, did you know that?!"

Sugar first, then salt. And then after talking with one of her new friends in the church café, it was suddenly God's will that we live together. It was God's will that we should resist ever being put into a machine. It was God's will nobody should get a look at her pussy, or anything else down there.

"Besides, Earl, it's against the law…just so you know."

So now she had the law on her side – don't ask where she'd dug that up from. But the sheriff, Tom Norman, looked it up in the law book for us. And fuck me if it wasn't there – Earl Merrik cannot have an operation if Betty Merrik doesn't want it too…As though it could happen the other way around…as if two people would *choose* to be tacked together. Who the hell would want that? Who the hell would want to share a bed with their sister for the rest of their lives?

I've never cried, pleaded or begged for anything so much in all my life. All useless.

So, since Betty had the backing of the law, and not least *Our Lord*, when it came to shafting Earl there would be no trip to the machine, no operation, no life of freedom. Just a whole lot of aggravation. Littletown seemed like a heaven-sent gift at first, but soon turned out to be a boring, white-picket-fenced hellhole.

Sometimes, she got me slamming my head against the wall with all her God-fearing wailing and visionary fretting. There are limits to what a person can take and once Betty was on a roll, nothing could stop her insane religious outpourings. God and paper angels rained from her lips, as she prayed aloud for us both. After all, if I didn't get to Heaven, neither would she. Up there, she said, we'd count as one. God's will.

I, on the other hand, am certain of one thing. That afterwards, after death, there's only black. Black, black, black. Totally over-rated black. It's waiting outside. With all the time in the world.

ECHOLS

Three of the Echols kids are waiting at the bottom of the church steps. For a long time, *they'd* been the town weirdoes. But that was before we turned up in Littletown. To the expressed delight of the youngest, Karin. Peddling furiously on a ridiculously big bike, long red hair flapping like a happy dog's ears, she'd cycled towards us one day soon after Littletown had taken us in from the cold – after we'd been offered lodgings in a vacant room at the old-folk's home they call Sugarcane View.

"What is it wiv you two?" she said, rattling on excitedly. "Did you fuck each other and get stuck? Go on, tell us!! Can't yer talk? Or are yer thick in the 'ead or summat? 'Ere Fatso...are you two stuck togevver?! You ain't old, is yer... oh yuck...you is a bit old..." Then she'd peddled off again on that gigantic bike. Pinched as usual from her brother, Hurst, without asking.

All the Echols kids have something wrong with their eyes, apart from Hurst, the second oldest brother, who's never to be seen with the rest of the gang and perhaps that's why, perhaps he's ashamed to come from a family with so many blind mice. Who knows.

Karin usually wears a patch over her right eye, not that this ever stops her from being on the move. All day long she peddles about on that bicycle, on a shameless hunt for the means to buy sweets – empty deposit bottles or lost change. Her healthy eye scours the terrain, while her other quivering eyeball spins round in its socket. And when she's desperate enough, she'll badger you into sending her on meaningless errands.

"Hey, mister, d'you like fizzy drinks? D'you want one? I

177

can go and buy you one. But I'll wanna swig too. What colour d'ya want? They've got yeller, red, green or brown. What d'ya want?"

"But I've got a drink already."

"Oh c'mon. That's nearly finished and then you'll want anuvver one, won't yer. Shall I get yer a yeller one, or a brown one...I dunno...'ow much dosh you got?"

Karin hates begging or currying favour. Apart from on a few heart-melting occasions, she is the worst-tempered, worst brought-up, least endearing creature you could imagine.

Entirely to my taste.

"Hey, Earl, what's up with yer sister? Is she sick, or what?!" she hollers after me now, impatient as ever, as I drag Betty across the church green. A bit of an exaggeration perhaps, to call it the "church green" – it's more a few steps with a strip of concrete and a bit of lawn on either side, leading from the church down to the street.

"Ain't dead is she?! She's been like that for ages, ain't she?" she yells from the pavement. Her big sister, Randi, steps forward and grabs her upper arm, face flushed.

"Be quiet, Kari," she says. "Sorry, Earl."

Randi's red hair runs in a plait down her back, against a blue flowery frock. I seldom see her these days, and never without Gunnar, her older brother. Generally on their way to or from home, after the new doctor's latest treatment of his bad eyes. He's been reduced to a sorry state. Over this last year he's developed some kind of eczema. His eyelids are covered in a rash, and not being the sharpest knife in the drawer – more like a toddler – he can't understand that he has to stop scratching his eyes if they're going to get better. The doctor pulled two metal tubes over his elbows, to stop him scratching them out. Then he almost sewed the poor kid's eyelids shut – all he has left to look through now, are two tiny holes.

Gunnar is known locally as Big Chief. Because every afternoon he's to be found in front of the Echols' driveway, doing what can only be described as a Red Indian War Dance. He hops in endless circles at the end of the drive, shaking and gyrating his upper body.

"Are you alright, Earl?" asks Randi, blushing a bit still at her kid-sister's behaviour.

"Yeah, sure!" I answer. "Fine!"

"And Betty?" She squints behind her glasses.

"Na, she's just takin' a little kip…" I say, doing my best to smile.

My gaze wanders, searching the street behind her – the town square and park, the passers-by. Somehow I expect death to be standing there. In the shape of a dark figure, perhaps. Or a black-eyed dog. But one thing's certain. I can feel its presence. A chill goes through me. Death has come to Littletown. Maybe it's busy with one of the old folk on Sugarcane View. Or lurking in the bushes, or under the tall trees in the park… waiting to get me. There aren't too many people in Littletown to choose from. If it's here, I'll soon know about it.

"Ere, you got any sweets, mate?" Karin's healthy eye scans Betty and me for any evidence of sweets. What does she think? That I've been sitting in church at some sodding party, stuffing myself with sweets?

I shake my head.

Immediately she starts howling. Her skinny limbs stiffen, almost trembling with indignation and disappointment. She clenches her fists, her lips go white and her good eye rolls skywards in exasperation, before she finally tosses her head, back and then forwards and sighs with her whole being.

"*Karin*," says her sister disapprovingly behind her. Gunnar is signalling that he wants to leave.

"Don't worry," I say, adding quickly: "I like kids." With

179

that I stretch my hand out to pat Karin on the head.

But as I reach out towards her, she flings her head back and grabs at my hand. And before I can catch my breath, she's sunk her teeth into me. She glares up at me with her one good eye, preparing to bite me again. Then thinks the better of it.

"Karin! Come here now!" says Randi, pushing her glasses back on her nose.

But her kid-sister scowling, stands motionless before me, my hand still firmly in her grasp, as though she's counting to five, her good eye fixed straight ahead at the lawn in front of the church. Then she holds my hand up and gleefully admires the little dents left by her teeth, before wiping the spit off it with her sleeve.

"I'm sorry, Earl." Randi smiles apologetically, moving towards her sister.

Karin turns and skips off, playing an invisible game of hopscotch. Randi reaches out to take her hand, but instead the kid darts off towards the enormous bicycle, overturned in the grass.

This bicycle must be the cause of countless rows in front of the Echols' house, when she finally gets back home after riding it into the ground in pursuit of sweets. If and when her brother doesn't find her first. And then after dinner, it's Big Chief's turn to make a rumpus. The Echols' parents' hair is as grey as it must once have been red. I'd be surprised if they've had a moment's peace in the last twenty years. But then, they're not such regular churchgoers as their kids...so perhaps they use these stolen moments to get some shut-eye or to fulfil their conjugal duties. Although I hope they take precautions, so they don't make any more weirdoes.

"Have a good day, Mr Merrik!" Randi smiles, and finally allows Gunnar to tug her away impatiently.

I open my mouth, but nothing comes out. Randi walks

away with her arm tucked under her brother's locked elbow and her little sister going full pelt on the bicycle some way ahead, red hair tossing from side to side.

Randi Echols. *Randi Echols*…If it isn't just fucking typical. Here I come, wandering out of the church door…and what walks along…what stops right in front of me? Everything I wanted and never had. Like a final taster, to really rub it in. The local town beauty. And I know it's impossible. Totally impossible. I shouldn't even think the thought…just make my way home to Sugarcane View and die.

She's barely more than eighteen or nineteen, and what would she want with a man like me? Particularly when he looks like he's about to snuff it? No…I should be too old to go imagining such things, but that doesn't stop me gazing after them…Randi with her slow swinging gait, hugging her brother close, and her cackling kid sister peddling in circles round them on her huge bicycle, bumping up and down the curb.

Life could have been so different, if you hadn't been tacked together with your sister, little man. Couldn't it?

Sure, it could. I'm losing them from view now, and I start my journey back to Sugarcane View – if I don't die somewhere out here in the twilight first – but then, after circling her brother and sister a few times more, Karin suddenly makes a u-turn and comes peddling furiously towards me, before swerving on the pavement in front of me.

"Me sister's wonderin' if you'd consider goin' wiv her to the pictures tomorrer," she says panting. The bicycle wobbles between her taut legs, as she straightens the waistband on her skirt.

"Tomorrow?"

"Yeah…you comin' or not, eh? I can't stand 'ere all day! Tell me!"

"Yeah…yeah. I'd love to go to the pictures," I finally manage to say.

"What yer gonna bring?"

"What am I gonna bring? Do I need to bring somethin' special to the pictures? For your sister, you mean?"

"Eh? Nah! Are you totally bonkers?! Are you gonna bring popcorn-chocolate-caramels-raisins-toffeeapples…well… what you gonna bring?! Are you gonna bring sweets?"

"Hmmm, I'll have to see what we can afford."

"Great. It starts at five."

And she's off again.

Betty's body seems heavier than ever, as I start the journey home towards Sugarcane View. It would have been nice to drop into the bar and get a stiff drink down me before I turned in. But it'll have to wait. Besides, I've still got a couple of bottles hidden from matron, at the back of the cupboard. Though, ever since the shock of waking up after a few days binging on booze and hemp, and finding Betty dead beside me, I've had difficulty keeping anything down. Liquid or otherwise.

I thought I'd go mad to begin with. I sat in silence up in our room and just waited, waited for her to wake up again, while the worst-ever hangover ebbed away. People don't often look in on us, but when the nurses or matron did occasionally poke their heads round, I was careful to arrange Betty so it looked like she was asleep. If they asked any questions, I told them to keep the noise down and asked them if they'd please bring some food up for us.

The last thing I wanted was a whole lot of fuss. I was alone at last, if only for a few moments. Besides, someone might get the wrong idea and think I'd killed her, what with all our quarrelling. Everybody knows I wanted to split from her. It wasn't a secret, and our rows made us pretty unpopular in the end. But I've not done anything to her. I'm pretty sure…why would I? But then I can't remember anything. Nothing. Just a paralytic stupor and those dreams when nothing happens until you wake up.

After a few days I got restless so I thought to myself that if there was any chance of her coming back to life, it would be in church. And my curiosity was getting the better of me, anyway So early one morning, I crept out and shuffled down towards

Littletown. I tied one of her ankles to mine, and propped her up with a plank down her back before we went out. It wasn't too hard.

I was alone for the first time. The streets were empty. All I could hear was my own breathing, my own voice, my own noises. So I hauled us as far out of town as I could, to listen to the birds singing and watch the sun rise. Totally alone and without as much as a dram in my body. And if a brook flowed, a brook flowed, it had nothing to do with God. For every second that went, every step I took, I either thought I'd die with her, or that my sister would wake up and everything would go back to normal. And with that, my new life, everything that was mine for a few brief moments, would be over.

I wanted to listen to the wireless, play gramophone records, go to the cinema, all the things Betty had always been too scared to do. Not the juicy pleasures – not the leggy girls or booze – but little things, the everyday things I'd denied myself. After all, they were the main things I'd given up to placate her. When it came to it, Betty was more frightened of a pathetic wireless set, than her brother having a drink or indulging in a bit of totty. She could keep an eye on that...she could see it.

But voices from a wireless, they were spooky. Witchery.

"I don't like those voices, Earl, I can't see who's talking," she'd say.

"Oh belt up! Can't you see I'm trying to listen?"

But I didn't have either a wireless or a gramophone in my room. And I'd get neither now. For fear of raising too many questions. And who'd risk going to the picture house with a corpse dragging after them? But then, when I did finally sneak in to find the wireless in the dayroom at Sugarcane View, and twiddled the knobs and pressed the buttons, a cacophony from Hell was unleashed. Crackling and wailing, music and contorted voices, floated in and out of the room, so I thought

I'd gone mad. I started hitting the box. And when the nurses ran to my rescue, to twiddle the knobs and press the buttons, all that streamed out of it was war. War. War. War. The world had dipped its hands in blood and was trying to wash the blood off with blood. So I begged them to turn it off.

And I crept into the church during a service, and tried, really tried, to stay awake. Easier said than done. It wasn't hard to avoid the pastor. He's so sick of us both already, he generally does his best to sidestep us anyway. What with Betty's endless fretting about her salvation, and my persistent attempts to raise support for Uncle Rust. Still, he's not bad for a priest. And if I met anybody else I just had to nod politely and move on before they asked any questions. Although, with the exception of the Echols family, I've barely talked to a soul since Betty died. She always did the talking round here, Littletown was her patch. I just wanted to get away. I wanted to get away from Littletown, and get away from my sister. Away from everything.

Though not like this. I'd only just begun to savour life, before misery descended. I looked at my sister's lifeless body. There was nobody there any more. I'd always had the feeling that there was nobody there – now there really wasn't. Nobody to listen to me, nobody to comfort me, or take care of me. The thought was nauseating. I got so scared it almost spewed out of my mouth. I tried to shake her. But she didn't wake up. And in the end I realised she wasn't coming back. That nothing in the world could bring her back. And since I knew she wasn't with some God – that she wasn't anywhere – I wished her back. Here with me. But it just didn't happen. For the first time I was really afraid. Completely nauseatingly afraid.

That night I crept around Sugarcane View until I found the meat cleaver. I'd already nicked a bottle of ether from the doctor's surgery. But I couldn't do it. When I'd finally manned myself up with the ether, my body turned to rubber and the meat cleaver slipped out of my hand like a bar of soap, again and again. Fingers like weak reeds.

Sugarcane View glitters in the dark, full of geriatrics, at the top of the hill overlooking the town. As I struggle up the hill, I think about Randi again. About how sweetly she spoke to me. And about her asking me to go to the pictures. Why on earth should she, *she*, ask me out to the pictures? Aren't there enough men, or boys, of her own age? At first I wonder if it's all just a set up. Perhaps Karin just wants to trick me into coming so she'll get some sweets. But if not...if not...what could it be then?

"You're fooling yourself now, Merrik my boy," I whisper to myself.

But, of course, it doesn't take much to get my imagination going. And before I know it, I'm imagining us together. Her and me. Alone. Not just playing fun and games like with the bordello's girls, but something real, something meaningful. A proper life. I picture us moving into one of the smart little houses, closer into town. Not that it needs to be very smart. But a smart little house where we might share a reefer or two. Randi and I. Where I could go to work in the morning, God knows what doing, some carpentry maybe, or even an office job, working as a middleman – whatever. Running a flea circus if Littletown permits it. If I could get some papers saying I'd been in charge of the cash at the bordello, that would be something. Earl Merrik has managed to run the odd business in his time, not altogether legal, but his head's screwed on right. And Betty could have a nice funeral with all the trimmings.

And before I know it, my quickened steps have carried me all the way to Sugarcane View and past matron, and I'm standing with my head in the cupboard looking for the bottles.

matron doesn't like drinking in the rooms, but she's turned a blind eye all the way. Apart from the odd remark, or a few stern lectures when our quarrelling got out of hand, she's never threatened to throw us out.

I uncap the bottle and take a swig. I dig out a sprig of dried hemp from deeper in the cupboard, grown from the seeds Uncle Rust gave us. And after wedging a chair under the door handle, I loosen my sister from my ankle and flop down onto the bed with a freshly rolled reefer.

"Oy, oy," I sigh in satisfaction. "That's better."

And I almost regret that I didn't drop into the bar. Plenty of people would stand a drink to spend time with a guy like me. The heat starts spreading through my body. And in a delicious rush of warmth, it suddenly hits me that I might be wrong. Perhaps I'm not dying. Perhaps this is just the beginning. If I just dared to open my mouth, and explain the situation to the right authorities, a new life might be waiting for me out there. Now Betty's gone. It certainly puts our situation in a new light…the doctor might think it's worth taking a look at us after all.

"Yeah, the situation's *dire*, doctor! A matter of life or death! Can't you see!"

I'm talking to myself. And now I see it all before me – Earl's big misunderstanding, like mist dissolving in the sun. If I could just make it to the next county with my sister in tow, or hold out until the next time he bothers to make the trip here. If he comes in the next day or so, for example, to see to the old folks, we could have a chat, and arrange an examination in one of those new machines. Things might not even be that bad, if we can just get a peep at how it all hangs together in there. It can't be that big a job. If they can patch up a man like Mr King, when he's chopped off both his legs, they must have had worse cases than splitting a couple of Siamese twins.

If I could just shake off this dead meat, I could start again. Is that so much to ask? To live a life, like everybody else? To be alone…with a wife and family?

And who knows, apart from my worn-down teeth and puny legs, I'm not the ugliest man to have trudged this planet. Nor the dumbest. If I could just dump this load, things would be different. Maybe it's not nice to talk about my sister like that, but fuck me – she is, if not dead, then as good as dead, so what should I say? Even if I don't snuff it myself, I'm not the most uplifting sight – some old geezer dragging about with the world's prettiest corpse.

The drink's lifting my spirits, and it comes to me that if I could get Uncle Rust here, he could write my memoirs. People have shown enough interest in Earl and Betty Merrik's past before, enough money's been thrown at us already, just to gratify their curiosity. I reckon people would be more than ready to pay for a book like that. With pictures and the like. Not the best pictures perhaps, with Betty in her present state but I think we could find a solution to that. I'd have to be quick though – it's not quite the done thing to be photographed with a corpse on your arm, all those flies and that racket.

"Wouldn't look good. Wouldn't look good. Yer hear me?!"

Nobody answers. And my left hand's started to go cold – it's gone to sleep again during the course of the day, sort of numb, I have to fight to move my fingers. Perhaps I should drink myself stupid, sniff down that ether, and get it all over with right now. Dig that meat cleaver out again, grit my teeth and chop this off before I start to rot too.

But half way down the bottle, I shake my head. Cutting Betty off won't solve a thing. They'll think it was murder. That Earl Merrik hit the bottle again, and things finally came to a head. Enough people have seen me lay into her. If I chop Betty off, nobody will believe me. Then the doctor will poke about in her privates, with all his instruments, and conclude that there's been a murder. And then they'll be at liberty to let loose on her brother too, and poke about in *his* privates... after they've seen him dance from the gallows. I could chop her loose and bury her in the woods...but how the hell do you explain something like that?

"My sister? No idea, yer honour. Woke up and she was gone. Probably one of 'er many suitors, yer honour. We were always gettin' letters, you see."

What a laugh. And, while I was at it, I could maybe explain to them how the hand ended up killing Mr King. But how the fuck do you explain *the thing*, if you can't cough up any evidence?! If we got examined by the doctor in one of those new machines, *then* we'd get evidence. If not, I'll get done for Mr King's murder. Strictly speaking, I was the one who held the knife on that fateful night. But now that I've got hardly any feeling in the hand at all, that might act as proof. *That*, plus getting our bodies examined in the machine.

Or...if I got Uncle Rust here, and he wrote my memoirs, or a testimony where I explained everything, without any frills.Where we came from, how we looked, how we came to Littletown, all the juicy details, and pictures and everything.

I put our clothes back on, and put the bottle away. I'm in a no-win situation.

TYPEWRITER

After splashing cold water on my face, combing my hair, and downing a handful of pills I nicked from the old doctor last time, I venture downstairs to chat with matron about the old typewriter I've seen in the room behind the counter.

"What d'you want with *that?*" she asks, looking up from her paperwork at last.

"Oh, I was just thinkin' of writin' down a couple of things. About me and Betty. About when we were small, and how we travelled the world...that sort of thing."

"Goodness, Earl, have *you* seen the world?"

"Yeah. I wanna write about it all...and the medical stuff... for posterity. The doctor reckons the medical profession are very interested. We might even make a bit o' cash on a publication like that...then you lot wouldn't have to keep us any more. We could pay our way...like proper folk."

"You mustn't worry yourself about that. And I don't need any payment for that bit of scrap. Just promise me I can read your book...if anything comes of it."

"Thanks, Mrs M."

"But you won't go writing anything bad about me, will you?" she says, smiling as she returns with the typewriter. "Nor Littletown, when they've taken you in and treated you so well?"

"Nah, course not," I laugh, my whole body prickling and itching, to get its claws on the machine. "I've only got good things to write about you and Littletown."

"But what's up with Betty?" She peers at my sister, eyes filled with curiosity.

"No idea...she sleeps all the time," I answer, pulling

191

the typewriter towards me across the counter. "So perhaps someone should take a look at her. She's barely awake long enough to get any food down, and then she's asleep again. It's a bloomin' hassle, that much I can tell you."

"Dear me. She's rather cold," says matron, stretching over the counter and placing a hand on Betty's forehead.

"Well…she always has been. She's the one with the 'eart, you see…so the blood can get chilly by the time it gets back to her. But it's fine when we're up in our room. I just chuck a blanket over her and she soon warms up. She'll be on her feet again tomorrow, I expect."

"Well, I'll send some food up to your room, and you can have breakfast in bed." Matron smiles and brushes the dust from the counter.

"Oh, bless you, you're an absolute angel," I smile back and grab the typewriter.

Escape from Bigtown

After getting the lead-weight thing up the stairs the first thing I want to get on paper is how our friends rescued us. That's what's most important. The rest can wait…how we were found, our travels, all the finer details. But when I've finally managed to get my baking paper (I have no other) down into the typewriter with my free hand, all I can think about is death. That Betty is dead and that I'll soon be following her.

My body's feels icy again, so I twist the cap off another bottle, break off a sprig of hemp, roll a reefer and light up. With some warmth down me again, I let my forefinger hover over the little letters on the keys. It's not easy to understand what they all mean, but I can use the ones I recognise, at least. Uncle Rust used to drum the alphabet into us, so I can remember most of it. I can even get through a newspaper if I have to though it's beyond me how he did it so easily. After what feels like an eternity – my head swimming with hemp and booze – I finally tug the paper out to look at it in the light of the table lamp.

```
Earl dont want nuthin to do wiv that deth
thinng...deth is Uglybugly...and weve got
nuthin to do wiv it. Nuthin...we jus sit eer
and luk after my sista. In the middal of the
blac nite.
```

Very impressive. But right now, death is not what I want to write about. I want to write about the friends who brought us out of Bigtown and to this mind-numbingly boring, but safe, Littletown.

Uglybugly

It was on that fatefull nite bifor Crismas
Eeve, meny years ago and the hole of olimpen
was quivring with ecspektation and Earl Merrik
was drest in his best – Spinks had bin up all
nite sewing a leotard from bits of material that Frehley had
lying around. Bright red and smelling of jasmine. And a crown
on the breast. A cape over his shoulders and a gold painted
crown on his head. Not that anybody expected us to do that
much, but we were up on the billboard – we were going to
participate and I was finally going to show my potential...
the star turn was going to get his outing. All my life I'd been
waiting for this moment. I was going to be a wrestler! Along
with the Giant Frehley and Cougher! But mostly with a dwarf,
of course, but still. If everything went well, nobody would
ever laugh at Earl Merrick again. Not after he'd been declared
winner of this mass brawl. The last man left standing.

My only regret was that afterwards, when all this was
over, we wouldn't get to stay in Bigtown any more. When
the big fight was over, it would be as though the earth had
swallowed us up...if things went to plan. Meanwhile, the
legless scoundrel seemed happy enough when he visited us
down in the changing room. In fact he was clapping his hands
with delight.

"Well, well, Earl, this surpasses all expectation. Just look
at that..." Perhaps he was being friendly in the hope we'd be
fooled into revealing our plans, but his ploy didn't work.

Mr King reached out a hand and felt the soft material.

"Maybe I should get myself one like that. What do you
think Tim?" he said, as he always did when I'd got something
new, or wore something smart.

"Sure, Mr King, sure." Tim looked over at us. I still wasn't
sure whether he was on our side, but I had no choice but to
trust him.

"If this is a success, Earl," Mr King continued, "we'll have to repeat it. And perhaps this might just earn you a little reward too. For all the publicity you've brought me. You're priceless, Earl. Priceless!" said Mr King glowing with satisfaction as Tim rolled him back up towards the stands.

The evening was soon in full swing. Starting with the lighter entertainment, including jugglers and contortionists, neither of which were really to the public's taste. Then – after the magician who'd been hired to replace the absent Dom Wilder, and who cut a woman in two and only just managed to reassemble her before the disgruntled public began booing – Frehley decided to move onto the main show. First with the dwarves in their elf costumes, whose pictures on the billboards had already won the public's hearts, before he finally introduced...like one trump card after the other, the most famous wrestlers from all over the country.

"Go! Go! Go!" yelled Frehley. Ready for action himself in his black leotard, he slapped all the wrestlers on the back as they ran eagerly out of the changing room. After checking the lists, he looked back at us with a grin and thundered off.

I held Betty's hand as we sat waiting in the changing room. With the public roaring in the arena above, Tim gave us a run down of what would happen as soon as the mass brawl began, and what to do when it was over. Then he put on his white leotard and leather mask and came to sit next to us on the bench. We said nothing, then he mumbled something behind his mask.

"What d'you say, Tim?" I asked.

"Try to keep a cool head, and it'll be fine...you'll see. It can be a helluva lot of fun while you're up there, so enjoy it while you can."

"Yeah, sure."

"And Earl...we might not see each other again after this...

195

but I want you to know it's been a pleasure...a real pleasure."

He got back up and stood in front of Betty.

"Betty, it's been an honour and pleasure." And with that he kissed her hand – her *real* hand.

Then he took both our hands, and said a prayer – brief enough for me to live with – before the signal we'd all been waiting for finally came, and we got up to join the fight.

The crowd scared Betty witless of course. First the massive din, then the sight of it all. Now, just when her brother was going to show the world what he was made of, she tried to back off. Now, when everything stood or fell by our getting up into the ring, Betty was having second thoughts.

"Oh my God...no!" she gasped.

For days, hours, and right up to the moment we left the changing room, she'd stayed amazingly calm. Now she was leaving scratch marks in the wall from terror and reluctance. There might be a fight going on in the ring – with hair, teeth and blood flying about – but the biggest fight that night was to get Betty out into the arena. She scratched and screamed, sobbed and hissed...and it took more than just me to drag and haul her along...Tim had to help. Meanwhile our friends played for time in the ring, improvising as best they could. Which led to something nobody could have forecast...

Every time a wrestler was knocked down, he got back up and went on fighting. They fell and got back up – fell and got back up. And Frehley waved them aside desperately as they kept charging at him. Cougher coughed blood and slumped against the ropes, before the dwarves and the Flying Latinos flung themselves around his neck in an effort to bring him to his knees. At least three men were fighting the Phantom... simultaneously...and in different places (though the crowd didn't seem to notice.) The bouncers had their work cut out keeping the public out of the ring. Even Mr King started yelling and demanding to be wheeled down to join the brawl. So the spectacle that finally met Betty at the entrance was miraculously gruesome.

The highlight that night had been the clash between Cougher and Frehley – the climax of some careful pre-match plotting. Frehley had started it by making some disparaging remarks about Cougher to the press. Vague criticisms at first, about the way Cougher fought, and hinting that he'd indulged in too many unsportsmanlike stunts over the years. Cougher was still his friend, but sadly this friend, was in danger of bringing the sport into disrepute. And so on.

"Anyway, I'm relieved he's thinking of retiring, and concentrating on the school," Frehley had said in an interview that was meant to be all about the wrestling school and their chosen charity.

Cougher had then called his own press conference to rail against these derogatory remarks. "Frehley's no friend of mine and if we meet at the mass brawl, so much the worse for him." Cougher pounded his fists on the table, flung a chair at the wall and stormed off.

Frehley's response had been swift – this time over the wireless.

"That guy is a fraud and a swindler. He's never fought an honest fight in his life. And I'll make this his last. Are you listening to me, Cougher!" he'd roared into the microphone, held up for him by the wireless man. "I'll crush every bone in your body and wring out your blood! This'll be your last fight! Ever!"

And by way of illustration, Frehley had wrung out a wet towel so all the water ran out of it.

"Feel that," he growled. "Totally dry, isn't it?"

"Yes, totally dry," confirmed the wireless man.

And then, when Radio Bigtown invited Cougher to answer

these accusations, Frehley crept up from behind him and the interview ended in a scuffle and torn clothes, before the two men finally collected themselves and vowed to settle their scores in the ring – like the true professionals they were.

But now the press really cranked things up. The whole town started talking about how Frehley had betrayed his old friend. But instead of apologising, Frehley just scoffed...

"Of course I'm bitter about that freeloader. I've slogged all my life taking care of the business, while that scumbag has basked in the spotlight. At my expense. But it's over now. It's over, I tell you! He'll be as bloodless as a mummy when I'm done!"

These scores had been settled in front of the public long ago that night, but with Betty balking in the wings, Frehley had to initiate a new drama in the ring. Suddenly he launched a violent attack on Cougher again. Never mind they'd just made up in front of everybody, and joined forces against the Phantom. Cougher looked so furious his eyes would burst out of their sockets.

"D'you see what he's doing to me?!" Cougher screamed in disbelief, turning to the gasping audience for sympathy.

And Frehley, cast now in the role of villain, when he was usually the good, dependable, irreproachable one, pounded into him from behind. Cougher shook his head and refused to fight his friend...this was just going too far...he fell to his knees in front of the giant and pleaded with outstretched arms. Meanwhile, the other wrestlers, seeing an opportunity to rest, stopped to observe the drama. Everybody had their eyes fixed on the two men in the centre of ring. But instead of accepting Cougher's plea for peace, Frehley grabbed his good friend by the neck and lifted him off the ground.

Then he sent Cougher to the ropes, over and over, so that Cougher spun to and fro across the ring, between the idle wrestlers. Until, finally, Frehley sent him to the floor with a blow to the throat. Cougher lay motionless. Frehley lay on top of him. Then, just as the umpire was about to hit the mat for the third time, Cougher managed, in one last strenuous effort, to throw him off and get to his feet. The audience couldn't believe it. Everyone shouted excitedly…

"Cougher – Cougher– Cougher– Cougher."

It was obvious who'd stolen the sympathy. And the louder the stamping, the more he woke up. Moments ago, he'd been begging for mercy, now he was raging. His whole body quaked with fury. He slapped himself around the face, clenched his fists and growled. Frehley backed off. Cougher laid a punch on him. Then another, and another. Frehley tried to hit back, but in vain. The giant started to totter as Cougher pounded into him relentlessly.

He staggered, and his big body plunged forwards. But just as everyone was expecting Cougher to let the giant crash into the floor, something happened to make this a truly, truly legendary fight…instead of letting him fall, Cougher caught hold of him with one arm between his legs and the other over his shoulder, and then turned the enormous body, seven foot two inches tall and forty stone in weight, round in the air before crashing him onto the floor. For the first, and definitely the last time, since he'd been a child, somebody had lifted Frehley off the ground. And all because we couldn't get Betty into the ring.

We watched on with disbelief – the hordes going wild above us – as we tried to get Betty to move.

"Yes but, yes but…they're friends," she sobbed, thinking everything had gone down the tubes, our escape from Bigtown, everything.

"Idiots!" she screamed.

"Betty," I said, "thing's ain't how they look…"

"Listen Earl," interrupted Tim, "can you do without Betty for a while?"

"Sure, but what the fuck d'you mean by that?! It ain't like you can cut her off with the magician's saw, y'know."

Instead of explaining, Tim tried to give Betty a smack to knock her out. You'd have thought it would be dead-easy, considering how regularly she'd passed out over the last year. But all he managed was to give her a big black eye. And it was enough of a blow, to nearly whip me off my feet. Taken by surprise, Betty screamed and clutched her head.

"What the fuck! Have you gone awol too, now?! Don't you touch me, you cock-sucking cunt!" she screamed. And with that we started down the aisle towards the ring, with Tim haring after us.

We stormed into the ring. The other wrestlers had come back to life, and Frehley was taking a breather, lying on the mat apparently lifeless. Betty screeched and thrashed about with her one available arm. I lashed out with my two, or that is, I could barely feel my left hand, but it seemed to have a motor of its own and it dealt one well-aimed blow after the other. Meanwhile Betty set to, even getting Spinks – in a costume that made him unrecognisable – into a Flying Mare. She pulled hair, kicked, bit and punched, while Frehley slowly got to his feet again. Then little by little the other wrestlers drew back, until only Frehley, Cougher, Tim and Betty and I were left, each in our corner of the ring.

Frehley and Cougher signalled that it was time to lay hostilities aside and fight an even greater shared enemy…The Phantom Wrestler. They stretched out the gigantic blanket they used for catching the Phantom. Tim threw one corner over to us, and Cougher and Frehley took a corner each too…and before I knew it we had a squirming bundle tied up on the floor

"Feathers and tar," yelled Cougher and Frehley with satisfaction. "Feathers and tar, damn it!"

It was beyond belief – we'd caught the Phantom Wrestler. From nowhere, an enormous human being lay inside the material, flapping like a fish. Of all the people in the world, we were going to get the credit for catching him. Finally! With the cord between our teeth, Betty and I scrambled to the top of the human mound and presented it proudly to the public.

"We've got him!" I yelled. "WE'VE GOT HIM!" But nobody could have heard me over the ecstatic commotion that filled the arena.

"I'm the Champ!" I roared, lifting two arms triumphantly into the air. "I'm the Champ!"

Now everybody expected the lights to go out. But they continued to blaze. Cougher and Spinks peered over at each other. And then down at the sacred entity we were about to demolish before us in the ring. If they lifted the cloth now, it would be the end to everything, forever. And with it, an end to the money, an end to the touring, an end to any possible comeback. The Phantom Wrester both gave and took – on the one hand this Phantom caused lungs to be filled with blood and knuckles to be broken, but on the other, he put food on the table, kept roads open…and the world open.

Cougher looked at Spinks. Spinks stared down at the sack and then back up at Cougher, who suddenly gave a deep sigh and slumped heavily against the ropes. And as he collapsed, he lifted one hand to his mouth, while with the other he fumbled with the cord.

Then he suddenly went to his knees, coughing a cloud of blood across the ring. For a second the Phantom was forgotten. The buckets of tar and pillows of feathers were forgotten on the floor. And all eyes were on Cougher…and then on Spinks… who let out a heartrending scream for help for his partner.

The blanket was empty...the cords loosed...the ring abandoned...the Phantom Wrestler had escaped again. And while Cougher created as much drama in the ring as he could, by pretending to be at death's door, Spinks called for an ambulance. There was pandemonium. And Tim ran up onto the stands to fetch Mr King and wheel him down to us, as they'd agreed. But up there, he got out a drawing pin he'd been hiding and punctured Mr King's tyres. And in the darkness behind him, out from the crowd crept Uncle Rust who emptied a matchbox of fleas over the miserable bastard.

Meanwhile we ran, together with Frehley and Spinks, under the floor of the arena, along the catacombs that led us out into the underground sewers, and from there out into Bigtown's backstreets, where Frehley's milk truck was waiting. Disguised temporarily as an ambulance, it was going to take us, and Cougher – who was apparently at death's door, but who nevertheless looked up at us with a tired smile – to our hiding-place.

COUGHER AND BETTY

Everything was big in Frehley's wagon. The bottles were
big. The glasses were big. The beds were big. The chairs and
armchairs were big. There were pictures on the walls from all
over the country. The prairies. Wide, open expanses. Huge
mountains. Pictures of people Frehley and Cougher had met
on their travels. Pictures of crowds, and the wagon festooned
with ribbons and flowers. Frehley and Cougher had certainly
seen and experienced a lot together. And this probably wasn't
the best hiding-place, but with such huge men it was hard to
find a practical alternative in town. Besides, the milk truck
couldn't have taken us far, ready as it was for the scrap heap.
So Spinks drove it back to the wrestling school, where there
was a Christmas tree lighting party to celebrate the success of
the mass brawl.

The burliest wrestlers were guarding the doors there,
with strict instructions not to let Mr King in however much
grief he gave them. If anybody asked, they had to nod and
explain that we were there, but at a private function on the
first floor for guests only, among them the Mayor. Behind the
thick curtains was a cardboard silhouette of Frehley, and if
the amputee got really difficult, the bouncers would let Tim
in, and Tim – who we were assured was on our side – would
walk up to the silhouette, before coming back out to confirm
that we were inside, but refused to come out. And that Frehley
had put his foot down. But as a precaution – in case Mr King
saw through all this, and put him under pressure to talk – Tim
wasn't informed of our whereabouts.

If we could have, we'd have fixed the wagon to a train there
and then, and rolled out of town. But there were limits even to

what Frehley could arrange, so all we could do was keep our nerve and exercise a little patience. And trust the big guys to keep guard. If things got heavy, they could handle it. Or so we thought.

Since we had to wait for the first train out of town, Frehley and Uncle Rust set about preparing the wagon. We'd talked privately among ourselves recently – in moments when Betty and Cougher had been absorbed in each other – and we'd agreed that if the opportunity ever arose, we'd arrange for the two of them to have one another. If nothing else, we'd set things up and see what happened. And now, more than ever, we felt the time had come for these two to enjoy a moment of privacy.

Frehley lifted one of the train seats and took out a large cloth. Used earlier to catch the Phantom Wrestler. He hung it up from one side of the wagon to the other. Then sticking a finger through the material, he made two rips that fitted perfectly over the bedrails.

Cougher was sitting in one of Frehley's enormous armchairs, his head resting in his hand. He started to blush.

"What are you lot doing?"

"Oh, just securing your rights to a private life," answered Frehley.

"Somebody's gotta ensure public decency," added Uncle Rust.

Betty said little, if anything, and stared at the floorboards of the wagon, her tousled hair framing her face. Her cheeks flushed and eyes shining like glass. Then, after I'd lifted us both up onto the bed, I arranged the material as a screen between Betty and me. Uncle Rust offered to play a game of noughts and crosses or poker, while Cougher and Betty organised themselves on the other side of the drape.

"D'you fancy a drink?" Uncle Rust asked Cougher. "Or

a bite perhaps?" After all these years the wagon was like a second home to him.

Cougher shook his head, downed a glass of water, and then went to the bathroom. Finished in the bathroom, he strode back past us, torso bare, not looking to the right or left, and slipped behind the screen to Betty. When everybody in the wagon seemed comfortably settled, Uncle Rust sat down to his needle. Clearly shaky, if not because of the day's turmoil, then because it was a long time since his last fix.

"D'you need help?" I whispered.

"No, it'll be fine," he answered, looking for a vein in his forearm.

"Steady now," I said.

"Oh...it'll be fine...really. More people die from bad dinners and a life on the streets, than morphine ever had on its conscience. And since Frehley keeps me from those two eventualities, everything'll be fine, you'll see."

With that he extracted the needle and wiped the crook of his arm.

"Now, where were we?" he asked, before mumbling to himself, "Ah yes...ah yes..."

With a glazed look in his eyes, Uncle Rust handed me a couple of cotton-wool balls to stuff in my ears, put on a gramophone record, rolled a reefer and held two closed fists out to me. I tapped the left, and got the first drag.

Moments later, I thought the wagon was on its way out of the station. Very quietly – we could have spared ourselves the earplugs, since not so much as a gasp came out of Betty – Cougher was busy taking Betty's maidenhead. Causing the whole wagon to sway from side to side. If it hadn't been for Frehley settling to sleep in one corner, and his weight acting as ballast, we'd have been seasick, it was rocking so hard.

And whatever Cougher did to Betty, I felt too...at least to a degree. Thankfully I was spared from experiencing it all, since not every bit of our bodies is interconnected. But some of his caresses certainly made their way to my side. And there I lay, goose bumps and shivers running through me. As they did it. For a first time, and a second, and a third. Cougher clearly had some catching up to do. And he was behaving like this was his last time.

Eventually I had to apologise and throw my shirt off too. It got so hot. Uncle Rust fetched us some water, and put a bottle out for Cougher too. After a while a big hand slipped out from behind the curtain to grab the bottle, and it was emptied in one swig. Moments later, I took the plugs out of my ears and heard Betty's and Cougher's satisfied snores.

It was done. And it was good.

UNCLE RUST

That night, our heroes were still unaware of the challenge that lay ahead, in getting us out of the legless pimp's clutches. But it was Mr Wilder – the magician with the big blue eyes who'd helped Frehley develop the trick of the Phantom Wrestler in the old days – who we looked up when we got to Littletown. On Frehley's instructions. And it was Wilder who arranged for us to stay at Sugarcane View.

We handed him the bag with the money raised from the mass brawl at Olympen, and Wilder read the accompanying note. He looked up at us, tears in his eyes.

"Frehley's dead too, isn't he?"

We nodded.

"Yes…as far as we know…" was all I could stutter, before the tears finally flowed. We could breath easy at last. We were among friends again, or so we thought.

A couple of weeks later a telegram arrived from Uncle Rust…

MONEY SHORT STOP HOMELESS STOP PROBLEMS WITH THE LAW STOP POLICE FORCING ME FROM PLACE TO PLACE STOP NO REST STOP IF WE SLEEP WE'RE JUST FORCED UP AGAIN STOP GONE ON FOR DAYS STOP WITHOUT SLEEP STOP LEGS ACHING STOP CAN'T TAKE MORE STOP NEED MONEY FOR TRAIN STOP WARMEST WISHES UNCLE RUST STOP

We went to Mr Wilder with this telegram, to ask his help – told him the whole story, from beginning to end. Explained how it had all been my fault, how I'd stolen money from the till, and how if it hadn't been for me Uncle Rust might have stayed off the needle.

"What…because of a flea?" he asked, from behind his desk.

"Yeah, 'cos of a flea. It didn't take more, as fragile as he was then."

"Look Earl, I know it's hard, but I don't think the climate's right for me to help Uncle Rust right now. There's nothing I'd like more than to help a friend of Frehley's, but it'll cause too much of a stir. I haven't got much slack, it was hard enough getting *you* into Sugarcane View…but a…a…"

"The climate? I think Uncle Rust could handle the climate alright, Mr Wilder."

"Hmmm, I'm not talking about that, Earl. I'm talking about local reluctance to taking in a…a man like that…We don't even have a proper alcoholic round here."

"Well, you've got one now," I chuckled, my forefinger pointing down over my head. But Wilder just stared blankly ahead with those blue eyes.

"We've got our fair share of hard drinkers, for sure, but they're all capable of keeping their act together. They wouldn't be put out by a little flea. They're too fond of their money…"

Wilder smiled sadly.

"What I'm saying is that these are tough times here in Littletown. Everybody's on tenterhooks. It'll just take one little spark, to turn this whole town on its head again. And after all the mistakes that have been made round here, I've neither the time nor the strength. I've got enough to do straightening everything out that's gone wrong here. This would probably just be used against me, I'm afraid."

"But if he did come, he'd probably sharpen up and be more than willing to make good – he could fix up the library, there's nothing he can't do. He'd have a swimming pool up and running before you knew it...or a sports arena...get the whole shebang licked into shape. And his running costs would be low."

"Look, Earl, I can't promise anything. Though if he shows up, of course, I'll see what I can do. But if you do get him here, he'll have to stay on the straight and narrow. It'll be impossible for me to give him my backing if he gets into trouble. It's a delicate situation here and I already have enough problems with the council, without being seen to shelter a...a...well, you know what I mean? However much I dislike it, I have to play by the rules. And the way things are right now, there are more important things to do than to take a man in who can't stay off the needle."

"I understand."

"But if he does come, *and stays* clean, he'll be more than welcome! Check with Tom Norman in the sheriff's office. If he vouches for him...the rest should fall into place."

Of all the guys who stood by us, Uncle Rust's the only one left. And it's thanks to us that he's in the shit if he's alive, that is. It was Uncle Rust who took the rap for us, sacrificed himself when no one else would. With all the crap a poor bastard can do in lifetime, who'd blame me for wanting to do at least one good thing before I die? So, despite Wilder's gloomy words, I refused to give up...I was going to get Uncle Rust here.

If it was the last thing I did.

I wake up with my nose landing on the keys of the typewriter. My ear is boiling hot from the bedside lamp, and I've nothing but a feeling of discomfort in my body – from the hemp, the spirits, and the miniscule amount of ether I managed to sniff.

"Are you awake?" I ask."

The room is completely quiet. Somebody's walking down the corridor – matron perhaps, or one of the nurses who's not gone home yet. There's a rattling of keys. The guttering is slamming in the wind.

Littletown glitters in the dark. All the little houses with all those frightened little people. I reach out for the bottle and open the window.

"The world's most deadly boring town," I mumble. I spit out of the window and lift the bottle to my mouth. My body's prickling all over. I turn round, again and again, as though there was somebody in the room. All the noises Betty made, that I'm so used to, are gone. Her breathing. The air bubbles that rumbled around, and seemed to erupted inside her. All the things that used to irritate me, have gone. Instead, it's as though something was clawing at my chest. I start at the slightest noise. It's as if there's still someone here in the room – just not Betty.

I take a drag on the hemp till my chest smarts, swallow it down, pull the sheet of paper out of the typewriter and shove another one in.

"So, you don't want me to write nothin' bad about Littletown. Eh?! Littletown, what's been so kind to us? Earl, what came with a moneybag and gave it to Wilder!"

210

Not that I really miss Bigtown much. Or rather, I do. But I wish we'd hooked up with Frehley and the gang first, instead of Mr King. Things might have turned out different then. We certainly wouldn't have ended up being stowed away in an old-folk's home, with people with barely a word to say for themselves. We'd have been out in the world, alive, happy... or as happy as-you-can-be happy.

The old-folks' home was called Sugarcane View, because, like most things in this town, it was founded by the confectionery manufacturer, Robert Smith. Having no heirs, he used every penny of his fortune to build the town up from scratch. Smith had run away from Bigtown too, in his own way. He discovered Littletown on the map and moved there, factory and all, out to where there was nothing. Nothing but a high street with a few shack-like businesses, open plains as far as the eye could see, and a lush forest on the hill where Sugarcane View was later built. The town didn't even have a railway. But things soon changed as Smith built the town up around his new sweet factory.

He cultivated the plains for sugar beet. And as the factory grew, and people arrived to take work, Littletown grew too. On Smith's initiative a new school was founded, then the old-folk's home and a town hall were built, followed by a library, a doctor's surgery, a sports arena, a cinema, a lake-side swimming pool, an orphanage and a holiday resort. This, and more, Smith bestowed on Littletown.

Not that he'd hear a word about it. When they finally raised a statue to him, he refused to attend the unveiling ceremony. But by then, he was so old and frail, that they managed to force him down from Sugarcane View – where, after selling his villa and donating the profits to a good cause, he'd insisted on spending his last days alongside his retired factory workers.

So they rolled him into the town square in his wheelchair, and there they unveiled the statue of him in the same typical pose as they printed on the sweet wrappers – bushy haired, walking stick in one hand and the other raised in greeting.

REACH OUT YOUR HAND, IF YOUR CUP BE EMPTY
IF YOUR CUP IS FULL, MAY IT BE FILLED AGAIN.

It said on the plinth. Although, later, when disaster hit Littletown, somebody would creep down in the dead of night, and chisel it off again.

"It is I, who should thank *you*," he said at the ceremony, in a quavering voice. Then refusing to say any more, he pushed the microphone away. The crowd, who were standing there waiting for a much longer speech, clapped disbelievingly, and the bewildered band struck up.

A few days later Smith died peacefully in his room up in Sugarcane View. He'd bequeathed the factory to the town, on the understanding that they should continue to share the profits, as he had.

After all the good that man did this must have been his sole error.

Soon the whole town were at loggerheads. They almost scratched each other's eyes out over the inheritance. Maybe the old man had gone a bit soft – after all, the most sensible thing would have been to choose an heir, anybody at all, or to shut the whole shebang down. But then, maybe it's wrong to put all the blame on Littletown's citizens, since as soon as news of Mr Smith's death got out, the big business tycoons came in from all over the world. And scumbags that they were, they were hell-bent on selling everything, lock stock and barrel, to fill their coffers.

After a massive campaign – financed, according to Wilder, by these tycoons – Carl Caigen was voted Mayor of the Town. Until then, Caigen had been best known for running illegal breweries in the next county and smuggling his moonshine in on the quiet, without ever being caught. Now he greeted the press, with arms aloft and a victorious smile, with no upper lip, and started holding forth about *change*.

The first thing he wanted to do was to shut down the orphanage that Wilder ran. It had, in his opinion, brought nothing but trouble.

"It's nothing but a breeding ground for all the budding criminals we've been mollycoddling," he thundered.

He promised – not that anything ever came of it – that Sugarcane View would benefit from the savings made. Something that not only seemed to go down well with the old people, but the not-so-old too. He also thought it was time to spruce up the old courtrooms and tighten up the sheriff's office, because, privileged as it was, Littletown had begun to attract all kinds of riffraff. By this, he meant the seasonal labourers who came to work in the sugar-beet fields. Who, like Tim, had much darker skin than Littletown's citizens were used to.

Finally, he said it was time to sell the factory. According to him it was no longer viable. New factories had sprung up elsewhere in the country making sweets with cheaper (if not exactly better) ingredients than the Smith factory had to hand. Caigen wanted to sell it and invest the money in all sorts of novel things. And to get his proposal passed, he suggested the profits be shared between all the town's citizens. By this, he meant the original inhabitants. Those with the relevant paperwork at least, and certainly not any seasonal workers.

Then they'd each be free to distribute the money exactly as they pleased and to their own advantage. This, Caigen insisted, was in keeping with Smith's wishes. Everybody agreed at first.

Until they saw how much Caigen's scheme would actually cost, and how little would be left.

"These are new times!" said Caigen, with a solemn face. "We must think new! Think to the future!"

But when he failed to sell off the factory, he sold Littletown instead. Piece by piece. Not necessarily to the highest bidder, but at a price to suit him and his business cronies all around the country. They rushed in and turned the sugar-beet fields into cotton and tobacco plantations. The remaining plots of land were so small, that when there was eventually an increase in sales, the sweet factory had to source its sugar from elsewhere. And it's hard to say how things would have gone, if it hadn't been for this upturn in the factory's fortunes. After everything had been sold off, and all the profits had gone to the business tycoons, some citizens were so hell-bent on getting their slice of the cake, they sued the factory for making them diabetic. In fact, people began suing each other for the craziest things, which certainly kept Tom Norman busy at the sheriff's office.

In the end Caigen put forward yet another plan. He always spent copious time, as well as Littletown's small and diminishing funds, on making big plans. This time the idea was to move the factory closer to the farms that now supplied its sugar, and to turn the old factory into a prison.

"We've got plenty of people who should be locked up," said Caigen. "Besides, it'll stimulate the economy."

He suggested that any seasonal workers who didn't know how to conduct themselves, could sit there prior to deportation. Despite there being so few of them left. And when research showed that Littletown didn't strictly speaking need a jail, Caigen suggested they could bring prisoners in from other towns. For a fee, of course. Then Littletown could build hotels and cheap restaurants for their visitors.

At the thirteenth hour, Littletown's citizens realised that

Caigen had taught them a costly lesson. The town no longer belonged to them, or even to the scruffy and repellent seasonal workers. Littletown was now the property of well-dressed but invisible men, living in altogether different towns and houses. And it also came to light eventually, that Caigen had already bought up all the land for those hotels and restaurants.

"We stopped him at the last minute," sighed Wilder, as he brought his story to its end. "And even though I took over as Mayor, Caigen went on and sold the land back for a hefty sum. He ended up a very rich man. But if you think he's content with that, Earl, you'd be wrong...there's nothing he'd like better, than to grab his old job back. Though if he knew what I have to contend with..."

But except from the smart new courts, the sheriff's office, jail, and new factories that offered fewer and fewer jobs, Littletown was slowly but surely falling apart. The orphanage survived by a thread, the lakeside swimming pool was mouldering and its paintwork flaking, and the holiday colony had closed down long ago – mainly used by the deprived kids of Bigtown, Caigen had decided it was a charitable drain on the budget, and eliminated it with a stroke of his pen. At the school, that the kids now had to pay to go to, the textbooks were dog-eared and frayed. In fact, everything was old and tatty, apart from the rulers and rubbers and the like, that Caigen handed out each term, bearing his portrait and slogan. The library rarely got a new book. And unless you had money, a doctor was to be had only two or three days a week, because Littletown had to share a doctor now with the next county. And when the old doctor fell ill, it got even worse since the new doctor generally refused to travel to Littletown, unless it was something really serious.

"And if it's serious *enough*, they can come to me," he

reasoned.

And if it wasn't, they could treat themselves to a trip out of town to be rid of their ailments. Apart from the old folk up at Sugarcane View – the new doctor's marvellous with the old folk. Even if he does always make a dive past our room. But though Sugarcane View survived, it was never the same, and Caigen always found new excuses for not keeping his word. All in all, Caigen was little better than Mr King.

"D'you realise what a difficult position I'd be in," continued Wilder, "if people found out that I was responsible for taking Uncle Rust in?"

"I understand," I answered. There's no point discussing things with these people. Mr Wilder does the best he can, even if he can't do what a sweetie-man can.

"But…then again…if somebody else took him in and vouched for him, that would be a different matter. Ask the pastor, or the new doctor…or even the old one perhaps. But, Earl…do me a favour… don't mention my name."

Wilder opened the door.

"Is there anything else I can do for you, Earl?"

"Well, you could maybe have a word with the doc about gettin' us into one of them machines…"

Betty cleared her throat demonstratively.

"Or…perhaps not…forget it, Mr Wilder."

"Earl, I don't think you should be too hard on yourself. You can't be sure Uncle Rust's in such a bad way. Perhaps things have turned for the better. Have you heard from him lately?"

"Nah."

"That might mean things are better, mightn't it? And I'm sure he doesn't blame you for anything, if I know him right. Don't go reproaching yourself, eh?"

"If you ain't got no regrets, you ain't lived," I answered.

Wilder shrugged his shoulders.

I nodded politely and went out of the open door with the envelope of money he puts our way each month.

"Hey, Wilder…" I said. He looked back at me. "I don't think you should worry yourself so much over Littletown. It ain't your fault, is it?"

"I know," smiled Wilder, "but I can't help it."

THE TWIN

The sun is barely up when I wake up with my head on the typewriter. It feels like it's about to burst and it doesn't help when Betty's weight makes me keel over onto the bed and smack the back of it into the wall.

Are you awake?

Nobody answers. I bind our ankles together again and get up. Over in the mirror I see that the typewriter has left a black stripe on my hairline, from the ribbon that makes the letters on the paper, and the keys have stamped three circles and the letters G H U on my forehead.

After I've got us dressed I look at the typewritten pages from the night before. If I am going to die, I think to myself, at least this will be something to leave behind. Perhaps I can hand this testimony over to Wilder, or Tom Norman at the sheriff's office. It might even get Uncle Rust out of the corner he's in. A full written confession. With lots of juicy details, so as not to be boring. The whole story, if anyone will believe it. Perhaps it'll get in the papers. Or be used as evidence, who knows, to explain the misfortune Mr King led us into. And if I haven't been too hard on Littletown, perhaps they'll see Uncle Rust for the hero he is, and give him a break. Hell, I reckon I'll be as hard and truthful about myself, and the role I played.

Carefully, with Betty resting over me, I go down on my knees and gather up the sheets of paper that are lying all over the floor. At first, I think the pages must be lying facedown, because I remember how the words poured out of me last night. How, like in a dream, I'd watched my fingers fly over the keys and the pages spill out. But now, as I turn them over, I discover that most of them are blank. Blank, and ripped into

218

uneven pieces. The scraps that aren't blank have only a few words on them, here and there, almost impossible to read... until messages start to appear across the baking paper...

Dont screem dont showt, no mor runnun abowt

Get the lickor out...

If the bugs ar to hop it, the lady must pop it...

Hunger or thirst. the lady goes first...

Youve had it, yor old now Master Merrik

The dark is kreeping

Kreepies ar crawlin,

in erth and sand and worter an stone

in evrytihing known

they'll krack you like a louse in the end...

lett him staay, but mak him pay

an let him goe

on his high and mitey tippy toe...

"What the fuck's this??" I groan.

None of it seems to make sense. Just gibberish. Not one single story. Not even about Littletown. And not one interesting fact about Betty and me and our lives. Not even any of the juicier confessions I'd wanted to put down. Nothing about how we came into this world. Not a thing. Not one sensible word. Just when I was going to bring everything to light. Including the secret Betty had never let me tell. If only for sensation's sake.

It goes like this…Betty was born with a twin on the back of her arse. I was born with something like the stump of a tail, but this slowly retreated as we got older. Betty, though, never lost her twin. It's like a hole. A lump with a hole. In her lower back. And it was a very sensitive topic. If you caught sight of it and asked about it, she'd deny its existence, however obvious it was. If you dared, or, to be more precise, were allowed, you could fit a fat forefinger in. Lining the hole, in concentric circles, are several sets of miniscule teeth. And deeper still, clumps of smooth skin, before you come to a little tuft of black hair. It's hard to know what's behind this bed of hair. Betty doesn't like being tampered with. Nobody was ever allowed to get that close to Betty. Apart from Cougher of course, but he was a hero, a proper gentleman. A hero who knew how to conduct himself.

But now, when the time was ripe, with Betty gone and all, there was fuck all on these pages. Just ramblings and gibberish.

"That fucking saboteur," I whisper, and get the desire to jab something sharp deep into my chest.

AT THE PICTURES WITH THE ECHOLS

On the billboard outside it says "Haunted House" starring Mickey Mouse, there's a dreadful buzzing coming from all the kids in the shabby foyer. But the minute we walk in, silence falls. Barely batting an eyelid, Karin runs straight over to the sweet counter and slams her change down on the glass top.

"I'll have that one, that one, and that one," she says, her finger thumping the glass, before turning towards us and rubbing her hands with a gleeful grin. Every single rotten tooth stump coming to view in the glaring light of the foyer.

After the newsreel – bringing barely a shred of good news, mainly stuff about the war that was in papers Uncle Rust used to read to us, and that pours out of the wireless – the kids stream into the auditorium. The projectionist puts the first cartoon on, to wild applause from everyone. All except Karin, that is, who's polished off her bag of sweets already, and is in despair because she's been sat next to Gunnar – out of reach of the sweet-cone that Randi is patiently feeding him from, being as his arms are still locked in metal rods to stop him scratching. Karin starts groaning and chucking popcorns on the floor. One by one, with a stroppy expression on her face. Until suddenly, she gets up, marches over and makes a grab for my cup of soda. And since I refuse to let go, she leans over us, with her lips around my straw and her one good eye fixed on the screen.

Randi is red with embarrassment, and stretches over to stop her, but I shake my head.

"It's alright," I whisper, "she can 'ave a slurp if she wants."

"But…but watch out," whispers Randi, "or she'll just spit

221

it all back."

"Yer what?"

"Yeah, she's got a habit of spitting it all back first time, watch…"

But before she's finished her sentence, her kid sister spits the entire contents of her mouth back into the cup. Then taking the straw out of her mouth, she stirs it round a few times, tastes it again with a look of suspicion, before spitting everything out and stirring it again.

"Oh…Karin, please!" whispers Randi.

"But it's best like that," Karin barks, tapping the straw on the edge of the cup before taking another gulp. This time she swallows with satisfaction after she's sampled it for a moment.

"Ah…there," she says, and starts at a noise from the screen.

A harsh, rasping noise, like heavy machinery cranking up, comes from the screen, and then music starts up like a perky machinegun. I look down into my cup, it looks like she's poured sour cream or something into it. There are unappetising white clumps floating on top of the brown liquid, like it's separated. With my mouth going dry from the salty popcorn, I look up at the screen.

The mouse is out, battling his way through a gale. The words "Haunted House" come up in nice, soft letters. When this film came out I went to see it with Betty in Bigtown. The second the cheery music stopped, she went hysterical, and sat there screaming with her eyes shut for the rest of the film. And the fact she couldn't see anything made it even scarier. The people behind us kicked our seat while it rained with popcorn. In the end we had to leave. You'd have thought everybody would be pleased, but as we got up a horrified gasp went round the auditorium, and somebody shrieked in terror. Not Betty. But somebody else. We'd been sitting so close, of course, they must have thought we were up to something obscene. Now the audience was screaming, not at the film, but at Betty and me. Smothered in popcorn and sweet wrappers, not to mention, kicking and screaming, this two-headed monster rose. Then arms thrashing, the monster tried to squeeze past a row of old ladies and kids. Everybody was horrified, and there was such an uproar the film was stopped. Out we went, and from that day on, I never got Betty into an auditorium again. Once or twice we were allowed to sit in the projectionist's room here in Littletown, but Betty would still hassle me to leave. With all kinds of excuses. Either she had to go to the toilet, or something was worrying her back at Sugarcane View. Every bloody time.

Here I am, alone in this cinema filled with kids, with all this fucking life squirming round me, and nothing but death waiting for me, and a young girl sewn firmly to my body, unable to offer me one word of comfort. While the only friend I have in the world, who can put words to the things I can't say, is stumbling about in Bigtown with a needle stuck in his arm. I am surrounded by death. Death and nothingness. There's nothing, nobody there for me…

And as fate would have it, I don't get to see to the end of "Haunted House" this time either. I get to see the house with the big eyes that made Betty scream, the mouse getting lured inside, and then the shadow forcing him to play the organ. And the skeletons that dance to that spooky music. And, if I'm honest, it gives me the shivers…Here I am, about to die, and death's up there laughing at me just like that goddamn awful thing the two of us carry between us. The room up there on the screen, could be my room at Sugarcane View. And these are the selfsame skeletons that'll come popping out of me, to jangle and mess with me, when I get home. The skeletons start playing accordion with the radiator. And tap their bones to make music.

But that's as far as I get, because just then Hurst, Karin's older brother, storms into the auditorium. Despite the ghostly high jinks and horror up on the screen, everybody turns. Hurst surveys the room, then slips quietly into the row behind us, sitting in the last free seat. A moment later he leans forwards and whispers in Karin's ear, as she sinks lower and lower in her seat.

"My bike..." he whispers viciously.

As usual his sister's not been able to keep her paws off it.

I reckon this will be the cherry on the cake for all the other kids – first the film, and now the Echolses settling their scores.

"You fucking little whore," I hear her brother snarl. "Gimme the key to the lock, or I'll thump you one."

Meanwhile, throughout the film, Gunnar's been whimpering about his half-sewn, and more to the point, madly itching eyes, and quietly but determinedly trying to prise off the metal tubes the doctor fixed over his elbows. Now, just as Hurst is about to dish out another insult, or promise of what'll happen after the show if Karin doesn't behave, he suddenly gets a breakthrough. Gunnar, a pretty big guy, way bigger than his brother, has wedged one of the tubes between his knees and then yanked for dear life. And as Hurst leans forward again, he gives him a whapping great clout. Right in the face.

Gunnar barely notices that his elbow has hit anything, as with satisfaction he starts scratching his eyes. His brother manages to pull himself up behind him with a roar and clenched fists. Fists ready to plant it in the back of Gunnar's skull.

But he gets no further and keels over between the two rows of seats. In a second Karin leaps to her feet, and under cover of the confusion and chaos, grabs the sweet-cone, her one good eye flashing wildly behind her glasses.

"Ha! Ha! Ha!" she snorts.

A moment later she's out in the daylight with Gunnar. Randi gets up and follows them out, but then comes back. She gives me a reassuring pat on the arm.

"Karin's going home with him, it'll be fine," she laughs, throwing a final glance at her brother, lying in a slaughtered heap between the aisles.

There's a loud snore, followed by a long fart that makes all the kids howl with laughter, before they pinch their noses, and start booing and grimacing. Randi stays in the seat next to me. She polishes her glasses with a long-suffering smile and shakes her head. Her brother goes on snoring behind us, his black eye swiftly expanding. The screen could have been blank, for all I cared. Who needs films, when there's us and the Echolses? And as I look at Randi, who seems unfazed by anything, I can't help thinking how perfect she'd be. How totally, uncommonly perfect...

I sigh.

Distracted, I take a large glug of my miserable soda.

When I think Randi's not looking, I spit it carefully back out.

Sigh.

After the film we walk the same way for a while. Pretty soon her brother passes us with a hand over his eye, cursing. We amble along in no particular direction, with me dragging Betty behind me. Randi suggests we sit on a bench at the top of the park.

"Earl, is there something you want to tell me?" she asks suddenly.

"Eh?! No. What d'you mean?" I ask.

"There's nothing you want to talk about?"

"No...That mouse was a laugh tonight, wasn't it?"

"Yes, sure."

"And Gunnar flattenin' Hurst...sorry to say...but that was pretty damn funny too."

Randi smiles.

"Reckon people got more than their tickets' worth."

"But what's up with your sister, Earl? D'you wanna tell me?"

"Oh. That...right."

And here I was getting fancy ideas...hell.

"The whole town's talking about it. But nobody dares ask you. So what's up with her?"

"I dunno," I answer.

"Isn't it time you got her examined or something?"

"She's dead," I whisper. "Ain't much to be done."

"Are you sure?"

"Yeah. I dunno if you know...but my sister never liked bein' examined. Reckoned it was ungodly. And she had the law on her side too."

"Hasn't anybody looked at her? Hasn't anybody even asked?"

"No. And like I said, I don't reckon she'd have liked it. I reckon most people 'ave got a whiff of something, but it ain't easy to question a person what's clearly at death's door. And when they do sometimes have the guts to say somethin', they go along with whatever I tell 'em. I dunno, maybe people just ain't really bothered. I thought I was gonna die yesterday, but then I didn't. It's been dragging on, but if I don't do nothin' I'll be snuffin' it too soon, no question."

"I can take a look at her if you want?"

"Ain't no point." The tears are rising in my throat. "There's no point, we're done for, plain and simple, done for. And what can you expect from a pair like us? We ought never to 'ave existed...we're a medical impossibility from the start."

"Because you're a man...And Betty's a...?" asks Randi.

"Precisely," I answer.

"And Betty's definitely...? There isn't any doubt?" She asks again.

"No, no doubt whatsoever," I whisper, with a lump in my throat.

Randi sits for a while in silence, saying nothing. Then she takes something from her pocket, gets up and walks around the bench to Betty. She puts a pocket mirror to Betty's mouth, then presses her throat, before putting a hand up under her jumper and then sitting down again.

"I know she's cold. Matron said so too. She's cold...but it might just pass."

"I'm so sorry," she whispers, taking my hand. "I'm so sorry, Earl."

The tears gush out of me. I try to tell her everything, everything I've tried to write down and not managed, but the words come out in such a jumble I give up, and we sit in silence, my body quaking like I'm about to die of cold. Without a word, Randi moves closer to me and puts her arm round my shoulder.

How long we sit like that, I don't know. Hours perhaps. For a moment I drift off, and all that's left of life in Littletown are the streetlamps, a window or two, the slamming of mosquito-net doors, when a shooting star suddenly scuds over the town, and over us, as she sits here with her arm around me in the dark.

"You've gotta make a wish, Earl," she says quietly.

"Nah," I say, wiping my nose on my sleeve. "I don't believe in that stuff. My sister believed in it, and look what good it did 'er."

"Well, maybe you should then, just for Betty's sake?"

If I was going to wish for something, the first thing that would come into my head would be obvious – I'd wish that Betty and I could be separated. It's that simple. I just want to live. I don't want to die. Not at all.

But then it occurs to me that if I'm going along with this nonsense at all, I may as well go for something big. Something bigger than Betty and me. Something bigger than Littletown and Bigtown put together.

So I wish for peace on earth.

It makes sense that if the world's alright, Betty and I will be alright too.

"Peace on earth," I whisper.

"You mustn't say it out loud, or it won't come true."

"So, d'you hear what I said?"

"No...but almost," smiles Randi.

Just then, I notice that weird, sickening feeling creep over me. I can't put words to it at first Then I notice that my left hand

228

is moving without me feeling it, and without me controlling it. I have to grab it firmly with my right hand to hold it still.

"I'd better be going back up to Sugarcane View," I whisper.

I'm about to get up from the bench when Tom Norman glides up in his patrol car. He tips his hat at us. It gives me a bit of a jolt. He must have turned the motor off and let the car roll in our direction on the gentle slope through the park.

"Randi...Betty...*Earl*," he greets us and walks round the car.

But the car starts moving off again. Tom throws himself round and dives in again landing on the front seat with a solid belly flop. After fumbling about in there with the car gliding on, he finally grips something and the car stops with a jerk.

With a red face he strolls back towards us. A little flustered, but with his usual warm smile.

"How are things?" he asks, with a nod.

"Fine thanks, Tom," answers Randi, without getting up from the bench.

"Heard Hurst got into a bit of scuffle at the cinema earlier?"

Randi laughs.

"Yeah, with Gunnar, but he'll be fine. He'll just wake up with a stonking great shiner tomorrow."

They laugh. Tom says yes, yes, a couple of times, distractedly, then turns to me.

"And how about you, Earl, eh? How's things? You're not bothering this young lady, I hope."

"Oh no, no, I hope not," I mumble.

"And you're not to tell this young lady too many tall stories," Tom grins. "You can save those for me...I know how to poke a few holes in them."

I'm not too sure what Randi makes of all this *young lady* talk, but it doesn't seem to impress her.

"Everything's fine, Tom," she answers, with a quick nod.

"Jolly good!" nods Tom. "Any other news…?"

Two's company. Four's a crowd. I get up from the bench. Even if Tom's not playing his cards to his best advantage, but I can't bear the embarrassment.

"Can I give you and Betty a lift up to Sugarcane View, Earl?"

"Nah. I think I'll manage, Tom. Don't worry."

However tempting it might be, it really wouldn't be stylish to end a date with a police escort up to the old-folks' home.

"It's been lovely to see you, Randi. I've enjoyed every moment."

"By the way Earl," says Tom, "Matron's complained about noises coming from your room."

"Noises?"

"Growling noises – you haven't got a dog or something have you?"

"A dog, Tom. What the fuck would I do with a dog?"

"I just had to ask, that's all, Earl."

"Sure, Tom. But a fucking dog?!"

The doctor's been here asking after you, says matron when we finally get home. But I don't stop to listen. I walk right past her with a brief nod, and go straight up to our room, keeping a tight hold of the hand all the way. I push everything off my table, stuff the whirring hand firmly into a sling and sit down at the typewriter with the bottle beside me. *My Memwars* I type with my free right hand, noticing as I do that I've grown rather suspicious of the typewriter after last night's events. With each key I press, I seem to get a taste of death in my mouth. But I'm not going to let myself be fooled this time. I'll check every damn word that spills out of this machine, and I won't hit the bottle so hard. It doesn't need to be long...but I want to be totally sure that every word is written by Earl Merrik. Nobody else. And certainly not *the thing*.

```
My Memwars. Went to the pitures with the
eckols. Saw the fiml weare micky mous
Escapes biggtown.
```

My forefinger gets sore and sweaty from typing, from time to time it slithers over the keys so the cuticle gets shoved up. I give up. Then it comes to me – a kind of poem or song.

```
Stars
C the stars
R nt thay butiful
Wen u is happy
Wen u r sad
```

```
Wen u smil
Wen u crye
We n you love sum boddy
Wen yous angri
The stars is ther e all the time
Cudent u  abit love me thn?
For eve r?
```

"Ha! I yell at the idle hand. "Y'see that. Y'see that?"

Pleased with myself, I lift the bottle to my lips. For the first time in a long time, I sense victory in my grasp. With my arm in a sling and a warming bottle, I'll do it. It may not be much, but I'll get something down. I'll write like I'm smoking out the bandits. Everything will come out. And not only that, I'll give them what for, the lot of them, and I'll take Littletown down with me. Fucking self-satisfied Littletown and its citizens who shove babies in the wood burner in the cold. And who can't even share the warmth, when the baby finally starts to burn.

BETTY AND THE MACHINE

I'd followed Wilder's advice eventually. I went to everybody I could think of in Littletown to get Uncle Rust here. The first person I tried to get on side was the old doctor. I thought I'd kill two (or maybe three) birds with one stone. Firstly, I'd butter the doctor up so he'd vouch for Uncle Rust. Secondly – without giving too much away – I thought it was time to get us into one of those machines to get a look at *the thing* that's made life so difficult. And lastly, I reckoned if we found *the thing*, we could also find out, once and for all, whether or not Betty was the one with the heart.

"So, nobody's ever examined you before? Nobody at all?" The doctor looked at us with big eyes.

"No, never," I lied. "We've never 'ad the time."

"Lord above, that's extraordinary. And what'll it cost me to have such a mystery served up on a plate, eh?"

"Not a lot, doc. A bit of help maybe – quids proko – for a mate of ours. If the doc gets my meaning?"

"I get your meaning alright, Earl," said the doctor, with a smile and lighting up another cigarette.

And our first week at the old doctor's place was fine. We'd go up to his villa in the late afternoon, after surgery hours. I'd heave us both up onto the couch, and we'd sit up there, legs dangling, until he was finished with us. He worked tirelessly, writing all his findings in a folder that grew bigger and bigger. He seemed pleased to have such a thrilling specimen of humanity visiting him for investigation. And, at first, Betty let him do all the tests he wanted.

In the second week things started deteriorating. We

crossed into the neighbouring district to be put into one of the machines. That was before Betty got the law on her side (not to mention our Lord), and before Tom Norman looked it up in the law book for her. Having said that, she'd always found the idea disturbing, and I'd only managed to get her to agree, because she was sick and tired of my boozing. But by the time I dragged Betty to the doctor's surgery again, she began her habitual whining. This time buttressed by Our Lord and the law. And when the plates came out of the machine black, Betty presumed it was nothing less than God's will.

"He wants it to fail. We shouldn't meddle with things that don't want meddling with. It's not right to go spying inside a person's body. Yuck, no. I can't bear the thought of some machine looking right through us again," she sighed.

"Yes, but Betty dear," the old doctor grumbled. "This isn't any hocus-pocus, really it isn't. It's just mechanical, like looking through a telescope."

"Well, that's not right either, if you ask me. Besides, I'm so scared of machines. And since I'm here, I'd like to make it clear that I don't think it's right for a doctor to cut you up after you're dead either. And that's my honest opinion."

"Don't listen to 'er doc. She was alright about it a few days ago, and she'll come round again."

He asked us to come down from the couch.

"Betty, could you take your clothes off, please."

"Exactly 'ow much does the doc expect Betty to take off?" I asked.

"Everything," smiled the doctor. "Every stitch, so I can get a proper look at you both."

"Yeah, right...I don't think that's a good idea, doc," I answered. "She ain't too keen on being fiddled with down there, mister. I can't guarantee what might 'appen."

"Don't you think Betty can decide that for herself?"

Betty said nothing.

"Believe you me, doc, it ain't the easiest thing in the world to get Betty's kit off. But if you really want to look at her pussy, perhaps there's one or two other things you'd consider takin' a look at too…if you've got the time, I mean."

"Like what?" The doctor took off his glasses and rubbed the knuckle of his forefinger into his eyeball. His patience had already started to wear thin with my chatter about Uncle Rust. We'd touched on the theme a couple of times and he'd always dodged it.

"Well, perhaps you could take a look at the little issue of my friend."

"Are you talking about that junky again, Earl?"

"Uncle Rust, yeah."

"You're suggesting we make a deal?"

"Yeah, you know…somethin' for somethin'…quids proko…if you get my drift."

"Look, Earl, we've been through this, it's not something I can do. He's a criminal. It's a legal matter. Not exactly a medical problem. You understand? This isn't my area. It's a matter for the law."

"You could give Uncle Rust some pills. You could do it legally. Then he wouldn't 'ave to be a criminal at all…right? Then he'd have something to build on. Then you could put him on a cure maybe…he could cut down gradually…one pill a day or somethin'?"

"Quite possibly, Earl. But I don't want to. I don't think there's more room for sloppy standards."

The doctor stuck a cigarette in the corner of his mouth, lit it with a match, shook the flame out brusquely, and then stood perplexed, looking for an ashtray.

"I see. But fair do's, doctor. There's ain't gonna be no more tests, if we can't discuss the matter of Uncle Rust. And to be honest, I'm sick of all your sermonising, mister. I think Betty and I might just go home again."

"You ungrateful little worm!" snarled the doctor. "Just tell me one thing – what's so important about that pathetic man?"

""Aven't you 'eard the story, doctor? Uncle Rust's a hero. Without 'im we wouldn't be sat here now – my sister would've been forced into whoring at the bordello, and you certainly wouldn't have got to squint at us and brag about your medical sensation."

"Who the fuck d'you think you are? Alright, so one of you is a tranny. And I still don't know which. Which of you likes dressing up. What the fuck's so sensational about that? I'm sick of all your tall stories, Earl. So drop your trousers, and I'll clarify things for you, once and for all!"

"Didn't we just know it…!" I said to Betty, laughing. "Off with yer trousers, and the doctor will clarify…!"

"Listen here, Earl, haven't we always been good to you? Haven't you had a roof over your head? Isn't it nice here in Littletown? Why are you so hell-bent on dragging a type like that here? D'you really have to drag the rest of the circus with you? This paltry contribution to science is the least you can offer as payback. Don't you have warm clothes on your back? A roof over your head? Food in your belly?"

"Just remember Earl Merrik came 'ere with a not-so-small moneybag, doctor. And if it's really so important to the doctor and to science to peer up Betty's privates, I reckon he should be willin' to spare us a little of his time. If the discovery's worth anythin' at all."

"But, Earl, don't you understand? Do you like living like this? Like some weird bug? Wouldn't you prefer to be free?

Wouldn't it be great if you could help find a solution…a treatment…a cure? Think how many other bugs like you the world could be freed of, if we knew how?!"

"If it hadn't been for Uncle Rust, I wouldn't be 'ere – that's all I know."

"What makes you think a snivelling little bug like you can save the whole world!?"

"Just tell me somethin'…"

That was how I started, kind of – *tell me somethin' doctor…*

"…I dunno about you, doctor, but I reckon we're all bugs, sir. Or built from bugs somehow. It's just that some of them *bugs*, sir, grow to be ugly bugs. Ever found that *yourself*, sir?"

"Oh, I'll get my claws in you in the end, Earl. You won't live forever, you'll see, you'll finish up here with me in the end, like almost everybody here in this town. Though you shouldn't go thinking yours will be a normal death….Mister Merrik."

"No doctor, I don't expect we'll have a normal death. But we won't turn up 'ere again, not if I can help it. I'd rather sell our corpses t' the Devil himself than t' science, if I have to. At least *he'd* give us a fair deal. He'd have helped me with Uncle Rust no hesitation, I swear. And as for *sloppy standards*, doctor! With the doctor reekin' so strong of brandy and ether, perhaps it's no surprise the plates came out black."

The doctor went red. His eyes bulged from his head like a taunted bull. He sat motionless, apart from the tip of one finger that vibrated against the tabletop.

I dangled my legs over the edge of the couch, and we eased ourselves down.

"Creep!" he said. "Snivelling bug!"

"At least I'm not a *cowardly* bug, Mister," I said, filling my pockets with ether and anything else I could lay my hands on, while in his fury, he tore everything he'd written into shreds. The entire folder. Black plates and all.

After this run-in with the old doctor, Betty probably thought she'd be spared from talking about these things ever again. But the old doctor fell ill shortly afterwards, and then I started to hammer at the new doctor's door...without much luck. When we did finally get to talk to him, he was busy with what he called *matters of grave import*. He always dives past our room in Sugarcane View. And when we go to visit him, he generally leaves us to sit in the waiting room for hours. Unless he's at a loose end, and only then, do we get to go in. We can sit all day sometimes, waiting, while the rest of Littletown hurries in and out.

"Hello, Earl! How can I help you?"

As a rule he doesn't look up from his newspaper, though his voice is friendly enough.

"Well, I just wondered if the doc could..."

"Are you ill, Earl?"

"Nah, not ill exactly, but..."

"If you're not ill, I can't help you. I've got plenty of other people to see."

That's all I ever get out of him. And that's on a good day. No talk about the machine, and certainly no talk about Uncle Rust. Otherwise, we just see him dashing out of the surgery, his coat draped on one arm and his hat raised in brief greeting, before it lands back on his head. And Betty's quite happy.

"That poor doctor must have more to do than to stare at people's insides. Leastways, people like us, quite healthy otherwise."

BETTY AND THE PASTOR

As I started to hit the bottle harder and harder, it was Betty's turn to seek help. Not that I was drinking so much because I really wanted to, it was more an attempt to drink some sense into her. And, as I've said, when Earl Merrik takes a drink, it's party time for Betty Merrik too. Not as much as for me, but she certainly feels it. And by the end, I was hitting the bottle at regular intervals, day and night, in an attempt to get her to see things from my side – to see that it would be better if we weren't stuck together. That she could have her life and I could have mine.

But it can't have been easy for her, with me being so pesky, trying to make her cave in. On Sunday mornings, for example, when she wanted to go to church, and her brother was still plastered from the night before. It must have been some ordeal to drag me along. And when she finally did get me staggering into church, there was no guarantee I'd stay awake. It can't be much fun with your brother snoring on a church pew next to you. And once I'm off, I sleep like a log, too. Betty was not best pleased.

"Sitting here with Our Lord and all the congregation watching us," she hissed. "And if either of us looks in need of the pastor and God, it's you, Earl Merrik. So you're the one who should stay awake."

In the beginning the pastor told her how pleased he was she'd come, and tried his hardest to be understanding and welcoming. But Betty still said she felt like she was dragging something from Hell into the church. Not that I doubt her love for me, she loves her brother. But as everybody knows, I'm

239

not exactly easy to live with. Littletown's too boring for me, the only thing that makes it bearable, is the drink. And with me attached to her, she found it almost impossible to make friends. She wanted to sing in the choir, but that wasn't on, at least not with Earl pissed and squawking his head off, with his sheet music upside down, and his worn-down pearly whites. Betty tried to sign up for some charity work, but when we overheard someone saying how weird it was for such a *charity case* to want to do charity work, Betty cried inconsolably for days.

Littletown is nice enough really, but nobody talks *to* you, only *about* you. And everybody walks about scowling. The town's disappointed over how it's turned out. All they ever talk about is how things once were, when everybody cared about everybody else and there was always enough to go round. Everybody thinks everybody else in Littletown is spoiled. So, instead of talking to each other, they go around scowling, without a word. Walls between them.

And when Betty sought help from the pastor because of my behaviour, he tried to reassure her that although she was obliged to walk, side by side with me, it wasn't certain we took the same path.

"I don't mean to offend you, Earl."

"No worries, pastor."

"But I assure you, Betty, that according to the church's teachings Earl is responsible for his own actions. As you are responsible for yours. If Earl gets blood on his hands, so to speak, it doesn't necessarily mean that you do…not that we're not talking about such grave transgressions, I'm sure."

"No, of course not," answered Betty.

"We've all heard that story about the *flea*." The pastor smiled, as though he'd had to think long and hard, to come up with such a witty remark.

"But pastor, suppose I did 'ave a smidgeon of blood on my 'ands. And suppose it was for 'er sake? What then? How would that be? Accordin' to the church, I mean. Flea's blood aside…"

The pastor wiped the grin off his face, and scratched his head.

"That all depends, Earl. I'm not sure…it's not easy to say," he said, before ducking the issue and dishing out more ecclesiastical guarantees for Betty's soul. But despite all these guarantees, she continued to fret as soon as we were alone.

"If the pastor's a good man, mightn't he also be a kind man, who just says these things to console me?" she whined.

And although she continued to meet the pastor, she began praying ceaselessly, for God to give her a sign of His forgiveness, asking Him to reveal Himself to her and give her a sign, an assurance that the worst wasn't awaiting her. But when this sign failed to materialise, she started droning on about *the thing* too – *the thing* that we generally left unmentioned. And not only to me…but the pastor too.

"Sometimes I'm woken up at night by Earl, sitting on the bed staring at me with a bottle in his hand," she said. "That's when I think it's not Earl talking any more…but it…*the thing*. And it says the most horrible things in this scary voice. You'd think the Devil himself was sitting there talking. Sometimes he wakes me up and orders me to get up and fetch him something. A glass of water, or something. But that's impossible! If I get up, he has to get up too. But that's what he doesn't seem to understand. And then he'll just laugh.

"Little Betty…Little, Little Betty," he says, sneering at me, and in that weird voice and everything… *"Get me some water! Get me some water, you silly tart!"*

The pastor stared down at his shoes uneasily as she talked, then over at me, then back at her with a sceptical look.

"And then," Betty continued, "with his face all twisted, and using the filthiest language I've ever heard, he gets angrier and angrier...until he decides to get up and fetch it himself. Then he just jumps up from the bed without any warning. Sometimes he even flings himself out of bed when I'm asleep. So I wake up with him dragging me up and chucking me round the room while he looks for something. With no consideration, as if I'm not there. And then I get flung into a washstand or a table or a chair..."

We'd broken a vase during one of my night-time bouts. A vase and a hemp plant in its pot. Her feet got so badly cut up on the bits, we were bedridden for over a week.

"When he's like that, I can see that it can't possibly be Earl. His eyes go black and empty. He's as sweet as only Earl can be during the day, but the minute he hits the bottle, *the thing* comes out."

I shook my head at the pastor, who clearly had no idea what to say to all this. The Devil himself in Littletown...no, he wasn't going to believe that.

"But I can't really say for sure if the bottle's the cause – no matter how much Uncle Rust took of that evil stuff, he was never nasty or bad. He was a good man through and through. A good man who only ever wanted the best for everyone... and when he had a hard time, Cougher used take him to Frehley's wagon and nurse him better again...Cougher...poor Cougher...who lost his life in my arms." Betty had begun to cry. "If only we'd come to Cougher first...instead of that evil old pimp, Earl sold my soul to..."

I rolled my eyes, and rotated my finger warningly at my temple, before gazing despondently out of the window.

"But Betty, my dear," the pastor interrupted, offering her a hanky. Now she'd raised the subject of Uncle Rust, he was doubtless frightened I'd start on it too – then he'd have a two-headed monster talking him witless.

"Betty," he repeated, "I wish I could be of assistance, but this really isn't something I can help you with. But if you want Earl to stop drinking, I know several places he can go to, and I'm very happy to give you a lift one day...though right now, I've got a lot on. Get Earl to give up drinking, and you'll see that this...whatever it is...will disappear too."

"Thank you, pastor," I said, gliding off the pew with Betty after me. "Thank you ever-so much for your 'elp, sir, but I think the two of us should be gettin' home now. A bit 'ungry, you see."

The pastor flashed me a grateful glance and placed a hand on Betty's shoulder.

"Everything'll be just fine, you'll see," he whispered.

"It's almost so I can't bear to go on living. Every day I ask Our Lord for help, but it's almost, almost like I can't bear this life any more. I just want to go to paradise, and see our parents at last."

The pastor nodded. I laid my hand on the door handle, my body shaking from want of a drink, and Betty cried. I was prickling and itching all over. Betty turned to him.

"Sometimes...just sometimes...I think it would have been best if Our Lord hadn't forced us to live together. That's when I most want to die. Then I wish we were separate. Though not forever. I want to go home. Home to my mother and father in Heaven. But if I'm responsible for him too, I'm scared he'll drag us both straight down to Hell...and that makes me feel dreadfully, dreadfully sad."

Those were her last words to the pastor before she went

away. And she talked a lot about it. We didn't get much sleep or rest. And all I did was drink and roam about town looking for somebody to help Uncle Rust. But maybe the pastor's guarantees helped somehow. So she just gave up and died just a few weeks after we'd visited him that last time. But although Betty chose not to live any more, I didn't, I wanted to live – I *want* to live, and see the world, much more of the world. But it's impossible now, it can't happen. She's abandoned me here, with this unbearable yoke.

Alone, with *the thing*. And I'm pretty sure now that I've seen it – *the thing* – since coming to Littletown. And when we were fleeing from Mr King…running at Uncle Rust's heels out of Bigtown. When everything went black. And we just ran blindly. A shadow. A swarm of creepy crawlies moving under the skin.

Blud.
i had blud on my hands blud on my shoos blud on my shurt in my nales down my shoos blud evrywere. The old man lay ther for days. Erl washed the blud off his shirt off his shoos his hands his sista but cuddnt get the blud off evrythin. betti cryd, erl cryd like a kid to. so thay layd the old man in the bed and tuk mony and travld a long waay and came to Biggtown and met mista kink. Got blud on his hands from mista k ink blud on hands for his sista and eskapd to litletown stinks nobdy helps...

Blud blud so much blud screemd the bruther and sista in ther sleep.

THE DREAM

As I drift off to sleep, almost without noticing, a dream I've had before about Uncle Rust comes back to me. The same dream I've had many times since we got here. In this dream I lift Uncle Rust up from the ground. We're out for a walk, Betty and I, sort of bored in the sunshine, with nothing much to do. Littletown is as boring and uneventful as ever. And he's just lying there, on the ground, staring up at me with a smile.

"It's about time, Earl," he says, "the frost's biting into me."

"I'm sorry, Uncle Rust," I answer, leaning over him.

And when I go to lift him, he is as light as anything, and I carry him all the way to town. Everybody is standing there waiting in the Town Hall Square, Tom Norman greets him with a touch of his hat, the pastor nods, Dom Wilder peers at me with those big, watery, blue eyes, ready with a speech in which he'll say that little Earl Merrik managed to do something that nobody else could. And this time, Randi Echols is there waving at me from the crowd, and even Caigen has turned up, and the doctor is ready and waiting with his bag and syringe.

"We managed it," I say, "we managed it!"

"I always knew you would," says Uncle Rust, "I knew it would end like this. You're a good man Earl Merrik. A good man."

In the middle of the night, surfacing from this dream, I'm woken by a clacking sound and eventually realise it's coming from the typewriter. On the paper are the words:

```
It wil tern owt al rite Earl. nuthin te wurry
abowt, evrythin will be alrite...
```

245

SISTER

I lift you up. Place your arm around my neck. Carry you around the room. Find a towel and flannel. Prop you up, jolting body against body, so there's a cracking of ribs. Undress you before pouring water into the washbasin. The room is in chaos, paper everywhere, a broken flowerpot and soil on the floor, the rain came in the window last night. I tripped over the flowerpot and now it lies under the bed. I comb your beautiful hair with the one hand, pull the comb slowly through your hair and watch as it spills through my fingers. Perhaps I should have got one of the nurses to put it up for you, the way you do it, I don't know, I've never combed your hair before. I remember you used to sing as you took your morning wash – different melodies floating from behind me as I watched your naked body in the window pane.

"Are you awake?" I ask.

You don't answer. I shove the sponge under your armpit, stretch over and let you dangle forwards, your dress folded down around your waist. I let the sponge moisten your small breasts, turn your body and bring my hand as far down your back as I can. If you sang now I'd sense it in my fingertips, but I feel nothing, just death, a black darkness fighting its way back and forth between us. I lift you up, pull your dress off, and find your new clothes. Then I bind our ankles. I am so sorry, so terribly, terribly sorry. But you don't need to be frightened any more,

"You aren't heavy. I won't drop you."

THE PARCEL

I've just finished washing and dressing us both when there's a bang on the door. I wait. Another bang.

"Who's there?" I ask cautiously, looking around the room. The room is flowing with paper, bottles, hemp tobacco and worse.

"Karin Echols. And if you don't bloomin' open up quick, I'll take this Christmas present and go."

I turn the key and open the door carefully – then giving it a little shove, she's in. Before I've even closed the door she's sniffing around the room with a look of revulsion. Pinching her nose, she almost sticks her face through the typewriter. Her whole head follows as she struggles with her one good eye to read what's on the page…letter by letter.

"Wassat then?"

"My memoirs."

"Why've you stuck a roll of baking paper in there?"

" 'Cause I don't have any proper paper."

"What's memoirs?"

"Memoirs. Nah…well I just thought I'd write about Betty an' me, an' our lives. But however much I type, all that comes out is a load of old crap."

"Hmmm. Is it true you murdered someone?" For a moment her long red hair is still, as her good eye peers over at me across the patched one.

"You what?!" I ask.

"Randi says we shouldn't ask…and she says Betty's dead too…and she ain't sure if you're a man or not…but she says it makes no odds 'cos you're kind on the inside and you'll prob'ly die soon too…"

I stand there gawping. My first instinct is to give the kid a clip round the ear, but I find myself smiling instead. She hands me a present.

"Here! It's from my folks," she says, dumping herself down on the unmade bed. "They want you to come for dinner after church."

"Really?" I laugh. "When?"

"After church, I said. Are you deaf? Well, ain't you gonna open it?"

"What?"

"The present. You dumb or what?

"I dunno. If it's a Christmas present perhaps I should save it, so as not to offend your folks."

Suppressing a very deep sigh, she perches quietly on the bed for as long as she can manage, before breaking the silence again.

"But p'raps…p'raps you won't live that long?" She looks at me gravely. "An' I heard in other countries it's normal to open yer Christmas presents today. And you ain't from around 'ere, are yer?"

"OK. But if we open the present *now*, could you do me a favour?"

"Depends what…"

"Nothin' much. A *little* favour, if you know what I mean…"

"Well, what is it?!"

"Well, I'd be ever-so grateful if you could be bothered to do Betty's hair."

"No probs!" she sighed, "but then you've got to bloody open it."

Easing herself back onto the bed, Karin waves us in front of her. With a suspicious grimace she shoves her legs out and wraps them round Betty's hips, before sticking her fingers gingerly into her hair.

"We'd 'ave earned a packet at the circus now!" I laugh, as a tickling in Betty's neck sends shivers down me.

"What d'yer mean?"

"Nothin', it's just we'd make the scariest cripple the world ever saw...three pairs of legs...three bodies...an' a whole heap of arms."

I tweak her toe where it sticks out between Betty and me. She yelps.

"Well, you'd better bloody open yer present now...or I'll tell everybody you forced me to do your dead sister's hair. How d'you wannit? Plaits or a bun?"

"Plaits," I whisper.

I reach out for the present, and with Karin's uninvited help I take off the shiny paper and ribbons. As I guessed, it's a box of chocolates. Heart-shaped, and with the picture of Robert Smith in his bowler hat that they'd started printing on the lids not long after he went to his grave, along with the inscription from his memorial, embossed on the shiny paper:

REACH OUT YOUR HAND, IF YOUR CUP BE EMPTY
IF YOUR CUP IS FULL, MAY IT BE FILLED AGAIN.

I manage to get one chocolate, before Karin starts snapping them up – carefully, with her fingertips, as though Betty's hair had made her hands grubby. Then with her mouth stuffed happily with chocolate, and her fingers entwined in the hair, she sings a tuneless melody to herself, impossible to catch. And as she nods in time to this hopeless humming, she twirls her feet in front of her contentedly. I close my eyes, enjoy the sensation of her fingers on Betty's neck, let the chocolate-taste linger in my mouth.

"Did yer enjoy that?" She peers over at me, her face still filled with chocolate.

I nod.

"Great! I'll take the last one then." And with that she reaches out and gobbles down the last chocolate, before quickly fastening Betty's plaits. A second later she slips off the bed.

I laugh.

"In fact, it was the best chocolate I've tasted in my whole life," I say, trying to keep up a smile.

"Good!" Karin smacks her lips.

"...and perhaps the last..." the words tumble out of me. And before I can do or say anything the tears well up in my eyes like last night.

Karin peers guiltily at me with her one eye, then perches on the edge of the bed, and sits there thinking, head bowed. Suddenly she sticks her hand down into a pocket in her skirt, and smuggles out a chocolate bar in pretty paper.

"I've been savin' this," she whispers.

"Oh?"

"Yeah, for Christmas Day. But you can 'ave it."

"But what'll you have at Christmas?"

"Fuck that. I'll just have t'go and find some return bottles, or nick some from mumsy. P'raps they'll give me another one. The shop's full of 'em."

"You sure?"

"Yeah, go on, take it, Earl. Honest."

...Earl Merrick memwoirs Crismas stole sweeety from litle kid who did his sista's hare. Sista is ded as ever but he still gets goos bumps on is skin from her hare bein don.

Fuck, I think, and blub some more.

"Ta very much," I say, wiping my face with my sleeve.

"Yeah, well...make sure yer come round fer dinner, or they won't believe I came round 'ere."

I nod and stick the chocolate bar into my jacket pocket. When I look up again, she's already gone from the room...the echoes of her steps skittering down the corridor.

I sit on a park bench, a stone's throw away from the church, killing time before the Christmas service. My left arm and hand are numb again, worse than for ages. For a moment I think it must be death creeping in, and I sit here on the bench bracing myself.

"So it's comin' at last," I think to myself, picturing how we'll be found…the twins on a park bench…the brother clutching a chocolate he's nicked off a kid.

What a fucking tragedy. And it's sure to come out in the papers.

And still not a word from my mouth about the fate we were dealt. I look around, as though this'll be my last glimpse of this world. A grey-blue sky, empty streets, my breath like smoke on the air, the empty park with those fucking irritating crows squawking in the naked branches.

"Caw! Caw! Caw!" I screech back…as if that's not the stupidest fucking thing a numbskull ever uttered. "Just forget it!" I continue, thinking how that must also be the most idiotic thing a poor sod could think of saying.

"I repent!" I yell. "I repent, so I lived, I existed, are you satisfied out there, eh?" I mumble.

I mumble…and suddenly I'm aware that my body's still warm, the blood racing round. It would be weird for death to arrive in the middle of so much activity…surely. The hand has started rummaging in my jacket pocket now, plucking at fluff, then straightening my trousers. And when it stops it sits pointing straight ahead, like it was talking to someone. And that's liveable with, I think to myself – it's worse when it stops

252

altogether and I'm left waiting for its next move…

So I'm not dying after all. What should I do with my time?
What can I fit in? A sudden impulse gets me up from the bench,
but I immediately sit us carefully down again.

"Nah, ain't no point," I whisper, trying to calm myself. But
before I know it, I'm back up on my feet.

And now I'm knocking on the door of the new doctor who
has an office in the same house as the old one. Last time I'd
got it into my head to try him, he wasn't there of course. So
I ended up at the door of the old doctor. He supplements his
pension now with the odd consultation for a small fee. But
when I'd knocked, I just heard him swearing from behind
the mosquito net and barking that it was Sunday and what he
called his *stand-in* wouldn't arrive until Tuesday.

Nobody answers this time. But as I walk back down the
drive, I turn to the sudden sound of the mosquito net slamming.
The home help comes into view with a mop and bucket.

"Well I never…it's Earl isn't it?" she asks. "Not seen you
in ages, where've you been hiding?"

"Well, I've been sitting up at Sugarcane View as usual,
mouldering with the old folk. Though I poked my nose out
yesterday and went to the picture house with the Echolses and
stuff."

"With the Echolses? Well, that was a bit of a to-do, I
expect," she laughs with the whole of her big, fat body, and her
enormous breasts spill before her as she shoves the mosquito
net up with her mop and empties the bucket down the drain.

"Yeah, you bet. Gunnar thumped 'is little brother with 'is
elbow so he passed out between the rows. Brilliant, if you ask
me."

"Come to pester the new doctor this time, have you?" she
says, managing a quick smile before dumping the bucket

down. "But Earl, how's your sister? She don't look too good."

"That was kind of the point of seeing the doctor," I sighed. "I heard he'd asked after me up at Sugarcane View yesterday so I thought I might be able to see 'im at last."

"If I know you right, you'll end up arguing about that uncle of yours. But Earl…something ain't right here, even I can see that! You've gotta get her over to the next village and let him look at her."

"Yeah, yeah…I don't reckon there's much point…she's dead."

I clamp my hand over my eyes to hold the tears back.

"Ooh. We'd better send for him then – he's bound to come when we tell him that."

"No, don't bother yerself. She's dead. And if I ain't mistaken, I'll be dead too before the evening's up. We're stuck together, so there ain't much to be done. It was idiotic to trail up here to begin with."

"But Earl," she whispers, dropping her mop.

"*Adieu!*…Mrs…Mrs…" I can't remember her name off-hand, so it gets a bit embarrassing. "*Adieu!* You've been ever-so kind and it's always been nice to meet you. You're a good woman. *Adieu!*"

I leave before she can say more. Betty's feet bump along the pavement with a scraping noise, as I trundle down past the villas in the avenue that ends at the park beside the Town Hall and High Street. At the end of driveway of one of the smart houses, I see Caigen, carrying crates out of his car. I greet him cautiously as I pass by. He smiles broadly (without any top lip again). Then some way on, I turn around and walk back.

"Hey!" I yell. "Caigen!"

Caigen has his back to me, but turns sharply and looks at me in terror, before putting on a stiff smile.

"Hello there! Ern...Arn...*Ernst* Murrick?...Ernst?" He shoves one of the clinking crates back into his car.

"*Earl*," I say, correcting him.

I get straight to the point and outline my mission – my reason for intruding on him like this in his driveway. I tell him about Uncle Rust. A rough sketch. I tell him how I only have a short time left. Ask if he can think of any solution. He seems genuinely interested at first, smiles and nods. But somewhere along the line he loses interest, gives a heavy sigh and holds his hands up in front of him. In the end Caigen stands with his chin in his hand, leaning that fat arse of his against the car.

"Nope, nope. I can't do anything for a man like that. Nope."

"But it's for a good cause...and you could do with a few good causes, couldn't you?"

"Well, I'm not sure wasting time and money on a pathetic junky is a good cause, Earl...and you can just forget that flea circus business."

"They ain't the sort of fleas that go on people," I try to explain.

"But Ernst...what was that you said? That Dom Wilder knew him? Wasn't it something like that?"

"Well yeah, he knows him...but Wilder's a bit busy right now...there's enough to do in Littletown with the climate being what it is, and he..."

"So Wilder knows this flea layabout quite well? As a friend, I mean...?" Caigen scratches his chin and stares at me. "And Wilder...d'you know perhaps if he's ever had similar problems? Whether he's been...well...you know what I mean...when he lived in Bigtown?"

"They might be friends, but I don't think..."

"Right...I see! Here, Ernst, have one of these."

Caigen opens one of the crates and thrusts a bottle at

me. I recognise its shape instantly. I've knocked back a few of these in my time here in Littletown. But to get one from Caigen personally is new for me. He's got enough middlemen. It's rumoured that after losing his job as Mayor, he not only returned to his wicked ways, but that he took over as the local kingpin, after the previous kingpin – a defence lawyer no less – popped his clogs last winter. Shortly afterwards, this kingpin's son died too, after successfully defending Caigen's flunkey in a long court case. So now, Caigen and his flunkey – a one-eyed scumbag – run the show. And, I don't know why, but I'm offering Caigen a chance here. A chance to wash some blood off his hands. A chance he clearly isn't interested in taking.

"No thanks." I say. "I'm off down to Tom Norman's now. I wouldn't want to stink of spirits in the sheriff's office."

"Oh, blow that. Here, take one for Norman too," Caigen answers, taking a sly glance at the neighbouring houses and further down the street. Before I know it, he's given me a hearty slap on the back and I'm stumbling off with two bottles of his moonshine. But I've not reached the end of the garden before I hear the clanking. The clanking of chains, and panting. Something heavy pounding into the ground. Faster and faster. As the chains hit the pavement.

I turn just as the mongrel sinks its teeth into Betty. It growls, tossing its head from side to side.

"Fuckin' dog!" I shout. The dog grabs my sister again and shakes her limp body so hard that my bottles fall to the ground, one of them smashing on the pavement.

"That fuckin' dog!" I scream again.

"Norhus!" bellows Caigen, before he rushes over – to my surprise – to deliver a sound kick in the beast's belly, making it curl up with a yelp.

"Sorry, Ernst, that wasn't the intention. Sorry…you must

take another one, of course."

"Another what?"

"Another bottle...I'll get you one."

"But he bit my sister!"

There's a trickle of blood running down Betty's ankle.

"Dear me. We'll soon have that sorted with soap and water."

"But she's dead!" I whisper.

"Dead? But my dog only bit her foot."

"Is that your dog?! I thought it was God's hound."

"Yeah, sure, it's my dog," whispers Caigen. "But I don't think your sister can be dead just from a little bite." He reaches out and gives Betty a gentle pat on the shoulder.

"Hello there. Are you alright?"

"She's been dead for days."

Caigen eyes me suspiciously.

"Really?"

"That's why I wanted to get things sorted for Uncle Rust. She's dead and that means I'm halfway to being dead too. There ain't nothin' can be done."

"Ah, now I understand. Old Norhus here must have gone for the smell. That's only to be expected...don't you think... what with dogs being so sensitive to smell? That explains it."

Caigen scoops up the whimpering dog and makes comforting noises as he scratches it under the ear.

"Anyway, Ernst, you just wait here, and I'll fetch you that bottle..."

"Bottle? I don't want no bottle. I came for help."

"Yes alright, alright. Look, I'll go and fetch that bottle... and then maybe you can drop by later in the week, and we can talk about these things. Maybe I can organise a court hearing or something...so you can tell your whole story. Then it'll be on the record. But you'll have to tell us absolutely *everything*...

including about Wilder. What d'you say, Ernst?"

"That's no good – I'll be dead by then! Don't you get it?"

"Alright. I'll see what I can do. If I cast around a bit I might…just might…be able to get a judge to look at the case in a few hours."

Caigen smiles and gives my shoulder a squeeze.

"Do you really mean that?" I ask hesitantly.

"Yup, I most certainly do," answers Caigen, before adding in a whisper, "but it's crucial that you tell me *everything* about Wilder's involvement and…"

"Nah…forget it," I say, picking up the unbroken bottle and dragging my sister after me. "Just forget it."

"Hold in there, Ernst! We'll sort something out, you'll see!" Caigen yells behind me, the dog straining on its leash in front of him. "Hold in there!"

TOM NORMAN

Tom is standing on the steps outside the sheriff's office with a cup of coffee and a pastry, surveying the High Street and occasionally cocking his head as if he's listening out for something. He chews, then pauses, eyes fixed on the pavement before him.

"Hi Tom, what's up?" I ask.

He doesn't answer at first...he chews, listens, then chews again, before finally meeting my gaze over his coffee.

"Morning Earl."

"What's going on?" I ask again.

"Nothing really...hard to tell...just a feeling that won't go away."

Tom lifts his coffee to his mouth again, and stares stiffly at a car gliding slowly behind me. Somebody must wave at him eventually, because Tom raises his cup and mimes the words *Happy Christmas*.

For a long time I thought of Tom as a mate. We'd talked one evening when he gave me a lift up to Sugarcane View, after one too many. He seemed like a guy who appreciated a good yarn, and unlike the pastor and the doctor he was more than patient. Perhaps because he didn't have too much to keep him occupied in Littletown. What with it being so quiet, and Tom being the bachelor he is, it's turned him into a bit of an old woman.

Seeing as we got on so well, I'd drop by on a Saturday – when he was a bit pissed and in a good mood – and tell him stories about Bigtown and our travels round the world. Tom seemed to enjoy these stories to begin with at least. He liked hearing about the city and the wrestlers, gawping at my tales about Frehley and Cougher. And I'd make sure that I slipped it in, that I, and not only Cougher and Frehley, had been something of celebrity in my time. And I'd tell him what I could about my conquests at the bordello. Though, since Tom was the law, I was careful to disguise its true location – making out it was on the other side of the Pond. He'd take pleasure in poking holes in my obvious boasts, all good-humouredly at first.

"Come off it, Earl, we don't buy that…have you heard this guy?" he said, turning to his assistant and laughing, as we were shared a drop or two.

"I hear him," mumbled his assistant, "I hear him."

"Come on, Earl…you're not telling us these broads let a guy like you loose on them? But that's against nature?! If not physically impossible!"

"Well, if the sheriff just opened his eyes, he'd see a medical impossibility sittin' right here in front of 'im. Alive and kickin'! And anyone what's alive, wants to do what the livin' do…I might be spliced together with my sister 'ere, Tom…but I ain't dead!"

Tom laughed. I pushed my paper cup forward and he topped it up, and smiled – that warm smile that the local ladies oughtn't to have been able to resist. But then, whenever I steered the subject onto Uncle Rust, he'd instantly get more evasive and sullen. He liked hearing about the flea circus, the fights and the bordello, but his interest waned as the juicy bits got fewer and further apart. Recently, when I'd dropped by, he'd mostly stared into space, expressionless.

"So, what d'you reckon?"

"Sorry?"

"What d'you reckon?"

"About what?"

"About Uncle Rust…"

"Who?"

"Uncle Rust…"

"The guy with the flea circus? What about him?"

And just as I was about to tell him everything again, he'd interrupt and find some lame excuse for breaking up the party. Moments later I'd find myself back out on the steps. Or I'd be left standing there, as he grabbed his hat, got into his patrol car – piss-drunk as usual – and drove off like a scared rabbit, blue lights flashing. Then he'd either sit there in his car in the middle of nowhere, presumably swearing at himself and fuming over the fact he'd befriended this crippled windbag, or we'd have one of those embarrassing situations where I'd find him a bit later, his arse solidly planted on a stool at the local bar.

"Office hours, Earl. We'll talk about this in office hours," he'd mumble, without looking up from his glass.

Anything to avoid discussing Uncle Rust. Nothing helped. It was water off a duck's back. He just sat there, slurping on his coffee, cheeks getting redder and redder, as he tipped the contents of his hip flask into his cup. Until in the end I had to run out of stories. Though new ones would pop up along the way, and I've often fallen to the temptation of adding a bit more, and a bit more, though never laying it on *too* thick.

Sometimes when I realised he was losing interest, I'd find myself tempted, in desperation, to tell him how Cougher had had his way with Betty that Christmas. But Betty would have gone spare and never talked to me again or been talkable-to. So I had to keep that juicy morsel to myself. The other problem was that I had to omit so many essential details. I couldn't reveal too much however much I wanted Tom on my side, I didn't want to go dropping people in it with the law. Leastways, not people who had helped me.

But the time for these stories is over now. Tom's no idiot, but he's not the sharpest knife. He does his job, and that's it. He's Littletown's sheriff. That's what he's good for…that and pulling the odd string or two…if and when he wants.

Horse Trading

"What d'you want? Long time since you came by…"

For a moment Tom's face relaxes as he stuffs the rest of his pastry into his mouth, and peers at me expectantly.

"Nah…just wanted a chat."

"Hmm, I don't know, Earl. I've got a lot on today." Tom moves the half-chewed pastry around his mouth, his cheek bulging as he talks.

"On Christmas Eve?" I ask.

"Yup."

"Here in *Littletown*…?

"Yup!"

"Like what?"

"Nah, you know…*stuff*…paperwork."

He brushes the crumbs from his thighs. "Things look calm enough on the surface, but I swear something's gonna dump itself in my lap before the day's over. Feel it my bones… something's brewing…"

"Caigen asked me to give you this." I hold the bottle out.

Tom shakes his head, grins then empties his cup into the flowerbed. He opens the door and beckons me in. Lifting the counter in reception, he shows me through to his office.

"So Caigen asked you to give me this, eh?"

He lowers the blinds.

"Well, he gave me two actually, but then his dog took a bite out of my sister and the other one smashed to the ground…"

"So that's why she's looking so moody. I'd have given you a lift up to Sugarcane View, but I've already had a stiff drink or two, so you'll have to forgive me…" He winks.

"No problem, we're going to church later, anyway."

Tom leaves the room. On his return he shoves a cup in my hand.

"So, what can I do for you, Earl? What kinda story are you planning to foist on me today?"

"Nah…I dunno. Stories and *stories*…I thought I might come and give you a kinda testament. If that's somethin' you'd like, I mean. 'Cos I've been thinkin' that if you 'ad somethin' down on paper, it might be worth a bit. I tried all night on a typewriter up at Sugarcane View, but it don't seem to come out right."

"A testament?"

"Yes, you see…we ain't on top form…me and my sister. So I've come to tell you that I'll be snuffin' it soon. And as you prob'ly realise, there won't be too many people to inform, so I hoped you might take the time to look up a mate of mine. To organise my effects and the like, I mean. Get the formalities out the way."

Tom sat in silence for a moment, sucking on his top lip.

"Why did you have to come running to me *today*, Earl? I mean…it's Christmas Eve. Couldn't it have waited? There are three hundred and sixty five days in the year, surely you could have spared me today of all days? As I've said before, it's not my area, not my task to…"

"Things are pretty *touch and go* I'm afraid, Tom."

"*Touch and go?*"

"Yeah, and I thought with my condition bein' as it is, it'd be your duty to get hold of 'im. It must say somethin' about that in that book o' yours. The law must say that when a poor bugger's dying he gets granted a wish or two."

"Well, if you want anyone to take a look at that dog bite, I can try to see to that. And if you want to report Caigen's dog,

I can do that too. But do we have to get the whole cavalry out right now?"

"No, we won't need the 'ole cavalry, and the dog bite makes no odds. But if you could get a message out to my mate, I'd be more than grateful."

"And what *mate* might that be, Earl? To be perfectly honest I'm in no state to run messages today…"

"I reckon you know who I'm talking about, Tom…and I'd like it done before I snuff it. Then he might 'ave time to help me with the book I've started. Something which might – by the way – be of enormous medical importance. Just ask the doctor."

Tom nods, trying to look impressed.

"But more than anythin' I need a friend right now, Tom, 'cos I'm dyin' and someone's gotta get my affairs straight. And 'cos there ain't nobody else to comfort me in this goddamn-borin' town."

"Well yes, Earl, this is a small town."

"Yeah, ain't it just…"

"Yes, it is…But if we're talking about the same man as before, he's a *criminal* Earl. And I've already told you, I don't want any criminals here. We've got enough already, I've no intention of letting more in. Simple. But are you sure you've set the right vice to the right man? It'd be a damn sight easier if he was just on the bottle. Then he'd have no trouble finding some buddies here in town…But I really don't know how it would be with any damn *junky*."

"We don't like to call 'im that, sir," I say, clearing my throat. "To us he's…he's…" But I daren't even say his name, for fear that Tom will fly out of the door again.

"I know, but it's still difficult, Earl. It's difficult with these criminal types. He can come here if he really wants, of course…it's a free country…and there's nothing to stop him… if you hadn't made such a bloody fuss nobody would have turned a hair…as long as he stayed clean. In fact, it doesn't really bother me personally, Earl…but thanks for the tip."

Tom laughs with a shrug of the shoulders, then sighs.

"Can't imagine he'd find anything here, though. I mean… who'd employ a dope-head?"

"Well he's clever with a pen and paper…and light on his feet when he wants. I expect you know…he's been a *factotum*. And if the doc could give 'im some medicine…" I add, trying not to get over-excited. "Proper medicine…so everythin' was legal. And then maybe once we've got him 'ere, and if he liked it, he could take our room at Sugarcane View…Christ knows he's old enough and he needs it as much as anybody."

I'm nodding so eagerly, Betty topples slightly forward and starts slipping. I shove her up again.

"I'm not so sure," says Tom, "that I need a gofer on some crazy medicine running around in my town, Earl, legal or otherwise. Can't see us advertising for one either. But don't you think he'd soon get bored here anyway?"

Tom smiles, and takes another swig of tepid warmth.

"Nah, not that bored," I persist. "It'd be fine, honestly. He could take a look round the library, for example."

"Sure, but I don't know about a damned junky, Earl," sighs Tom, turning in his chair with a grimace. "We don't think it's right to have a man like that roaming around here…not when he can't stay off the needle."

"We?" I ask. Tom looks over at me and nods…the royal we…

"You're a hopeless romantic, Earl. I might like your stories, but they don't exactly hold water. To be honest, I think you're just trying to sneak another bum into town with all this talk."

"Another bum?"

Tom pulls his chair closer into the desk and places his hands on it.

"Now look, Earl, I like you. I think you're a great guy. But do you have to be so bloody melodramatic? As far as all this claptrap goes, I suspect you've dreamed the whole lot up. I think you've sat up there at Sugarcane View with that hemp of yours – which, by the way, the matron asked me to mention to you – thinking up ways to get one of your drinking mates into town."

"Give us a break, Tom, it ain't like that..."

"Oh, really? Look, I know you're lonely, but it's a bit much to barge in here on Christmas Eve, making out that you're dying, just to get what you want?"

"Y'what? Lonely?" I say, giving a nod in Betty's direction.

"You know what I'm saying...don't pretend. And I can tell you right now, this'll be as much help as your other tall tales. Why should I promise to let some bloody junky into my town to drag all the usual problems with him? Why should I give a man like that free passage? Do you really think I should fling my arms wide open and hand over the keys of the town to another of your sort? Christ, Earl, can't you just be grateful we let *you* stay, instead of driving you straight to the border? Do you have to drag the whole bloody circus after you?"

Tom shoves his chair back from the desk, and takes another swig.

"Alright. If that do-gooder magician we've got for a Mayor, promised me the resources so we could do more than just cushion people...perhaps I might see things differently and agree to this act of charity, but no...no way."

"Tom please..."

"I just can't see why you'd sacrifice everything for this

bum. What's he done for you that's so wonderful, eh? And out of everybody in Littletown, why are you sniffing round my arse? It's ridiculous. And not my territory at all. You've got the wrong man, Earl...or at least the wrong department. In fact, Earl, I'm the one man you should avoid. You should lie low... but you don't seem to quite understand that."

"Oh?"

"Oh, come off it, Earl. This is a boring little town as you said."

"And so?"

Tom gets up, closes the door to the reception, and sits back down at his desk. And continues in a low voice.

"Well, when someone like you turns up, or to be more precise, when a pair like you turn up – one looking totally done-in and beaten-up, and the other covered in blood – people talk. I shouldn't have to tell you, but it's cost me dear to turn a blind eye."

As always Tom's puts his finger on the weak point of my story – the stuff I can't fill him in with – because it's what Uncle Rust did for us, that he'd get in trouble for if I revealed it. My debt to him is what's gagging me. I'm on a lost mission. Tom doesn't want a criminal here. Doesn't want his town infected. And in a way, I'm relieved it's over. I've tried. And that'll have to do. I've tried, it's over, and there's nothing more than death left. I'd have liked to lay all my cards on the table, but I don't dare. It's not possible.

"Because, Earl," Tom went on, "that's exactly what I've been doing here. And it's cost me, let me tell you, not to dig deeper into all this – to sit and pretend I liked listening to your stories out of mere curiosity. So, please, with it's being Christmas and all, either put all your cards on the table and tell me everything I've not already guessed for myself – *without* the fancy packaging – or hold your tongue, walk out of that door and enjoy the time you have left at Sugarcane View. I don't know exactly what you've been mixed up in, but I have some idea.

We sit in silence for a moment.

"Alright, let's make this easier for you…who put you onto the idea that you should come sniffing round me."

"Wilder," I mumbled, hesitating.

"OK. And who d'you think came into my office on the day you arrived in town?"

"Wilder?"

"Wow, Earl, who'd think? Right in one! I think you deserve another drop…"

"…with it being Christmas and all," I add, to save him the trouble.

He looks up holding the bottle out.

"So how much does it cost, really, Tom?" I ask, as he takes the first swig.

"What?"

"To turn a blind eye?" I drain my cup in one, as Tom sits motionless, a look of bitterness crossing his face. Then he laughs.

"Everything has its price, Earl…everything has its price. But don't come here and fuck with me…please."

He smiles, yet his eyes are stone cold. There's a prickling in my fingers, one of my feet is shaking, and I try to restrain it. Betty's body starts shaking and threatens to tip over again.

"Earl, Earl, Earl. I really hope the day never comes, but believe me, all I have to do is to lift the receiver and you'll be sitting in the clink. But why would I want that? You're already sitting behind bars. Perhaps you haven't noticed it, but you're…well, you're like a dog on the end of a chain, Earl.

You can't run far."

Tom ruffles his hand through his thin hair and rolls his neck. He lets out a heavy sigh, then takes my cup and tops it up.

"Come on, Earl...I know you...I know your kind. You're not doing this out of friendship or love for this junky. You're just hell-bent on seeing how far you can stretch the elastic. You run away from Bigtown, and then, when you get bored, you get these mad ideas and you just want to see just how far you can take things...to see if you can shaft the mean sods you're obliged to associate with. But let me tell you, it won't stretch any further, Earl...you pulled the elastic too far long ago. My patience is at an end. And what happens when you pull elastic too far...eh? What happens, Earl?"

"It snaps..." I mumble.

"Exactly. So my question is, *why?* Why are you poking about in this shit bucket, if you can't take the stink? As far as I know, you haven't even got your papers in order. For all I know you're risking deportation, so there's got to be a reason..."

I look up.

Tom looks at me sternly.

"I dunno..."

"Really?"

"Maybe because I think it's the right thing to do?"

"OK. Could you kindly tell me what that bum did for you? What exactly do you owe him? If you even know. And don't go telling me it's about that fucking flea because something'll snap, and you'll be out on your arse."

I nod.

"So I'm asking you again. Something tells me you can't give me an answer, but I'm asking anyway...aside from that pathetic flea story, exactly what has he done for you? What do you owe that bum? Spit it out."

"Listen, Tom, ain't you never been the cause of somebody else's bad fortune? In some way or other, I mean?"

Tom gazes up at the ceiling for a moment, as though he needs to think before answering.

"No, Earl. Not really. No. And as I said, that flea story is all that's missing before my foot plants itself up your backside."

The Thing and Mr King

It was still dark when I woke up. Cougher was cold. Uncle Rust was slumped in front of the coal burner, dozing. His head sank slowly, before nodding back up again. It was hot in the wagon, and I was thirsty and exhausted from being groped by Cougher half the night.

"Oh boy..." said Uncle Rust, squinting across the wagon. "Cougher's snuffed it!"

We managed to roll Cougher to one side, and got Betty on her feet and respectably dressed. At that moment we heard a noise on the gravel outside. Tim's head came into view as he walked past one of the windows. Frehley was already at the door and stood waiting at the top of the wagon steps. Betty and I followed with Uncle Rust close behind us.

"Wotcher, Biff!" I heard Frehley shout in a friendly tone. That was all he managed to say before he came crashing backwards through the doorway again. As he fell, something in his body seemed to give way, and there was cracking noise in his ribcage. The huge weight Frehley had carried about every day of his life, seemed now to crush something inside him as though his bones were splintering as his body met the floor.

Mr King had planted a sledgehammer in Frehley's kneecap, and Tim was trying to grab it from him now. But the legless bandit – who was, despite everything, no lightweight – managed to take a second swing with it and smash him in the belly. Retching, Tim sank between the sleepers. Mr King's wheels ground into the gravel as he turned his wheelchair towards the doorway. With the next blow, the sledgehammer caught Frehley on the jaw, before sinking into his chest. With the sledgehammer planted so deep, and out of Mr King's reach, Frehley managed to get a good grip on it and fling it to the back of the wagon, and then drag himself inside the entrance by his arms.

"Christ, I'm back in at least," he gasped, trying to sit up. It was true – if he'd gone down outside, nobody would have been able to get him back on his feet, and everything would have been lost. Leastways, without Cougher to lift him.

Mr King craned his neck and peered in through the doorway. His face was red and swollen from the bites of the fleas that were crawling all over him. With bloodied fingers he smacked his cheek, then squeezed the life out of a little flea, as he glared angrily at me.

"Hello, Earl. So this is where you are. And there was I looking for you all over town...You know what, Earl," he continued, still catching his breath, "there's something I forgot to ask you..."

I nodded. Mr King went on.

"Tell me, Earl, have you heard the joke about the third hand?"

Mr King sucked on his top lip, tasting sweat and blood. Then, as his tongue worked around his mouth, he opened his jacket and the handle of a large knife came into view.

"The point with the third hand, Earl, is that..."

He got no further before Tim, who was back on his feet, loomed up behind the old amputee and grabbed him.

"What the fuck?!" bellowed Mr King. "Let me go!"

"I'm sorry, Frehley..." said Tim, looking over at Frehley as he struggled to keep Mr King in his grip. "I'm so, so sorry..."

Mr King stretched his arms up behind him and tried to claw his way free. But Tim had the upper hand.

"No need to apologise, Tim," said the giant gently. He coughed, and there was a gurgling in his ruptured ribcage, before he went on. "And Biff, we can still sort this out. You hear me? We can find a solution."

At that moment, my left hand – *the* hand – pulled me after it. Through the wagon and out of the door. Where the knife came from, I have no idea…Frehley's kitchen perhaps…but suddenly, before I knew it was stuck in Mr King's throat. It crunched in his larynx. Mr King who'd reached his arms out behind him to wrench himself out of Tim's grasp, crumpled.

I screamed.

The hand pulled out the knife.

I screamed again.

Mr King screamed. Then the hand rammed the knife into Mr King's throat again, and everything went quiet. I looked up, my hand still whirring of its own accord in front of me. The cripple who was holding his throat, looked down at his sliced fingers.

I looked at my hand.

And we stood there, with not much to say, until the hand flung away the knife.

"It wasn't me!" I whispered. "It was the hand. It wasn't me. It was *the thing.*"

Mr King stared at me. Tim stared at me. Then we all stared down at the hand, twisting, turning and finally closing in front of me. Mr King sat clutching his throat, his other hand hanging limply at his side, and gashes in his shoulder pads revealing hacked tendons.

"Earl, you idiot. Now there's no way back," yelled Frehley from inside the wagon. "We'd have sorted this out somehow. Damn you!"

"It wasn't me," I repeated, shaking the hand to get the

feeling back. We stood there, paralysed. Mr King stared at me disbelievingly. Steam rose from his gaping throat and blood streamed from his mouth. And with eyes filled with dumb fury, he listened as the dying Frehley issued instructions about what was to be done with his body.

"Sorry you've gotta hear this, Betty," Frehley said, "...but Bill...this is what you gotta do...you and Tim take Biff and carry him into the bathroom and finish him off...and when the wagon-train gets going tomorrow...you gotta chop him up and throw the bits along the tracks...make sure the pieces are small enough, and chuck them as far as you can...best of all, in these small lakes outside Littletown."

Frehley turned towards Mr King in his wheelchair...

"Biff, this ain't meant badly. No hard feelings. I've always said, live and let live. But right now, there's other people gotta live, not you. And Uncle Rust...you'll have to take the rap for *this*..." He drew a hand along the length of his broken body. "Tell them you killed your friend in a quarrel."

Mr King tried to laugh, but a hissing noise rose from his throat as the blood spurted through his mangled fingers. And then he went quiet again, a malicious expression on his lips.

"Why me?" asked Uncle Rust – not in any attempt to squirm out of it, but just to get it straight.

"Because...because Earl can't go to jail. If jail doesn't break him...if the law doesn't crush him..." gasped Frehley, "...one of Mr King's cronies will...guaranteed. Everyone will know who Mr King's nemesis was...and an accident like Earl can't walk alone in Bigtown."

"And Mr King, I didn't come here alone, either," Tim interrupted, "but the others scarpered when it got too hot for them."

"There, you see...the twins won't see their old age if they

stay in Bigtown…and not in some jail, with a price on their heads. Bill…you're getting' old and you can't run a wrestling school…Spinks and Tim can, they're youngsters…but not you, you're old. There's a bit of cash for you, don't worry. I've made a will. You take the rap for this. Mr King will be gone…and that'll please most folk…but it'll be another thing explaining me away…"

Frehley coughed again and for a moment his eyes seemed to glaze over. Then he opened them wide, as though struggling to shake the sleep off.

If the cops don't get a result on a plate," Frehley continued, "they'll start pokin' about…if they've got time on their hands…or smell money. But the cops like it easy…it's happened before and it'll happen again. So long as everything fits neatly…they don't give a shit about the details…however obvious they might be.

"And you, Bill…I'm sorry to say…you fit like a glove…. and if we fix things…it'll look like self-defence…and then we're not looking at a long stint."

"OK, Frehley, I see your point. A little time in the clink probably isn't the worst thing that could happen to me right now."

Betty was crying. The giant stretched out a hand and patted her gently on the head.

"Hey, sweetie," he said, "sweetie…" he stroked her hair and asked Uncle Rust to fetch the sack of money for the children's home in Littletown.

"You two have got to get away…but here, take this and give it to Dom Wilder in Littletown. There's a letter for him in the bag that'll take care of everything…Can you manage that, Earl? And here's your prize money for tonight. You gotta look after your sister now, and keep well away from Bigtown until you hear otherwise. Understand? Stay in Littletown until you get word...it's not gonna be safe for you here."

He threw the bag to me.

"And, Bill, you take the milk truck and drive it as far as you can, and then you'll have be at the next station after Littletown..."

Holding the bag we hugged Frehley. He gave us a smile, blood round his mouth.

"Jesus, I'm starting to look like Cougher," Frehley whispered, red streaks between his front teeth. All the teeth in his right jaw had been broken by Mr King's sledgehammer, and blood was gurgling up from his lungs. He wiped his mouth and looked at his fingers for a moment before waving us off.

"Come on now, get going," he said finally with a faint smile.

And with that, Tim hauled Mr King up into the wagon and shut the door. All we heard was a death rattle as Tim and Frehley presumably finished him off. And for all I know that was exactly what they were doing, all according to Frehley's instructions. More than that...I don't know...not about Frehley, or Mr King, or Spinks or Tim.

But one way or another, Uncle Rust got us here...in the milk truck or somehow or other...everything just went black...and when I woke up, we were in front of the Town Hall in Littletown...and I've tried my best to remember...and so has Betty...but all I remember between our waking up and the murders in the wagon is everything going black...black... completely black...and my legs going of their own accord... my body prickling all the way...and the hand raised like a dowsing wand...a torch in the dark before us...and Uncle Rust running behind...lungs squeaking...on spindly, uncertain legs.

In complete black.

Tom is sucking on something invisible between his front teeth and leaning over his desk.

"Well...have you given it some thought, Earl?"

"Yes."

"So what's it to be? Am I getting the typewriter out, or are we taking a trip to the church?"

"Well, you don't need to get the typewriter out, at least."

"Fine! There's just one thing I want you to write on your forehead and think about when you've calmed down. If you get the urge to really irritate me in the near future, Earl, just consider how I could have used all this...*if* I'd really wanted. And for a poor sod like me that's some temptation...I could have used all this to make my life as a small-town sheriff way more comfortable. I could have been quite a hero."

Tom points at the safe in the corner of the room.

"There's a tidy stack of banknotes in that safe. We have, of course, kept your little contribution – every bit helps. But all the banknotes in the cupboard over there are covered with bloody fingerprints...and even though I'm not sure where the banknotes come from, we both know whose fingerprints they are...don't we?"

I nod.

"And if I'd wanted to use it, Earl, it would have opened a few doors for me, I can assure you. If nothing else I'd have had my moment in the limelight, and perhaps I'd have finally hooked one of the ladies round here...Randi Echols, for example. God knows there were nights I lay awake and thought of nothing else but getting my teeth into that little number…just ripe for the picking."

"Yeah, Randi's nice," I mumble with my eyes to the floor.

"Don't hang your head so low, Earl. Not now you've finally seen who's on your side in Littletown. You know who your real friends are now, don't you?"

I nod.

"And presumably you realise who's kept you alive, eh?"

"Littletown…?"

"Exactly. Every single person in Littletown has chipped in. Everything has a price, and that contribution that you saw fit to put in the cash-box wasn't too impressive. I reckon you stacked more than enough away. But we haven't demanded much in repayment, or given you an earache about it, have we?"

"No…"

"So, all in all, you have to agree we've treated you pretty well."

Tom rotates his coffee cup, sighs and looks over at me.

"But d'you know why, Earl…?"

"No, not really…"

"Because we feel sorry for you…or for Betty mostly…and if I put you in the clink, I have to put her in too. You put me in a legal dilemma. If you'd come here on your own, you'd have been under lock and key ages ago. And I'd have been in Randi's knickers."

He laughs. Then his face twists into a smile.

"But seeing as Betty was part of the package, we all thought that that would be wrong. As pointless as it's impossible. And it would have been equally wrong to send the two of you back to Bigtown. Something tells me, you wouldn't have lasted long there either…"

My shaking finally makes Betty tip forward. With a jerk

of my shoulder I get her up again. But it just gets worse – Betty's head flops back instantly, and mine feels like it's about to implode. My knees are jumping, my throat's burning, and a string of snot is coming out of my nostril. Meanwhile the third hand is jerking with increasing rapidity.

"Not that it looks like you'll last too long *here* either. Look at you! You're as white as a corpse, and that hand of yours has been going spastic since you got here…"

"Look, Tom…I just want my mate to come 'ere…I could die any minute…and I ain't got no other mates…" I whine. But Tom's not taking a blind bit of notice…he's enjoying the sound of his own voice too much…and the liquor.

"Just relax Earl. Like I said, you have friends. And if your chum had really wanted to come here, he could have shown his face long ago. There's not a lot you can do, whatever. He knows where you are, doesn't he? Perhaps he wants to be in Bigtown, or wherever the hell he is, and perhaps he's there because he can't stand more of your bullshit, Earl…or perhaps he just wants his slice of the money."

I nod.

"And, if you think it's just blood money Littletown's slipping you…I can open that safe door, like I said, and show you banknotes that really *are* soaked in blood. And anybody who wanted a slice of that would be pretty desperate, if you ask me…and certainly not somebody I'd want anything to do with."

I nod, head bowed.

"But what's with your sister?" Tom holds the cup away from his mouth. "She's not said a word today."

"Yeah well…she's just takin' a nap." I say, getting up and wiping away the snot with my sleeve. My legs have stopped shaking, but now they've gone to jelly.

"Really?" Tom looks up at me.

"Yup. Don't suppose you've had much to do with Siamese twins, eh?" I laugh through gritted teeth.

"No-o-o," says Tom, scratching his head with a pencil, before suddenly stopping and putting it down, to massage his temples.

"It's totally normal," I mumble, " 'appens all the time…one sleeps and the other one gets on with stuff. Can't be messin' with what the other one's doin' all the time, you know. But she liked you, Tom…*likes* you. So she's probably appreciated bein' 'ere, even if she's taken a nap this time."

Tom's eyes widen, his gaze softens.

"Sorry to have been hard on you, Earl. No harm meant… But the truth hurts, as you know."

"No worries, I've suffered worse…"

Tom smiles warmly again.

"Get someone to look at that bite, Earl. And take it easy for a couple of days…you look like you need it."

"But you do realise Tom, it ain't actually possible?"

"What?"

"A man and a woman, together…like me and her." I say, my forefinger swinging like a pendulum between Betty and me. "It just don't 'appen. So it ain't like things always add up…is it?"

"Jesus…you don't say…*impossible?*"

The air blows heavily through his nostrils. The room must stink of liquor. Halfway out of the office door I turn back, pick up my paper cup and empty it in a single swig. The mix of coffee and liquor warms me and clears my head, while a satisfying post-tears sensation spreads through my body. I hiccup, once, vacantly, then leave the office as the third hand starts to shake even harder.

"You know something, Earl," he says as he follows me out, "if you just try hard enough to pretend certain things don't exist...it sometimes turns out they really don't...things melt away...cease to be...more often than you'd credit..."

"Like what?"

"Like allsorts. Your friend for example. It's just a matter of daring to let these things go. And the truth is, even if I was a bit hard on you just now, I've appreciated your stories, really I have – true or not. So if you think life here in Littletown is a lie, I promise you that life in Bigtown is an even bigger lie. And if you think life here's a trial, I suggest you'd do better to try and let go – forget your old life."

"Because?"

"Because then you'll realise that all these people that you see on their way to church, aren't the devils you imagine, Earl. You'll see that we're really good people. That we're angels, all of us. It's just a question of how you look at things. Let go and forget, and you'll see – the devils will turn into angels again."

Tom smiles and winks.

"Happy Christmas, Earl," he says, following me to the front door. The sharp wind blows his wispy hair out of place.

"Yeah sure, Happy Christmas," I answer, and then whisper: "I hope you all fuckin' rot in Hell...all of you...great and small."

"You what?" he asks. His glazed eyes scour the houses and street corners, there's a dog barking somewhere. Its baying wanders through the quiet streets before the church bells start to ring.

"Nothin' nothin' to concern yerself over, Happy Christmas, *Mister* Norman...

Randi is still holding my hand when I wake up to the roar of the organ, and realise that I must have been gone some time. The congregation rises, and the pastor strolls towards the church doors. Randi lets go of my hand and follows her family. I stay behind and try to pull myself together. Shaking the sleep off, I gaze up at the church roof.

"Well, Big Guy, you 'ad your chance," I whisper. "And I suppose that's it now. We're through, you and me..."

Eventually I manage to stagger to my feet and limp down the aisle, with the hand pointing straight ahead of me. If this isn't bloody typical – I can't go for dinner with the Echolses with this spastic dowsing wand, it would be scandalous, however kind and patient they were. Almost without me doing anything, my legs slow down. So Christmas Night will be spent up at Sugarcane View after all. It's just so fucking typical. Except, of course, that this'll be the first time I'll sit there completely alone.

"Earl," says the pastor, "Happy Christmas Earl."

"Happy Christmas," I answer.

"How are things?" he asks.

"Oh, alright. A bit topsy-turvy, but alright."

"It's great you dropped by...we're not exactly used to seeing you as a regular churchgoer."

"Nah...well, to be honest I've not always been that keen. Betty often wants to come, but...well, you know how it is with me and churches."

"You've certainly been attending more frequently lately, Earl, so who knows...perhaps things are on the turn..."

The pastor looks at me quizzically.

"But *how* are things with your sister, Earl? She looks a bit listless."

"Well, I ain't sure really."

"You're usually the one who drops off in the service," he says, with a wink. "Be honest now, Earl...tell me...how is Betty really? A few people have noticed that she looks a bit out of it lately."

"Oh, that's just 'ow things are with people like us sometimes. Sometimes the Good Lord almost snuffs us out, and then – like in that big book of yours – he breathes life back into us. I'm gettin' hardly any sleep nowadays, so things even themselves out. But I dropped off during your sermon just now...and that was like heaven!"

The pastor smiles.

"That's the way it is, bein' one of God's fancies," I laugh.

The pastor nods and I wish him farewell. Halfway down the church steps I turn back, although I know it'll be in vain.

"Pastor," I say.

He has shut one of the doors, and is reaching out for the other.

"Yes?" he says, looking down at me.

"I was just wonderin'...we might not be 'ere in the New Year. Trouble with our health, you see. And I've got this friend, y'know, over in Bigtown, so I was just wonderin'..."

"I think we've had this conversation, Earl."

"Right..."

"And I don't think there's anything we can do. You'd be better off talking to Tom or the doctor."

"I've talked to Tom...and the old doctor's too ill to do anythin'...and the new one ain't never available, so..."

"I'm sorry Earl, it's difficult...really difficult. But is there anything else I can help you with?"

"No."

"Look after your sister, Earl. And Happy Christmas."

And with that the pastor closes the second door. Slowly, I start down the steps. But stop halfway. Somewhere in our bodies, the pumps are suddenly going nineteen to the dozen. My throat tightens as though an elephant had sat on my chest. With each gulp of air a whistling sound comes from my throat. I feel dizzy and grab the handrail. Then it comes to me...*this is it*...I think to myself...*it's goin' to happen now*... A moment later I hear a metallic, clanking noise rushing through the streets. Then silence.

Complete, utter silence...and just seconds from everything going bang...I feel it in my whole being...as though the earth was tinder-dry and ice-cold all at once. Betty is hanging heavily from me...and it's a split second from something happening... something's happening...*it's* happening...it'll happen... now...to Earl Merrik. It is happening now! If I only knew where it was coming from...but I know now that I'm not going to collapse....I feel it...but I sense there's something nearby... it's nearby...like something fluttering above my head...I turn my head, but I can't see shit...but if the Heavens tore open and lightning drove me deep into the earth...down to Hell even... it would be better than standing in this filthy, bitter wind... waiting. I feel like I'm about to explode...as though hell is breaking out of me. The right hand whirrs, without sensation, as I try to steady it with my good hand. But it's beyond control.

And I'm so bottomlessly, bottomlesly, tired and sad. And you God, you really know how to piss on me sometimes. Betty's as dead as a kipper, and I'm equally fucking done for, and nobody gives a shit about Uncle Rust. And it's Christmas for fuck's sake! Everybody I know is dead, and all I wanted was a friend, so as not to die alone. There was I thinking that if I could do just one good deed, then somebody might look down on me with mercy. But no. You fucking cunt. You enjoy grindin' your heel into us poor little creatures, don't you?! Is that really how you like to entertain your bastard child on his birthday? Is it?

"Come on then!" I bellow suddenly…it just comes over me…I clench my fists and shut my eyes and it rages inside me.

Come on then…Give me your fuckin' worst! I think to myself. Is this pissin' wind all you got? Is it? Why be so fuckin' miserly? How about some rats and beetles and splinters of glass and powders to make yer itch an' itch all over? How about some bugs under yer skin, and snakes round yer toes? I want alligators playing the accordion, houses howlin' with hollow-eyed skeletons, gorillas beating their breasts and dogs snapping at yer heels between organ music. Give us a proper display. A flash of lightning. Let our hearts be clawed out of our breasts. Let the earth close over us. You've always given me a double helping otherwise in life…and now I'm finally making my exit…surely you could dish out a bit extra…More!

"Come on!" I yell for the second and then the third time, "Come on!"

My chest is wheezing and people are turning round on the other side of the street, keys in their hands, on their way to their good dinners and smart houses overflowing with angelic kids and presents.

Randi just manages to step away from her flock of siblings, and put a foot on the first step.

When Betty screams.

It goes quiet.

Then another scream. I scream too, and fling myself round to see where the sudden sound came from.

"Put me down, put me down!" Betty screams, feet dangling over the edge of staircase. But I'm already spinning round on one leg, screaming with hoarse lungs and trying to lift her up.

But in the midst of our customary puppy-waltz we tumble down the steps, and right in front of Randi I plant my face in the railings, so my front teeth burst out of my mouth with a gush of blood.

"Me teef," I groan with split lips.

With my hand over my howling, gaping mouth, we pirouette along the pavement, legs like rubber. It's as though we're both pulling and tugging, each trying to get the other one off, before we finally skid across the lawn between the pavement and the road, and then I just manage to get a foothold and spin us around, before something heavy hits us from behind, throwing us high into the air.

We're flying. Everything is silent. We float through the air. And as we float there's a cracking sound, as though we'd been hit by lightning. And I feel light and heavy, like never before.

Then I meet the earth. Earth and stone. Blood, earth, stone.

GOD

I wake up in a huge white room. It's like some poor sod has painted the whole of Littletown white. Everywhere white. And when I try to look out into the edges to see if there's any darkness...some shadow or twilight...it's soddin' white there too.

"I am God," says Betty.

"Yer what?!" I say.

"I am God, and I was there all the time. Where you couldn't go, I carried you. And when you felt lonely, I was there."

"So it was you...all the time."

"Yes. All the time."

"Where's Betty then? If you're God and not Betty, I mean."

"Betty doesn't exist."

"How can she not exist, when I've seen her?"

"It's me you've seen."

"OK, *God*, what now? What's gonna happen to me now?"

"You're going to Heaven."

"Now? But I don't wanna go, I wanna be on earth and be free, just for a bit. Please Betty, God, please, let me stay on earth a bit longer..."

"No, you've got to go to Heaven now, little brother."

I'm woken up by the most terrible noise. A shrill, guttural noise. As though someone was being murdered. A dog whining for mercy. That and a fucking great fuss and commotion around me. When I open my eyes I realise that it's Betty screaming, with the pastor bending over her and the congregation standing around her. And in the background I can see Randi doing her level best to calm Gunnar down who's in full swing with his war dance.

"Everything will be fine," the pastor says. "You'll be alright, Betty."

"Yes but…yes but…*Earl*," Betty sobs.

My head feels heavy, I can barely open my eyes, far less move my head. I'm not even sure if I'm breathing.

Yes, I'm breathing. But faintly. A faint moisture on my lips.

"I'm sorry, Betty, but I think Earl's passed away. But you'll be alright – things don't look too bad," says the pastor.

Fucking idiot, I think to myself. Fucking dickhead. It's not enough that he can't see I'm alive, but he's chosen to give her the bad news right here and now. Bloody half-wit. Christ, I've wasted my time these last weeks…God's messenger, my arse.

"Hey, pastor-fucker. I don't suppose you'd consider givin' Earl Merrik the once over too?! Or is it too much to ask you to lower your gaze an inch to look at this worm?"

Nothing comes out of my mouth. Just a sensation of damp warmth, coming maybe from the blood that's pumping out where my teeth used to be. There's an icy, hellish itching and aching in my throat and the roof of my mouth. Not that I can do anything about it – my tongue lies thick and heavy, like it weighs a ton. I can't even push it forward to feel the gap between my teeth.

"Yes but...yes but..." says Betty.

My sweet, wonderful sister thinking only of her brother at a moment like this.

"You must lie still now, Betty,' says the pastor.

"Yes but, he won't be *saved*," cries Betty again, "I thought his soul would be *saved*."

The pastor stares into the ground with a grave expression. He looks over at me, then down at Betty again, and then at the tips of his fingers.

"Hmmm," he says anxiously.

"He won't be saved, and now he'll go to Hell. And he'll take me with him. He'll take me with him too, don't you see? That idiot will take me with him!"

Far away we can hear the whining of Littletown's ambulance...as though there was anywhere to take us apart from the mortuary.

"He's gonna take me to Hell with him," Betty rails.

"Now, now, there's no need for that sort of talk," Tom Norman says gently, his face red.

"Down to Hell! Don't you understand anything?!" Betty wails. "Why didn't anybody do anything? I tried to say. But nobody wanted to listen. Nobody! He wasn't kind to me, and I tried to tell people, but nobody would listen. Not even you, pastor."

"I'm sorry, Betty."

"He's got blood on his hands. And you knew it, Tom, you knew it!"

Tom shakes his head and tries to wave back the crowd.

"Blood on his hands..." she goes on. "And he's smeared me with blood too."

Self-righteous little cow. She can't fucking talk so loud. She's as much to blame as me. She just stepped back and let her brother do all the dirty work. Chicken. We both know who's really to blame – that damned *thing* inside us. That's what guided the hand. The lump of hell inside us. But when the chips are down, all she cares about is that she doesn't want to go to Hell. Betty doesn't want to pay the price for all the good times. Not that we'll go to Hell anyway, we're not going anywhere...apart from the mortuary and six foot under.

Suddenly I see it all. And that cock-and-bull dream about Betty as God. Humbug! Humbug! Laugh yourself sick. What a fucking joke!

With a strange grunt rising from deep in my throat, I finally manage to lift my head from the tarmac. Clumps of sticky blood spurt out of my mouth. I crane my neck, and my eyes travel over my sister's body. Then I let my eyes poke about in her flesh, to see if I can find it, to see if *the thing* is anywhere to be found. But I can't see it. Not in me – not in Betty. And suddenly I get the notion that all this is because I didn't wish hard enough on that shooting star over Littletown. Deep, deep down I didn't wish for peace on earth at all. Because, when the chips were down, my only wish was for Betty and I to be apart.

And this is the price to be paid. Fair deals. I push the thought away. Claptrap. Claptrap and shooting stars.

Betty is crying, but nobody's listening any more. The foot-draggers and dawdlers among the congregation who've been having a feast, peering at my body with craned necks and squinting eyes, step back with a gasp as another gurgling, grunting sound escapes my mouth.

As you'd expect, I find my trousers round my knees. And not far away, the second eldest Echols boy stands pointing at me with a bloodied finger and a grin that freezes, then vanishes.

It's hard to believe he'd resist the temptation. For all I know, the whole of bloody Littletown has investigated Earl's privates by now. And those who haven't are probably on their way by cart or automobile to get their slice of the action. Christmas or not. After all, it's what they've been waiting for all this time! To see if they've been paying for the genuine item, with all their alms. To hell with them! To hell! Now they'll fucking see!

Earl Merrik rises. He's raging. Raging, but free. It'll take more than a flash of lightning to put paid to this man.

"He's alive," says Tom.

"You bet!" I try to shout, but only air and a whisper come out.

"Well I never," gasps the pastor.

"Humbug!" I croak. My voice is clearer now, but cracked. My lips are swollen and dry. I force myself up into a sitting position. A sigh goes through the crowd.

"Ladies and...and gentlemen..." I mutter. "Just throw your coppers in the cap..." I grab for my trousers and ease them on, bit by bit. Tom comes over and sits on his haunches next to me with one hand on my shoulder.

"Leave me alone," I growl, my fingers groping for the gash where Betty and I have been ripped at the seams. "Where is it?"

"What?" asks Tom.

"Where's *the thing?* Mr Bugs?"

"Where's what?! You should lie down for a bit, Earl. You don't look too good. We'll have you in the ambulance any minute now."

Tom tosses his head towards the sound of the clapped-out motor pushing its way through the crowd.

"Where's the third man? The Jack-in-the-box?" Without

looking down, I point at the gash in my body where Betty used to be. "I ain't got much time, y'see. I just fuckin' wanna see it...him."

My tongue moves around inside my mouth, gathers the spittle and blows out a sticky clump of blood, as I try unsuccessfully to spit.

"What going on?" I hear the pastor say.

"I don't know. Earl was asking about some sort of bogeyman, I think." I hear Tom, whisper.

"A what?"

"A *bogeyman*. I'm not sure...but something like that."

They peer down at me.

"He was right...'ere...!" Almost out of breath again, I point first at myself, then over at Betty, who's lying with her back to me, her torn shoulder exposed to the air. I poke one finger in my gash and then hold three fingers up at Tom. The pastor stares at me, as if something's falling into place...first at me, then at Betty. Then his gaze travels from the pool of blood I've left in the road, and up a long trail of blood and gore that continues over the curb to the left. And then further over the gentle slope towards the villa that belongs to the doctor, who has now lumbered in this direction to view the wreckage of our bodies.

Red in the cheeks and reeking of brandy, he is investigating something with his walking stick, something in the pool of blood next to me. All in the name of *medical science*, no doubt.

"What are you saying? Are there *three* of you?" Tom bursts out almost like he's seen stars.

"Huh?" the doctor turns.

A thick strip of blood, almost a foot wide, is making its way up over the lawn, and then further in under the thick, tangled bushes by the fence leading to the veranda. The size of a rat, or a small cat. For a second, the world seems to spin, but I could swear I see it squeeze itself under the doctor's veranda. And if it's what I think it is, it must be the vilest thing I've ever seen.

"Under the veranda…" I gasp, hauling myself to my feet, before the unexpected lack of counterweight from Betty's body sends me to my knees again.

"Well I'll be damned. I knew it, just knew it – fucking knew that some bloody problem was gonna land in my lap today," whispers Tom as he stomps up the slope, pulling his torch from his belt, before he loosens the grating and moves crab-like under the veranda.

"What the hell's Norman doing?" The doctor is limping, poking his way forwards on his stick towards Betty, when a scream reverberates over the neighbourhood. The air rips, as if somebody was strangling a newborn baby.

He's caught it! That's my first thought. But I should have known better. Tom's so pissed he'd be hard pressed to find his own shadow. And true to form he comes bumbling out from under the veranda, turning off his torch and shaking his head. Then, as he tries to put back the grill, he skids on something and falls onto his arse, getting a huge wet patch on the back of his trousers.

"There was nothing there…leastways, no bogeyman. Sorry Earl, but I really do think you should lie down for a bit."

"I don't give a shit what you think, Tom! What about that trail o' blood?!" The strain of shouting, makes the world spin again. My mouth prickles like I'm gonna puke. My thighs are shaking.

"I…I don't know, Earl. Maybe it was a cat or…a dog… you know…perhaps it dragged something with it. We haven't talked to the woman yet…to the driver."

"*Dragged something with it?!* Fuck me, Tom, y'really are

somethin', y'know that?"

I start laughing. Down on all fours, blood and spittle running out from between my split lips. Partly perhaps at the strange lisping when I try to speak – like the words are kind of chopped at the ends. Or perhaps at my own naivety – I've been lying here thinking this whole event was down to a flash of lightning, and it's clearly just a car that's taken me down. But I'm laughing mainly perhaps at that idiot Tom, who, when it comes to it, hasn't got a tactful fibre in his body...who knows. But I'm alive. Despite everything. For a bit longer at least.

And Tom, who probably hasn't got the slightest notion that I'm laughing at *him*, turns to the others and whispers.

"Did you hear that scream? Caigen's dog must have caught a cat or something. Thought my blood would curdle." He shivers, then, as he tries to stuff the torch back into his belt his right leg suddenly skids out from under him.

"Damn you, Norman...you clumsy idiot. Look where you're going!" The old doctor shakes his walking stick.

With the stick waving furiously after him, Tom flaps off with a look of incomprehension, like a gunned-down crow with his arms thrashing in the air and a chunk of flesh, or whatever it is – presumably something from Betty or me – stuck neatly under his shoe like a skate. His heavy torch does a few whirls in the air before slipping out of his hand. It plunges past the head of the doctor, who leans stiffly to one side, past the pastor, who hardly registers it, and then flies into the windscreen of the car behind us, which instantly starts rolling towards the fountain in front of the Town Hall.

And Tom, who's finally got his balance, stands disbelievingly with his hands over his face, before making a dash for the car. Only to start skidding again, as though he still had a skate on one foot, hopping awkwardly now and then to wipe off the gunge that's stuck under his shoe from Betty and me.

Finally, one of the other guys flings himself into the car. And the chase is over. Tom wipes his shoe clean, shirt tails hanging out, arse soaking wet, trying to catch his breath.

"Rot in hell, Tom!" barks the doctor. You nearly killed me with that thing. You clumsy idiot, are you drunk on duty?!"

Ignoring the doctor, Tom wipes his sweat on his sleeve.

"Sorry, Earl," he gasps, "there wasn't anything there, honestly, though maybe a cat's stolen a piece of meat and dragged it up there, or something…You were gone for ages, I think the ambulance broke down three times on its way. We looked after Betty most, because she came round first. And you…well, you looked kinda dead, Earl."

Tom puts a hand on my shoulder.

"And now, I really think you ought to lie down or I'll have to force you. You don't look too great, Earl. Please, Earl, lie down for a bit. Then maybe we can talk about that poor old bastard of yours…maybe come to some arrangement…"

"Tom…ain't no point offerin' a dead man bread…Just leave me be…please…!" I hiss. I try to get up, and nearly tip over again, but this time I manage to get my balance.

"Where are you going?" says the pastor.

"He's walking!" says Tom, behind me.

"Oh, just let him go," growls the doctor. "It doesn't look like he'll hold out long anyway, then you can pick him up in an hour. Unless the kid's got more surprises up his sleeve."

"He's walking!" repeats Tom, ignoring the doctor's growls.

He'll have a good yarn to tell now, at last. Perhaps he'll stop sitting behind that desk, knocking back the liquor. Perhaps he'll get out a bit now. To tell the thrilling tale of how he was there to see Earl Merrik die and rise and walk again. Perhaps he'll finally get into a few of those girls' knickers from the neighbouring county. I don't care. I am free, maybe not for long, but right now I am free. With each step I take, I am walking to freedom. And I'll keep walking. Walking as far away as I can away from this mayhem.

What amuses me most now, is how I've always believed I didn't have a heart. That's what they told us when we were small, the people that looked after us, the doctors who examined us. They all said I didn't have a heart and that Betty was the one who looked after mine. But I obviously do have a heart. How else could I put one foot in front of the other? I've had one all along. And now as I stick my hand into the gash, I can feel it pumping, there among the sinews and muscle and bone. It's totally clear to me now. It's the only thing that is clear. Crystal clear.

I don't need a machine to prove it. I have a heart. And I am alone. Alone like never before. I am walking, and I am free. I am walking…and for a few minutes…or seconds…or however long this lasts…I am free for the first time. And I see it all, like a shot through the head. I am everything. Everything looking at everything. I am the universe that sleeps, that dreams through my eyes, before it wakes again. Earth that overthrows earth. I am the world, together with everything that can crawl or swim or walk. I am the earth, the planets and stars that sleep or watch us with our own eyes. I am everything that sees and dreams and joins the banquet, as it laughs at itself and its notions, utterly piss-drunk. I am everything…and everything is just shit. I am Hell opening…I am the banquet. I have been dreaming, am dreaming, and now I am waking up at last. I've been going around thinking I had no heart for all this time! Stupid, stupid, stupid Earl.

I fish out Karin's chocolate from my half-torn pocket. Mindless, I try to bite off the silver paper, shivers go through my teeth and jaw, but as soon as I've crammed the square of chocolate into my mouth I start suckling like a piglet.

I trudge onwards through the streets. With chocolate and blood around my mouth, Betty's absent counter-weight making me reel off balance. Turning to chase away the crowd that's followed me, I almost do a double spin on my own axis. My ears are ringing, and it feels like a thousand tiny fingers are prising my eyes open to let in the light.

And all I can hear are the footsteps behind me. Footsteps and the rustling of clothes. And Gunnar who is dancing in the silent crowd. The whisper of the trees spreading above me, birds that rise from the branches as we approach. My lungs are whistling again.

Then I stop. Put the remains of the chocolate-stub in my pocket and try to laugh with a viscous film of blood and slime and caramel over my gaping mouth. A stone's throw below, I see Betty on her way into the ambulance. I've walked in a circle. One walk around the block is all this dead man could make. Not much to write home about.

Then I hear the rasping of claws and the clanking of a chain.

"Ernst." Caigen smiles at me, his dog snarling before him.

I look at him.

"Ernst, I've got this friend...he's a judge. D'you think you might..."

But instead of stopping I walk on, swaying, onwards – with the crowd and the Echolses dragging along, and Gunnar dancing at the rear – back towards the waiting ambulance. I arrive just as they're pushing Betty into the back. Wilder walks towards me. He smiles.

"Earl, it's time you lay down now."

He puts a hand on my shoulder. I exhale. The pastor begins to pray.

"Mumbo-jumbo." I hiss. "It's all just a dream…a drunken dream."

I am here. I am not here.

I try to get up. My knee gives way, my body crumples and slides into the ambulance. I land with my torn shoulder against the ambulance floor.

I am here. I am not here.

"My sister," I sob. "My sister…"